LOOKING OUT

By the same author

MZUNGU'S WIFE

LOOKING OUT

Philippa Blake

THE BODLEY HEAD
LONDON

A CIP catalogue record for this book is
available from the British Library

ISBN 0 370 31304 6

Typeset by Computape (Pickering) Ltd, North Yorkshire
Printed in Great Britain for
The Bodley Head Ltd,
31 Bedford Square, London WC1B 3SG
by Mackays of Chatham PLC

First published in 1989

LOOKING OUT

One

'What is it, Liam – is it a boat or is it my mother-in-law?'

'It's one of Handel's sheep!'

'Can't be, Handel's sheep don't hang in the sky.'

'That's the sea, pillock.'

'Hold it the right way up, Liam.'

'That's no boat, that's Mrs Evans.'

'Mrs Evans the mermaid.'

Liam joined in their laughter. It was Friday night. Handel's farm hands had made up a team to play darts against a group of tourists. They weren't the picture-buying kind of tourists, neither old enough nor wealthy enough to take a landscape home as a souvenir. These were youngsters with rucksacks, staying in the village, bed and breakfast where the 'Vacancies' signs hung furtive in a downstairs window. Or a bed in The Swan, a drafty room over the bar, with the smell of fish on the breeze off the quay.

The late spring day had given way to twilight. In the public bar the smoke-stained ceiling lowered as dark as the scarred oak panels that lined the walls. The regulars sat on wooden benches against the wall, or on plain hard-backed chairs at the scrubbed table in the centre.

Liam propped his picture against the bar. It had been a night such as this – innocent, joining the easy laughter around the bar – just such a night that he had slipped in, found himself part of a thing, without looking to see what it was.

A night like this, with an unsold picture propped against the bar, the end of the day that he had found the car gone, Henry Alland's sleek phallus no longer in Matilda's drive. And Ruth gone – without a word, just the running back along the lane, the child whimpering in the pram, leaving him nothing.

The winter had been hard, bleak; ice in the outhouse in

Smithies' yard, snow in the fields, Handel's sheep dying in the drifts. Hard winds confined him to the studio, hunched under the electric light, painting the jagged-winged cormorants that huddled out on the Head, thinking of Ruth, of the warm fold of her thighs where so briefly he had laid his hand.

Handel kept his lambs close until the weather changed. Pale bundles in the far field, grey against the snow, too small to see unless Liam walked across, water running into his boots, ears whipped blue by the wind. Not until the end of March did the snow begin to melt. Handel's lambs came nearer, playing like puppies, splay-legged, tumbling in the small undulations of the grass. The sun warmed the chalk. April brought a bloom to Matilda's chestnuts, a slow unfurling of yellow-green leaves that hung like limp-fingered hands as their fat candles of blossom grew up from the stems. Liam painted the lambs and the trees, scampering shadows among bright new leaves.

'There's nothing like a warm spring, eh?' Handel chuckled at the picture. 'You'll get a good price for that one, if you ask enough.'

Liam grinned. 'I hope you're right.'

'Mrs Handel's got the spring in her too.' The farmer leaned against the gate. 'Been having a spring-clean, turning out the kitchen.'

'That's hard work, then.'

'But not all work,' said Handel. 'She's got her eye on a new cooker, you know, one with the oven in the cupboard.'

Liam shook his head, wondering how it would be to keep an oven in a cupboard.

'She says you can have the old one for a fiver.'

'Five pounds?'

Handel nodded. 'It's bottled gas. It'll do better than that coal thing you've got in here.'

'It would indeed.'

The farmer brought the cooker in his pickup, bumping across the back field with a bottle of gas, half used. Iron feet screeched on the stone kitchen floor.

'What do I owe you for the gas?'

Handel shook his head. 'Nothing at all.'

'I must pay you for it.' Liam put his hand in his pocket.

'The cooker's no good without gas. Half a bottle will get you started.'

'I don't want to be owing you,' said Liam.

'You owe me nothing but five pounds,' said Handel, firmly.

Liam handed him the five-pound note that he had in his pocket. 'Will you stay and eat with me? I've some parsnips to roast.'

Handel looked at his watch. 'I'll go and look at my ram while you're doing them.'

He came back, stamping the mud off his boots by the back door, as Liam took the parsnips out of the oven. Their heavy, warm smell filled the kitchen.

'The cooker works all right, then?'

'It does.' Liam grinned. 'It works a treat.'

Handel hung his coat on the door.

'Been cold up here has it?'

Liam nodded. 'January was bitter.'

'You don't get many visitors I suppose?' Handel scattered salt over his plate.

'You're the first since the summer.'

The parsnips were crisp and sweet. Liam opened bottles of beer and Handel talked about the lambing season just past, the high prices being fetched at auction.

Liam edged the conversation round.

'The tourists'll be back now, I suppose? With the warmer weather?'

'Some.' Handel nodded. 'Mind, these days most folk go to Spain for their holidays.'

'Still, the village gets busier?'

'Aye, a bit. The fishing's better anyway.'

'I suppose the Allands will be back?'

'To Matilda's?' The farmer raised a bottle to his lips. 'Not this spring.'

'They've not asked Mrs Handel to prepare the house?'

'No. Mind, every year Mrs Handel says she won't do it no more. She don't approve, see – holiday homes and that.' He nudged Liam, chuckling. 'She don't approve of you, neither. With your painting.'

Liam shrugged. 'Why won't they come?'

Handel emptied the beer bottle. 'Perhaps it's the wife don't want to.' He wiped his mouth on his sleeve. 'Who can say why a woman wants or doesn't want? Mrs Handel changes her mind with the wind. I take no notice.' He helped himself to a piece of bread and wiped his plate with it.'If you want to know, ask Enid Evans. She knows everything there is to know.'

Liam hurried down to the village. A light breeze caught his coat, swirled and paused, murmuring in the hollows of the cliff. The sun went in and out, a flickering brightness behind the clouds.

Standing beside her counter Mrs Evans held out a bunch of carrots. 'I don't know why I'm doing this for you, Mr McGuinness. My Glyn would have a fit if he knew.'

'I'll be five minutes, no more.' Liam adjusted the pad on his knee.'If you could just hold them still.' Her hands were rough and red, fingers themselves like jointed carrrots, arms marrow-like, thrusting from her dress.

'Is it for a painting, Mr McGuinness? Are you putting my carrots in a picture?'

'Not this time, Mrs Evans. This is just for practice.'

The shopkeeper sighed. Liam smiled to himself. They all wanted to be painted, no matter what they pretended. 'Drawing is like tennis, Mrs Evans, you have to keep in training.'

The shopkeeper shuffled her feet. 'How long will you be? My arms are aching.'

'Not long now.' His charcoal hushed against the paper, shading the shape of her apron.

'You'll have some tourists to draw before long,' said Mrs Evans.

'I hope so. I hope they'll buy some pictures.'

'Well, they should do,' said Mrs Evans. Your pictures are very good, my Glyn says.'

'No,' said Liam.'They are not good. They're terrible. But they're bread and butter, and I have to eat.'

'Will you sell any in Dover?'

'There's a shop – one of those framing places that calls itself a gallery – they've promised to take a few.' He used his finger to smudge the charcoal and wiped the excess on to the knee of his jeans.

'We could sell some here!' The little woman's eyes lit up.

Forgetting her pose she pointed to the wall.'We could make room along there.'

'The place in Dover is taking fifty per cent.'

'Fifty per cent! I wouldn't take as much as that.'

'How much then?'

'Hmm.' She stroked her chin. 'I'd have to ask my Glyn about that.'

Liam smiled and held out his drawing pad. 'There you are.'

She took the pad over to the light .

'Why it's not the carrots at all!' she cried.'If I didn't think it was for the sake of art I'd tear it up here and now.'

Liam grinned at her. 'Will you give me a pound of cheese for it?'

'I'll do no such thing. Not for that picture, it's rude!'

Liam took the pad back. 'I'll pay for the cheese, then.'

She cut a wedge from a bright yellow wheel in the refrigerator.

'Will the Allands be back at Easter?' His voice was ordinary, casual, giving no hint of the suspense that kept his free hand curled tight in the coat of his pocket.

'Did you not hear?' She laid a greaseproof sheet on the scale and put the cheese on it. 'Mrs Alland's had another babby.'

'A child?'

'Aye, a boy.' The shopkeeper put the parcel of cheese on the counter. 'I had a card.' She pulled a pink envelope from a clip of papers that hung from a nail on the wall. 'Here, it's all printed out, "Henry and Ruth Alland are proud to announce the birth of their son, Samuel David, born on the sixteenth day of March." ' She put the card back on the clip.

'They won't be coming for Easter, then?'

'I should think not – with a brand new babby. Not until the summer – perhaps not at all this year. Mrs Alland is no spring chicken to be having babbies at her time of life.'

The shopkeeper leaned across the counter, whispering, though there was no one else in the shop. 'They've been trying for ten years, you know. She's lost two since young Michael was born.' She patted the pockets of her apron. 'I gave her some advice last year. I told her it was the smog. No babby can survive that bad London air and with Mr Alland being so busy all the time. I told her to try again while they were here, by the sea, to give the babby a proper start.'

She beamed at Liam. 'I was right, wasn't I?'

Liam pointed to the shelf behind her. 'I'll take two bananas as well.'

'Ten years!' cried Mrs Evans, counting the change into Liam's palm.

He trudged back up Smithies Lane.

Ruth had told him herself of the miscarriages. Failures, she called them, bitterness pulling her lip into a line.

'One after another – and me, like a stranded whale on a rubber sheet.'

Because that was his way with things, not intending to hurt, but to show her that he thought of her words, Liam made a sketch in oils; a bleeding whale, stranded on the beach. Young Michael laughed aloud at the sight of it. 'Look, Mummy, it's a big fish all bloody!'

Ruth dragged the boy away, slapping his ears with rage.

He waited. Idled the time. Waited for the car; for the sleek, improbable limousine to come nosing down the narrow High Street. For the family inside, looking out, grey-faced through the tinted glass. For the woman who would sit in the front, unsmiling at the sight of him. For her shape, her poses, her unconscious loveliness; combing her hair in his house, bending to reveal the soft, full breasts drawn together under her dress.

He could see the place from Smithies; Matilda's Cottage set snug on the grass above the cliff steps, guarded by the proud chestnuts that looked out upon the bay, the small beach, half shingle and half sand, the grey sweep of the English Channel. On a fine morning a shadow could be seen on the horizon, a dark line that was France. It was said that, through a telescope, the time could be read on the Calais Town Hall clock. Liam had no telescope, and no interest in the time across the Channel. He had never been to France, never travelled the ferries that scarred the horizon. Never been anywhere but Ireland, and never would go there again. There was nothing left for him in Ireland. No mother to visit. Mary McGuinness dead before her time – from emphysema and exhaustion, from forty stone-cluttered acres, mean-limbed cows and an idle man. Dead, too, from disappointment in her eldest son, who had turned his back on the farm and painted pictures when there was digging to be done.

Liam looked away from the window, closing his eyes against the brilliant square of light. Never so disappointed as she would be now with his life, his painting, the home he had made in this huddle of stone, squatting in a hollow of pasture just short of the cliff edge. Smithies, it was called, after the previous occupant, a tenant farmer long dead, to whom old age had brought madness and neglect. Handel worked the land now, adding it to his own fields, and Liam rented Smithies, week to week, paying his rent over the bar in The Swan on a Friday night.

He had cleaned the place up; stopped up the leaks, turned the remains of a conservatory into a studio. A flock of sheep grazed beyond the wire fence that marked the boundary of the yard. They looked on, empty-eyed, as he replaced the glass, hung shelves to carry his pots and jars, boxes of charcoal, rolls of paper and canvas. Propped against one wall was his stock of pictures for the tourists, the ones Mrs Evans had admired: over-coloured landscapes, seaspray and seagulls. Against the other wall were his pictures of Ruth; the early impressions, quick drawings, oil sketches, all that he had managed to prize between her coming here like a child to a toffee tin, drawn against her will, and running back to Michael and the husband, complaining that she was too hot, too tired, too anything but patient.

She had smiled when he took her to his bed, her soft breasts turned taut and hard under his hand, but as he offered his body he saw her look at the walls of his room, at the web of cracks, shoes in a box, clothes piled upon a chair for lack of drawers. She had uttered her cry that was the sound of pain and not pleasure, and dressed again and hurried away, spoiling his plan.

'Why?' he cried. 'There can be no shame now!'

She buttoned her blouse. 'You ask too much. I have a husband and child to consider.'

'I ask nothing but that you sit in one place and hold still for me.'

'You take too much away!' And she was gone and would not be caught again.

Two

She arrived at teatime. The slam of a car door, a quick burst of radio noise from the taxi. Her clothes glared bright in the still afternoon: tight pink pants, pink gauze in her hair, a yellow sweater clinging to the outline of her breasts. A man mowing the lawn on the other side of the drive stared above the clatter of his machine.

'Hi, Mr Gaskin!'

While she fumbled for her keys, Mrs Gaskin opened the door.

'Suzannah?'

'Hello Gassy, dear.' Flying past into the hall, a flash of pink and yellow. 'Simon?'

A troubled smile. The same boy but older, deeply tanned from Hong Kong.

'You came all the way back?'

He shrugged. Shyly, Suzannah kissed his cheek. It was strange to kiss him. Her little brother, a grown man. Over his shoulder was her father, Cyril. She kissed him too. He was twice as old; his skin papery and pale, like crumpled tissue.

'I can't stay longer than a weekend. I have to get back.'

'All right, Suzannah.' He patted her cheek. As she kissed him, his other hand unconsciously patted her hip, felt the silky fabric of her pink pants. The sight of her took his breath away; his beloved daughter, bursting into the house, a bright, tropical bloom, strong and alive.

'Where's Mother?'

'In the garden.'

'I thought she'd be in bed. You told me – '

'She has a visitor. A young man from the hospice.'

'You're not sending her to a hospice?'

'No.' Her father cleared his throat. 'She wants to stay at home.'

'You're not to send her to a hospice, Daddy!' Suzannah had taken hold of his arm. 'People just go there to die. They give up hope.'

'That's what a hospice is for.' Simon's voice filled the hall. 'They're meant for the dying.'

With a small gesture, Cyril hushed his children. 'Your mother is staying at home. There's no question of the hospice.'

'Then why is the man here?'

'He's a priest, sort of.' Simon started up the stairs.

Cyril turned to Suzannah. 'Austin is a deacon, training to be a priest.'

'Is that his name? Don't I have to call him Father?'

'No, he prefers us to use his own name. He's very informal.'

'But why is he here? Mother isn't religious, we've never had priests in the house before.'

'He has been a great comfort to your mother.'

'Shall I leave them alone then?' Suzannah asked, with more haste than she intended.

Cyril ushered her along the hall. 'Go and say hello. She'll be so pleased to see you.'

Suzannah opened the door into the sitting room. Her mother was in the garden. Through the open french doors she could see garden chairs under a big white parasol. A man sitting beside her mother. He rose as she crossed the grass. Jeans and an open-necked shirt.

Suzannah walked slowly forward. Though the day was warm her mother wore a shawl, pale cream cashmere, that had been Cyril's present to her on their twenty-first anniversary.

'Suzannah?'

She had almost reached the chairs. It was only her mother's head that turned, swivelling slowly above the shawl.

'Suzannah, darling.'

Her hand felt the same, the long fingers strong and slightly coarse-skinned.

'This is Austin Keys.'

The deacon stood to shake her hand. 'Hello, Suzannah.'

He was tall. Automatically Suzannah smiled her wide, eye-lighting smile that could win hearts.

'We're having a cup of tea, I'm sure there's one left in the pot.'

There was something feeble in her mother's voice. Suzannah heard and dismissed it. She sat in the empty chair. 'Are there any biscuits?'

It was not just the shade of the parasol, the sun glaring through the white canvas. It was her mother's face that was white, shrivelled, grey about the mouth.

'I don't know, darling – perhaps in the kitchen.' Her hand rose from the table. A feeble gesture, as if its earlier strength had been a falsehood. 'Mrs Gaskin will show you the tin.'

The deacon was already rising. 'I'll have a look, shall I?'

He had gone, loping off across the grass before Suzannah realised that she had expected her mother to go, as she would have done in the past.

'I'm sorry, Ma. I didn't think.'

The hand waved again, fluttering from the table-top.

'It is so good to see you, Suzannah.'

Suzannah leaned across and kissed her mother's cheek. She could think of nothing to say. She could not say 'You look well'. Nor, it seemed, might she say 'You will be well again soon'. Her father's letter was quite explicit. Cancer of the liver; a swift, certain death. They must not think of hope.

She felt cold, as if a finger of icy wind had broken through the warm spring air. Henry was not with her, not even in her imagination. For a moment she was simply there, where she was, in the garden of her mother's house, and she could not imagine Henry sitting there. Handsome, clever, sophisticated, occupied with the business of being rich and another woman's husband, Henry Alland was not a man who would sit in the garden with a mother who was dying.

She rubbed her arms and kissed her mother once more. 'The garden looks very nice.'

Joan smiled. 'Did you see the laburnum as you came in?'

'Yes!' Suzannah nodded vigorously, unable to remember if the laburnum was a tree or a flower. She should have known, after all the childhood hours kneeling beside her mother (how large she had seemed then, how tall and safe in her wellington boots!), learning the names: laburnum and vibernum, hydrangea and hypericum, magnolia and myrtle. A litany. No Mr Gaskin then; Joan had kept the garden herself, even the lawn, mowed and raked and rolled it, going out in the dusk to move the sprinklers, the dry smell of garden gloves on her fingers when she came to kiss goodnight.

'The laburnum is a tree, darling.' Pale lips uncreasing as she smiled at Suzannah. 'The one with the yellow blossom by the drive.'

The deacon returned, a smile on his lips, rattling the biscuit tin as he crossed the grass, as if to say, 'I'm coming back'.

He offered the tin to Suzannah, chocolate bourbons and gingernuts. She selected a bourbon, glancing at his face. Plain and smooth, eyes of light blue, looking back at her, unblinking. Not as blue as Henry's eyes.

'Have one yourself.'

'Thank you.' The gingernut went in whole. He crunched rapidly. 'I must be going, my people will be waiting.'

'Your people?' Suzannah turned to him, ready to laugh. 'Is it a flock you have, or an army?'

His look was steady. 'Just some people who are sick.'

Of course, the hospice. She had another question but he was rising from the table, ducking his head out from under the parasol. He stood beside Joan's chair and took her hand. 'Goodbye, my dear. I'll try and pop in tomorrow.'

Suzannah waited. Her mother's eyes had closed, her head slumped forward. For a moment there was silence, her face contracted, transformed, lips pinched in, breathing in short, shallow gasps.

Suzannah started from her chair. 'Mummy! Are you all right?'

The priest shook his head, whispered, 'It will pass.'

Suzannah watched, appalled by their easy intimacy, the way her mother's hand clutched the priest's – as if she were surrendering something to him.

A full minute passed, a frozen tableau of the clutching hand and the priest's lips murmuring in prayer, and then her mother's voice, weak but audible. 'I'm so grateful to you, Austin. I'm so grateful when you come.'

He released her hand and turned to Suzannah. An ordinary face, smiling. She saw how young he was, barely thirty.

'Goodbye, Suzannah.'

Younger than Henry.

She began to stand, hesitating. 'Goodbye – '. Expecting him to say, 'Shall I see you in church on Sunday?' Already she had thought of her excuse. But he said nothing and when he had gone she could feel the coolness of his skin against her palm.

Ten o'clock on Saturday morning. The smell of bacon and eggs filled the house. Gassy's bacon and eggs, and sausages, and fried bread, and tomatoes, and the china stand of toast, steaming. Cyril ate nothing. He sipped his coffee, black, his face sleepless and dry. It was Simon who made the suggestion, having eaten his father's breakfast, and as if that extra food had made him stronger than the others, the suggestion that Suzannah had thought of and left unspoken, that Gassy had whispered to Cyril who had left it unanswered: that it was time to bring Joan's bed downstairs, time for Cyril to look to his own health, his own sleep, that might come more easily if his wife were not there beside him. After all, with her bed in the sitting room Joan could still be with them; the guest loo would be easier for her; she could watch TV and still be part of the family and after all . . . and the sentence trickled away.

Joan rested on Cyril's bed while he and Simon carried hers downstairs. The men stayed below to help Gassy tuck in the sheets and it was Suzannah who went back to fetch her mother. Feather-light, she leaned on Suzannah's arm as they descended the stairs, slowly, each step an effort of will. Suzannah saw the back of her neck, where she had not managed with the comb. The skin was loose, as if she were shrinking inside it.

At the bottom of the stairs Joan asked to sit down and reached for the little corner chair, opposite the clock. Suzannah could not recall anyone ever having sat in that chair. It was a hall chair, an ornament; tapestry seat and finely carved mincing legs; it had always seemed too frail for its purpose. And now her mother sat there, with the shawl she used to wear to read in bed, huge about her arms.

Suzannah wanted to move on, to finish the business, but

Joan had taken her hand. A gentle tug brought her down to squat beside the chair.

'Suzannah,' Joan whispered, 'Suzannah, I'm worried about your father.'

Her voice cracked out into the quiet hall. 'He's all right, Mother. You mustn't worry.'

'But who is going to look after him? You know how hopeless he is around the house, who will take care of him when I am gone?'

Suzannah cleared her throat. The soft material of the nightdress hung loose about her mother's shoulders. She could smell the fine sweet smell of her, her mother as she had always smelled, and overlaying it, the other smell, old and sour. 'Simon and I will look after him.'

Joan's eyes closed. 'But your brother must go back to Hong Kong, Suzannah. He must not waste his opportunity there.'

The conversation had made her breathless. She coughed weakly, and Suzannah took the opportunity to free her hands.

Three

They came that summer. Late in August, despite Enid Evans's words, they came. He watched from Smithies' window, the big car turning into Matilda's drive. One of the village boys had been over and cut the grass. Liam hurried down to the shop.

'They've brought an au pair!' cried Mrs Evans. 'Speaks no English at all.'

'Foreign is she?'

The shopkeeper nodded. 'Mrs Alland says she's to look after Michael more than the babby.'

'Have you any apples?'

Enid Evans pointed to the door. 'Over there. They're a bit soft. New crop's not here yet and you know how we won't sell French ones.'

Liam nodded. He tried to think of something else. Apples were all he could remember, Michael liking apples, the boy's prominent teeth sinking into the green skin.

'I'll just take a loaf, then.'

'Imagine,' said Enid Evans, reaching for a loaf of bread from the shelf behind her. 'They've only come for a week.'

'Only a week?'

The shopkeeper nodded her head. 'Hardly worth Mrs Handel's trouble.'

With sudden impatience, Liam reached into his pocket. 'How much do I owe you?'

'Just a pound.' She wrapped the bread and put it in a white plastic bag. 'You'll be wanting a wife and babbies yourself soon, Mr McGuinness. A man needs a family around him.'

'I won't find a wife in North Bay.'

She put the bag on the counter and rubbed her chin, stubby fingers following the contours of her face. 'But it's a nice Irish girl you want, one of your own kind.'

'That's it, Mrs Evans,' said Liam. He put the loaf in the pocket of his big coat and the doorbell pinged as he went out.

She was alone, pushing a pram along Smithies Lane, in the place where the road dipped behind the Head. A loose cotton dress, faded colours lifting with the breeze. Liam bounded towards her, bread bouncing in his coat. Had she been to Smithies, brought the child to see him and found the place empty?

He reached her, breathless, put a hand over hers on the handle of the pram.

'How are you, Ruth?'

She did not answer, would not meet his eyes.

'Well?'

Her hands felt cold, speckles of white under her nails; he watched her unclip the hood of the pram and fold it back.

An ordinary child; a pink face with a bubble in the corner of its mouth. He did not expect any feeling, but there it was, a wave of wonder that brought a smile like a child's own to his lips. He looked down into the pram, and then again at Ruth, and with great difficulty kept his hands from lifting the sheet, and putting his fingers about the fragile chest to feel the tiny movement of breath.

'Hello, little man.'

A hand wavered towards him, wondrously small. He took it in his own, warm and damp, soft nails against his palm. He looked again at Ruth, feeling the smile still on his lips.

'Sure, Ruth, he's a marvel.'

Her face was more lined than he remembered, her eyes more timid.

She nodded, unsmiling.

'Did you forgive me the whale, then?'

She nodded again, pursing her lips.

'And what did you call the little one?'

He knew, but wanted to hear the names from her.

'Samuel David.'

He nodded. 'Good names.'

'Henry chose them.'

'Ah,' said Liam, nodding again.

'Samuel was his grandfather's name.'

'Ah.'

The small fist slipped away.

'Where is young Michael?'

Her hand went to her hair, checking the pins that held it on the crown of her head. Liam sighed. Unconsciously, in raising her arm, she had reassembled a pose in which he had placed her once, arm up, rounding the line of her breast.

'Ah, Ruth . . . '

'He's out with his father.'

'On the beach?' Liam recollected himself.

'No. They've gone to Dover. The au pair wanted to do some shopping.'

He smiled. 'So you're alone?'

She looked at the pram. 'I have Sammy.'

'But you could bring him too, we can have tea together.'

'No.' She clutched the handle of the pram.

'Why not? Just for an hour?'

She began to push the pram away. He went after her.

'Please, Ruth. I have a picture in my mind, a good picture.'

He kept up with her, all the way to Matilda's Cottage, finally standing before her at the gate, blocking her path. 'Ruth! I ask no more than two hours. Just an afternoon. Don't you owe me an afternoon?'

She paused, looking down into the pram. 'Will you leave us then? Will that be all you'll want?'

Liam nodded, he took hold of her hand. 'Just an afternoon. Bring the little one, I need him too.'

She raised her eyes. 'Henry has promised to take Michael to the castle on Tuesday. Maria can go with them.'

Liam beamed. 'I'll wait for you.'

The afternoon, when they came, was cloudy, threatening rain. The child cried persistently.

'It's the smell of paint. He doesn't like it,' said Ruth.

They sat in the studio, on the hard chairs from the kitchen. Outside, Handel's sheep cropped the grass against the fence. Liam started sketch after sketch, a pile of feverish outlines: round-backed poses; swollen breasts; the faded hair falling from its pins. He tossed them aside.

'It's no use, Ruth. I have to have more time. It has been so long, you are so much changed . . . '

'Older you mean, and fatter?'

He shook his head. 'Nothing so trivial as that.'

She stood up, lifting the child on to her hip. 'I'll have to be getting back.'

He put out his hand, caught hold of her arm. 'They won't be home yet.'

'I must go. I must be there when they come.'

'But not yet.' He pulled her slowly towards him, gathering Sammy into the embrace. 'I have need of you, Ruth.'

'No!' She pulled away. 'I have to go to Henry. I shall lose him if I am not there when he wants me.'

'How will you lose him?'

She bent to seat the child in the pram. 'He has another woman.'

'He betrays you?'

She shook her head. 'It means nothing. This one is not the first.' She opened the door and he helped her lift the pram over the step.

'I wish you would stay with me.'

Ruth smiled, almost laughed. 'Liam, you are a dreamer.'

'Don't you think of it sometimes, how it would be?'

She shook her head, vigorously, as if to shake away the thought. 'Henry needs me.'

'Even though he has another?'

'She is nothing.' Ruth turned the pram and wheeled it across the yard.

He watched the swing of her skirt. The strap of her brown, sensible sandal thick against the whiteness of her ankle. 'I think you are beautiful.'

She looked back. 'Not any more. Look at me.' She gestured to her body. 'Henry says I have grown fat and grey.'

'He says that to you?'

Her smile was wan. 'Not in so many words.'

'But you are beautiful.'

Liam stood by the gate, his hands thrust deep into the pockets of his coat. He watched her body, angled over the pram, pushing it along the chalky road. Before they turned out of sight, he went after them, running along the road, catching her in his arms, folding shoulders and breasts and elbows into his open coat.

'Ruth, you must come back with me.'

She wriggled. 'Let me go.'

Her movement knocked the pram, diverting them both to steady it.

'Won't you come back with me? Just let me finish the drawing?'

She looked up. 'The drawing? – I thought you wanted . . . '

'I want both!' cried Liam. 'But if I must choose, I want the drawing. You and Sammy, mother and child. It will be a watershed, the first good work I have done.'

Her face screwed up, all its lines indenting themselves. 'That is all you care for, Liam McGuinness, your precious paintings!'

Her face was streaked with pink.

He took her arm. 'Ruth . . . '

Straightening herself, she pulled her arm free and began to walk briskly. The pram shuddered on the ruts in the chalk, shaking the flesh on her arms.

Liam could hear a car, still out of sight, turning up on to the cliff. Ruth began to run. The child whimpered as the pram rattled and bounced on the road.

He turned back to Smithies. There were lines in the yard from the pram wheels, the pile of new sketches on the table, a mug of tea gone cold.

They were gone the next day. The cottage windows closed tight, the stealthy, gleaming shape of Henry Alland's car, absent from the drive. Thinking it might be just the husband gone, returned to his office as he had done the previous summer, Liam went to the door. He pressed the bell and waited in the shady porch, expecting young Michael, shy with his teeth; or Ruth, smiling a little, with the new child, Samuel, held against her breast.

Instead it was Handel's wife.

'Liam, what do you want?'

'Have they gone, Mrs Handel?'

'The Allands? Of course they've gone. They went yesterday. What do you want them for?' Her dustcloth was the colour of marigolds.

'They've gone for good, then?'

'Until next year.' She held the door. 'Shocking I say it is. Him treating the place as a holiday home – it's not what Matilda wanted.'

Liam knew the answer, but still he asked the question, 'Who was Matilda?'

It was a trick he had learned, living among the villagers, to let them tell their stories, to smile and listen; to secure a place for himself in the village, and even in their hearts.

Mrs Handel leaned against the door frame. 'Matilda Alland? She's dead now, bless her. She left this place to him because he was the only kin she had. Not that he bothered with her much. He being a London man. She wanted him to make his home here after she was gone, but he's too grand for this little place.' She nodded. 'He's quite important, you know; a big man in the City, they say.' Her expression changed as she thought of it.

Liam nodded with her. 'They do say he is.'

'But Matilda Alland was a lady.' Handel's wife sniffed. 'I always said so. I used to do this house for her, too. And it was proper work then, every day. Now they only want me to clean when they've gone.' She was closing the door. 'Get on with you, Liam. I've Handel's dinner to get when I've finished here.'

Liam walked away. A stone skittered ahead of him. He gave it a savage kick and the stone lifted high, a dark shape against the bright sky.

It was that night, that same night down in The Swan with practically nothing in his pocket, a hasty landscape wrapped in his bag – of raggy-winged cormorants, and the scarred, oily-engined tubs tied up along the quay. It was that night he slipped in, caught, netted as easy as a fish in dark water . . .

Four

The smell of roasting lamb filled the house; a warm, ordinary smell, rich with comfort. Suzannah cut a sprig of rosemary from the kitchen garden and brought it in for Mrs Gaskin.

'Give Mrs Haig a sniff,' said the housekeeper. 'She's always liked the smell of it.'

She sat on the bed that had been placed where the sofa used to be, all the sitting room furniture squashed up to accommodate it. Joan was too weak to sniff, but Suzannah held the spiked green leaves near her face and she smiled.

'Can I bring you anything, Mother?'

Joan shook her head – a slow echo of her old gesture. 'But stay with me a while, it seems so long since I've seen you.'

'It's not all that long,' said Suzannah.

'But it's such a long time since we talked to one another.'

Suzannah looked out at the garden. Across the lawn the willow was in full leaf, trailing strands on the grass. The yellow-green leaves looked sick with life, spilling in their own shadow. Her mother would not see them fall. How does it feel, she wondered, to be dying? How does it feel for Daddy? Does he wish it would happen quickly, as one does at airports and railway stations, feel impatient for the parting to be over?

With practised ease, she turned away from the thought, closed her eyes against the willow, imagined Henry's arms wrapped about her, a warm, closing embrace. 'Darling girl,' he whispered, tucking her head against his neck, 'you are the most precious thing in the world to me . . . '

Joan's hand stirred on her arm. 'Darling, I so want you to be happy.'

Suzannah started. 'I am happy – well, apart from you being ill.'

Her mother continued as if she had not answered. 'Life is so short.'

'Don't say that!'

'But it's true, darling. We must make the best of it.' She made a small noise in her throat and Suzannah realised that this talk was a tremendous effort.

'Don't talk, Mother. You'll make yourself weak.'

The colourless lips moved on. 'I am already weak, that is why what I say is so important. Suzannah, the only thing that matters in life is love. Everything else is meaningless. Loving someone truly is the only thing that can bring you joy.'

She nodded, eyes averted, waiting for what might follow, but there was only silence and when she looked back at the bed her mother was sleeping.

She got up and went into the kitchen.

'Did she like the rosemary?'

Suzannah shrugged. 'She hadn't the strength to smell it.'

Mrs Gaskin shook her head. 'It's your father I'm thinking of.'

'Daddy?'

The housekeeper sniffed. 'How is he going to cope when she's gone?'

Suzannah frowned.

'You know what I mean.' Mrs Gaskin spoke without looking at her, her back turned, scrubbing potatoes over the sink. 'When Mrs Haig, God rest her, passes on.'

Suzannah leaned against the door. On the draining board stood a collander of new potatoes, scrubbed smooth like large white pebbles.

Mrs Gaskin sniffed again and took a tissue from the pocket of her apron. 'Eight years I've worked for her. Once a week to begin with, then twice a week for the last year. It's been every day this past month.'

Suzannah put out her hand and tentatively patted the housekeeper's shoulders, plump under their skin of stretched courtelle and apron. 'I'm sure Daddy will still need you to come, Gassy. He'll probably need you even more.'

Mrs Gaskin blew her nose. Suzannah went out into the hall. Through the crack between the hinges of the open door she saw the corner of the bed, incongruously white beside the dark bricks of the fireplace. No sound came from the room. She turned away, her feet climbed the stairs and when she reached the top she lingered, aimlessly, one hand smoothing the banister rail, feeling the solidity of the wood, glossy with polish, strong and sure.

In the garden of the opposite house a tent was being cleaned on the lawn. A family affair, women busy with sponge mops and buckets while the men looked on, checking guy ropes, running from the children in mock alarm, pursued by spongefuls of water.

Their cries drifted through the open windows, absorbed by the silence of the house that was itself a sponge, sodden with waiting.

Simon had gone to church with her father; to watch, perhaps even to pray, and to bring the deacon back for lunch because his presence would comfort her mother in a way, it seemed, that no one else could. She turned to cross the landing and stopped at the door of her parents' bedroom. The room was half bare, one bed without its twin, a wall-light poised above an empty space, marks in the carpet where her mother's bed had been.

Was this how Cyril saw it? An empty space where part of his life had been – like an amputation? Was moving the bed the same as checking in early for a flight, testing absence before it becomes absolute?

Suzannah ran down into the sitting room. Joan was awake again. She smiled. 'I thought you were in the garden.'

Suzannah knelt by the bed.

'What is it, darling?'

'Your bed isn't there,' she said, unable to prevent the foolish words.

'But it's down here, darling. I was keeping Daddy awake so we decided I should sleep down here.' A weak hand stroked Suzannah's hair.

Sobs broke from Suzannah's lips, loud and harsh. A thin, slack-skinned arm came out to draw her against a shrunken breast. Her tears made a black stain of mascara on the sheet.

'Suzannah, my little one,' whispered her mother. 'Daddy will be home soon. Dry your eyes and be brave for him.'

The sound of a car pulled Suzannah to her feet. She heard Simon's voice in the hall, and then her father and the deacon.

The men came into the sitting room and stood in a row, three suits from the church.

Speaking from her bed, Joan broke the silence. 'Was it a nice service?'

The three men answered at once.

'It was fine.'

'How are you, my dear?'

'It went well.'

Suzannah excused herself and went upstairs to change. She had worn a short skirt, unthinkingly – one of Henry's gifts, a bright band of colour well above her knees. It seemed too bright now, inappropriate for a priest, too alive for the dark suits and the waiting bed. A dress from her girlhood hung in the wardrobe, crisp flowers, pale and darker blue. She washed her face and put on the dress and took Henry's diamonds out of her ears.

Simon was knocking on the door. 'We're going to have a sherry before lunch. Will you join us?'

Suzannah took his arm as they went down. 'Gassy was upset while you were at church.'

'About mother?'

She nodded. 'I couldn't make out if it was the prospect of mother or of losing her job.'

They paused together on the half-landing, brother and sister alone together for the first time since she had come home. 'Gassy won't lose her job,' Simon whispered. 'She'll be more needed than before.'

'That's what I said. Perhaps we should get Daddy to reassure her.'

They set off again, still arm-in-arm. 'How long will you stay, Simon?'

Her brother shrugged, looking young again, his face dimpled with unhappiness. 'As long as it takes, I suppose.'

'I've got to go back tonight. I haven't got any time off.'

'Won't the bank give you some time off, some – what do they call it – compassionate leave?'

Suzannah faltered. It was Henry from whom she hadn't asked leave. 'This could go on for weeks,' she said quickly, 'I'll ask for some leave when the time comes.'

Simon winced. 'It's so bloody awful, Suzannah. I can't believe it's happening.'

'Nor me,' she whispered. 'It's like a bad dream.'

He let go her arm as they walked into the sitting room.

Cyril and the deacon were helping her mother outside. She had dressed, or been dressed, and now she settled beneath the parasol.

Simon went back into the house to fetch an extra chair. 'Gassy is an angel,' he said as he came out. 'She's changing the sheets.'

'She's a marvel,' Cyril agreed. There was nothing else to raise a glass to, so they drank to Gassy. Even Joan managed a sip before Austin rescued the slipping glass from her hand.

He had noticed that she'd changed. Suzannah saw him look up and, more than once, his eyes wandered back to look again. Catching him the second time, she smiled.

Joan touched Suzannah's arm, a flutter of weightless fingers. 'Lunch won't be ready for a little while. Why don't you show Austin the garden.'

Austin turned to her. 'I'd like it if you would.'

Suzannah swallowed her sherry. 'I can show you the path but you'll have to see the rest for yourself, I've forgotten all the names of the plants.'

The day was bright. A warm wind stirred the leaves and hazy sunshine lit the grass. He walked a step behind her, his arms stiff behind his back. 'I'd like to do a bit of gardening.'

Suzannah turned to face him. 'Do you have a garden of your own?'

He nodded. 'It's only a tiny patch, mostly weeds, I'm afraid.'

'Where do you—?'

'How long have you—'

They spoke and stopped in unison. With a gesture, as gracious as her mother's would be, Suzannah smiled. 'Please go on.'

'I was going to ask where it is that you live.'

'In London,' said Suzannah.

'Do you have a flat there?'

She nodded. 'I share with . . . someone else.'

'Oh?'

She would have lied; invented a girlfriend, or a gaggle of girlfriends, but for the look he gave her, his clear eyes resting on her face. Perhaps it was not his look but the sickbed in the sitting room, the dislocated furniture, the strangeness of this almost priest in the garden, that squeezed out the truth. 'Actually we don't share – he has another home.'

Austin nodded and they walked a few steps further. 'It must be expensive,' he said, 'managing the rent on your own.' She had stopped but he began to walk again, taking the initiative. They reached the pergola. 'Is it?'

Suzannah had forgotten the question, too absorbed in watching his back, the cloth stretched across his shoulders.

His suit was worn, the trousers slightly too short for him. 'Is what?'

Patting his chest, he made a little bow. 'Forgive me, I was asking how you manage the rent, but I don't mean to pry.'

'You're not.' Suzannah shrugged. 'The truth is that I don't have to pay the rent. The flat is his.' Her fingers played with the buttons on her dress and her tongue rattled on. 'I don't know why I've told you that. No one in the family knows, they don't even know his name. But it is quite respectable. I mean, we are in love and he's never had an affair with anyone else.' She looked up, expecting to find his face full of deaconly disapproval. Instead she found him listening, his head on one side, as if she were explaining a problem.

'What about you?'

'Me?'

'What do you? – How do you manage?'

'To live?' He hunched his shoulders and put on the voice of an old crone. 'I be just a poor man. Charity and cold gruel.'

'Stop it!'

He was laughing, the mask gone as fast as it had appeared.

Suzannah turned back towards the house. Catching her up Austin asked, 'Am I that terrible?'

'No! It was just . . . '

'Embarrassing?'

She looked into his face. His skin was very clear, the features large and regular. 'Are your conversations always like this?'

He shook his head. 'I have very few conversations with beautiful ladies.'

'Do people always confess things to you? Don't you ever talk about ordinary things?'

He spread his hands. 'I have no talent for it. In my kind of work you lose the art of small talk.'

They were near the house. Both had stopped, as if by mutual wish they could prolong their meeting.

'I'm sorry if I . . . '

'Would you like . . . '

They stopped.

'Please go on.'

'No, you.'

'I should like . . . ' Austin stopped again but Suzannah had not interrupted. 'I should like,' he began once more, 'it very much if you would come to lunch with me.'

'But you're a priest!'

The words were out before she could stop them. 'Damn.' She looked away into the garden. 'I didn't mean to say that either.'

His laughter was silent but she could see, through the corner of her eye, the slight movement of his shoulders.

'Now you're laughing at me.' She frowned.

'I'm not a priest yet. And even priests have to eat.'

'All right then.'

From the house came the scrape of a garden chair. Gassy was helping Joan to stand. Without a glance at Suzannah, Austin set off across the grass. She hurried after him, the heels of her shoes catching in the soft turf.

Simon came out as Gassy and Joan disappeared through the french windows. 'It's all right, you needn't go in. She only wants to lie down.'

'Where's Daddy?'

'He's carving the roast. He'll call us when it's ready.'

Needlessly Simon straightened the chair in which his mother had been sitting, then adjusted the angle of the parasol so that the chair would remain in the shade. Suzannah stood awkwardly beside Austin. There was a clump of muddy grass stuck to her heel. She looked at Austin's hands, broad like the rest of him, with a down of curled brown hair. Unpriest-like hands. It was hard to imagine them resting, so recently, on an altarcloth.

When all the chairs were straight Simon looked at his watch. 'Do you think everything's all right in there?'

Quite unexpectedly, something boiled up in Suzannah, as if her honesty with Austin had opened a door and everything she thought would come tumbling through. 'I shouldn't think so,' she cried. 'We'd hardly be standing here with a priest, if everything was all right.'

Simon clutched the back of a chair. 'Was it necessary to say that, Suzannah?'

She swung around, facing away from her brother and found herself looking straight at Austin.

'It's all so sudden!' she burst out. 'I can't get used to it! The last time I was here she was fine. I keep forgetting. Just now in the garden—' she glared at him – 'I forgot about it completely.'

Before anyone could reply, Gassy appeared in the doorway. 'You'd better come in and eat your lunch,' she said. 'Mr Haig has let it go cold.'

Five

It was Handel's farm hands who won. A roar of applause had followed the flight of every dart. The farmer himself sat at the scrubbed table in the centre, with Glyn Evans, who owned the shop and the two petrol pumps on the forecourt.

Liam ordered a half pint of stout and dug in his pockets for some change. The barman waved him away. 'I'll catch you next time you've made a sale.'

Liam grinned. 'Bless you.'

But the barman leaned across the bar. 'I can't let you go on the rent, though.'

'I know, I know.' Liam shook his head. 'I'll do what I can.'

'You must bring it in, Liam. Landlord'll be on to me for it.'

Liam propped his picture against the bar. There had been no takers for the sharp-beaked cormorants, for his painting of the oily-engined tubs on the quay. Tourists wanted gentle colours, matching pairs to go with their wallpaper.

'I don't suppose the painting brings in much.'

The man who spoke was a stranger, an outsider who sat in the corner, where the long bar met the wall.

Liam shook his head. 'I've had a bad summer.'

'Why was that?'

The stranger was tall. Despite the warmth of the bar, he wore his blue nylon anorak zipped up to the neck. As he lifted his glass, the nylon made a swishing noise.

Liam put his glass on the bar. 'I was waiting for something which didn't happen. It kept my mind off my work.'

'A woman, was it?'

'Maybe.'

'I'll give you a hundred pounds for your picture.'

Liam turned on the barstool.

The man placed his hands on the counter. The backs were coated with scar tissue, as if he had been burned. 'It's a good picture, but I won't pay more than a hundred.'

Liam took another sip of beer. 'It's not worth half that.'

'Why don't you buy me a pint and we can discuss it?'

'I can't.'

The man spread his fingers. Liam watched the play of light on the cracked and shiny skin.

He spoke very quietly. 'Would I be right if I said you're behind with the rent and you've an empty belly?'

Liam was still.

'All right, don't hurt your pride.' He called to the barman and ordered two pies on one plate. When they came he pushed them across to Liam. 'Help yourself.'

Liam's stomach rose at the smell of the food. The pastry was warm and flaky. It stuck to his lips and clung to the roof of his mouth. The man pushed his own glass across.

'That'll wash it down for you.'

When the plate was clean Liam said, 'I can't repay you.'

'Yes, you can.' The man spoke very quietly, so that Liam had to concentrate to hear him above the noise of the darts match and the middle table where Handel and Glyn had put a stake on a game of cards.

'You can work for us.'

'What sort of work?'

The stranger looked hard at him. 'We need a safe place.'

'Meaning?'

Without answering, the stranger beckoned to the barman and ordered two pints of stout. He said nothing until the beer was in front of them and the barman had moved away. 'Somewhere near the sea, with a man we can trust.'

'You mean Smithies?'

The stranger nodded. 'The situation is perfect, and you're the right man.'

'How do you know?'

The stranger took a swallow of beer and licked the foam from his mouth. 'Your brother suggested you.'

'Brendan? My little brother? What has he to do with you?'

The stranger smiled. 'Not so little now, he's grown into a man since you left the nest.'

Liam looked away.

Brendan. Youngest of the four. Liam's only admirer; the skippet in the background, biting his nails, willing to clean brushes and stretch canvas; believing in Liam's belief that a master lived among them.

In the bar of The Swan the noise grew louder. Handel's men slapped each other's backs and whooped as they ordered beer for themselves and the tourists who had lost.

'Where is Brendan now?'

The stranger smiled back but said nothing.

'Well?'

'I can't tell you that.' He finished his pint. 'Think about what I've said. I'll be here again tomorrow.'

Liam returned the next evening, half hoping not to find the

stranger. The pies were waiting for him on the bar. Beside the plate was an envelope containing twenty five-pound notes.

'I haven't brought the picture with me.'

The stranger shook his head. 'You can keep it, we have no use for a picture. Call this a down payment for your services.'

'What is it you want me to do?'

The man lit a cigarette. The collar of his anorak was open. As he moved his head Liam saw that his neck, too, was burn-scarred.

'We just want you to live quietly here. Keep a low profile.'

'That's all?'

'After a while, when we see how you behave, we might have a few little jobs for you. Nothing too difficult.'

'Dangerous?'

'Not if you're careful.'

'Was that how you got your burns, doing little jobs?'

The man's expression flickered.

Liam changed the subject.

'How much will you pay?'

'Enough for you to live.'

'How much?'

'How much would be enough?'

Liam took a bite of pie. 'I want enough for materials, and food – and rent.'

Remembering the rent he beckoned to the barman.

'Here's what I owe you.'

'That was quick.'

'You keep that landlord away from me, eh?'

The barman grinned, waving the notes. 'He'll never know it was late.'

When he had gone Liam turned back to the stranger. 'Why should you trust me?'

The man sat forward. 'Your brother has spoken for you.'

'And if he is wrong?'

The man was silent for a moment. 'It would go badly for him.'

Liam finished the pies and used one of the remaining notes to buy the stranger a beer.

His roll of canvas was dwindling. On the shelves of his studio the long tubes of paint lay flat, exhausted. There was nothing for the winter except potatoes and what he could bring on under the coldframe. He did not ask who 'they' were. He could guess. He knew he could guess, but did not permit himself to try. The offer was a gift from heaven and in the warmth of the bar, between the pints of beer, in the thick of the smoke and laughter and the flash of light on the man's burned hands, there seemed no reason to refuse.

After the third pint he said, 'Do I have to decide tonight?'

The stranger smiled. 'Finish your beer. There's someone waiting for us.'

Liam stood up. He felt slightly drunk.

Handel and Glyn looked up as he passed. 'Home now is it, Liam?'

He waved vaguely.

'Don't walk off the Head!'

He went after the stranger. The wind caught his coat as the door slammed behind him. An electric light hung from the wall above, illuminating the wooden sign of The Swan. The stranger stood in shadow. Another man had joined him. Both had their collars turned up. Liam remained by the door.

'Come on, man,' called the stranger. 'We haven't all day.'

'Where are you going?'

'Just come over here out of that light.'

Liam walked slowly towards them. The second man stepped forward. Liam's heart lurched as a pair of arms were flung about his greatcoat. The man was smaller than he, Liam broke free easily, grabbed the hands and pulled his assailant into the light.

'It's me, Brendan.'

Liam stared. Bright eyes, freckles, sharply pointed ears that he would have recognised anywhere. The rest was hair and beard, his little brother disguised as a man.

Brendan grinned up at him. 'How are you?'

Behind them the door to the bar was opening. Two of Handel's men lurched out.

'G'night, Liam!'

Brendan ducked into the shadows.

'Good night,' Liam answered.

He followed his brother into the dark.

'Have you a drop of whisky for your brother, Liam?'

'I might have.'

'It'd better be Irish.'

'It isn't,' said Liam. 'It's the cheapest blend you can buy.' He put his arm around his brother. 'Does your friend want to come?'

He felt Brendan shrug in the darkness. 'He's gone now.'

They walked briskly up Smithies Lane. Tiny flints reflected the starlight in the surface of the road. Liam had left a light on in his bedroom. 'That's it,' he said, as the light came into view, the outline of a house on the far edge of the cliff.

'That's your house?'

'I thought you'd seen it already?'

'Not me, the others vetted it.'

They trudged together along the lane, the smaller man struggling to match Liam's pace.

He stopped at the gate, looking up at the bulk of the house with its single lighted window. 'Perfect,' he said, turning to Liam. 'There's nothing else here? No neighbours?'

Liam laughed. 'Only Handel's sheep. It's a job to keep them out. They prefer my vegetables to Handel's grass.'

'Where's the nearest house?'

Liam opened the gate. 'We passed it at the top of the lane, you probably missed it in the dark.'

'Where the trees were?'

'That's it. Matilda's Cottage they call it, after the woman who lived there.'

'It's empty now?'

Liam opened the door and switched on the light. 'Except in the summer.'

Brendan was taking off his coat. He looked around the kitchen. 'Have you a woman in here, Liam?'

'Why do you ask?'

'It's so tidy, you'd think our Mam had been.'

Liam took a bottle of whisky from a cupboard. 'Do you want water with this?'

'Half and half,' said his brother.

Liam mixed the drinks and Brendan held up his glass. 'To our Mam.'

Liam raised his own. 'God rest her.'

Brendan drained his glass and held it out.

'Help yourself.' Liam filled a jug with water and put it by the bottle. 'I can't keep up with you, I'm full of beer.'

When his second glass was empty Brendan said, 'So you're going to join us?'

Liam was silent.

'Is that right?' Brendan persisted. 'You've joined the side of the angels?'

'I've joined nothing.'

'But you will help us?'

'Why should I?'

'Come now, Liam.' He held out his hand to touch Liam's shoulder but missed and caught the side of his face.

Liam stood up. 'Have you eaten?

Brendan sloshed more whisky into his glass. 'Not since dinnertime.'

Liam selected an onion from a basket by the door and chopped it into a bowl of cold potatoes. He added slices of carrot, a spoonful of sweetcorn from a tin. He put the bowl in front of Brendan.

'Have you nothing else?'

'There's nothing else in the house.'

Brendan pushed the food around the plate but did not eat. 'Things are pretty tight then?'

'You know they are.'

'I told them you were desperate – but it was just a guess. I didn't think there could be much of a living in the painting.'

'I get by.' He looked at Brendan's plate. 'Are you going to eat that or not?'

Brendan pushed it away. 'I'll eat it later.'

'You're staying then?' Liam asked.

His younger brother smiled. 'If you'll have me.'

Liam sat down and poured whisky into his own glass. 'I've been keeping the bottle for a special occasion. I didn't think of a visit from you.'

Brendan raised his drink. 'Here's to you, Liam.'

'And you.'

They drank. Brendan had dribbled a little into his beard. After a moment he grinned. 'You haven't answered my question.'

'What was that?'

'Have you a woman here with you?'

'You know I haven't.'

'What happened to . . . ' Brendan clicked his fingers. 'I can't remember her name!'

Liam laughed. 'That was years ago. There've been a few since then.'

'No one who stayed?'

'No.'

'No one important?'

Liam put his head on one side. 'The last one, maybe.'

'How important?'

Liam shrugged. 'Important. She went before I was ready. I was planning a picture.'

Brendan pulled a face. 'Is that all she was good for?'

'What else is there?'

'I can think of a few things.' Brendan giggled and gestured with his hands.

Liam pushed his chair back from the table. 'You can get that from any woman.'

Brendan raised his eyes. 'You haven't changed, Liam. Still the same, the artist, first and last.' He leaned forward. 'But for all the fine principles, the money would help, wouldn't it?'

'What money?' Liam had forgotten.

'That they'll pay you for the safe house.'

'I haven't said yes.'

Brendan's eyes opened wide. 'But you will, Liam?'

'I've promised nothing.'

'But you must!' He rose from his chair and came round to stand in front of his brother. 'I've told them you will.'

'You've told them?'

'Aye, well . . . I thought you would.'

'You thought? After ten years you thought you knew what I would say?'

'You're my brother.' Brendan gripped his arm. His voice pleased. 'Say you will Liam, it's such a little thing.'

'What's a little thing? You haven't told me what you want.'

'We just need a safe place.' He cast around, as if trying to find what was needed in the room. 'To store things. For people to stay sometimes. It wouldn't interfere with your painting.' He turned back and grabbed Liam's hands. 'They'll pay you a hundred pounds a month.'

Liam shook himself free. 'As much as that?'

Brendan saw his advantage. 'It could be more, once they see that you're all right.'

'What if I say no?'

Brendan's face collapsed. 'Don't play games with me, Liam.'

'Answer the question, what happens if I say no?'

Brendan squatted down, his eyes full of fear. 'It would go badly for me, Liam.'

'What does that mean?'

Brendan twisted his hands. 'I can't explain.' He began to pace up and down the kitchen. 'I've done things.'

Liam watched him.

'I've done things,' he repeated, shaking his head. 'Things I couldn't tell you.'

He stopped pacing and stood before Liam. 'I fucked up. The last time. They spent months setting up a job. They'd raised the money, brought in a specialist, all I had to do was keep a look out.' He twisted his hands. 'I fucked it up, Liam. I wasn't there. I was too afraid to go. Imagine? The whole operation aborted because of me. They came to get me. You know they're always looking for a Judas.' Brendan loomed in front of Liam, wringing his hands like a second-rate actor.

He pushed him away. 'Get on with you, Brendan.'

'It's God's truth!' Brendan's eyes grew wide. 'Do you know what they do to people like me?'

Liam sighed. The longer his brother stayed, the more like his old self he became. Their Mam had always said that Brendan would never quite grow up, that there'd always be a part of him waiting for playtime. She'd say it even now, seeing the man who paced the kitchen, nervous and afraid; Liam knew that if he said 'yes' the fear would be gone in a flash and Brendan would pour another drink and make another crude gesture about women.

He waited until Brendan sat down again and then asked, softly, 'Did our Mam know you were in this?'

Brendan looked up. 'What has she to do with it?'

'You wouldn't have been mixed up with this if our Mam was alive.'

Brendan poured more whisky into his glass. 'It's too late to think of her now. You should have come to the funeral. We all said you should have come.'

'Why? She was no longer there.'

'But you should have been there. You should have seen our Da'.'

Liam folded his arms.

'He got drunk after,' Brendan continued. 'With the aunties. When Father Patrick left Da' got out his mouth organ.'

Liam snorted. 'You wonder why I wasn't there?'

'It was . . . ' Brendan waved his arms. His speech had become slurred and tears threatened in his eyes. 'It was an abomination.'

Liam put the whisky bottle back in the cupboard. 'You've had enough, little brother.'

Brendan nodded. Tears flowed down his cheeks. 'You'll look after me, Liam. You'll do as they say, won't you?'

Liam spooned powdered coffee into a mug. 'I've no milk. You'll have to drink it black.'

Brendan wiped his face on his sleeve and lifted the mug of coffee to his lips. Liam rinsed the glasses and put them on the draining board. 'If I do this job, Brendan, will they leave you alone?'

Brendan nodded earnestly. 'That's the deal. If I could find them someone to trust, a safe place on the coast, it would – well, balance the debt.'

'A hundred pounds a month, you say?'

Brendan nodded. 'They wouldn't want much. Just the use of the house now and then, a few jobs, nothing big.'

Liam stared out of the window. A hundred pounds a month would pay Smithies' landlord, buy paint, canvas . . .

He put Brendan's mug in the sink and turned on the tap. 'Do you want to sleep upstairs?'

Brendan ignored the question. 'Will you say yes, Liam?'

'All right, all right.' Liam banged the mug on to the draining board. 'I'm going to bed now. If you want to sleep there's a bed in the room above here.'

Brendan grinned as he went up the stairs. 'I knew you would.'

Liam turned off the light and undressed in the dark. Through the window he could see the plain sweep of grass that covered the cliff and, beyond it, the faint gleam of stars on the water. No sound came from the kitchen.

He woke late, with a dull headache from all the beer and whisky. Brendan had gone, leaving only the empty mug and the bowl of food, uneaten.

Two days later a brown envelope came flapping through the kitchen door. No letter, but a small wad of used notes, neatly folded inside. More than Brendan had promised. Liam put the money in his pocket.

A month later, on the same day, another envelope arrived, and again the next. A regular payment, like a salary cheque. When the cold weather came he took himself into Dover and ordered a paraffin heater for his studio. The fumes mixed with the smell of paint, the snow melted off the roof. Contented, Liam settled down with his sketches of Ruth. The brief outlines of the child. She would bring him again. In the summer he would be quicker with his brush.

But the spring came and Ruth did not. All summer the cottage lay empty. Ruth did not come and he did not see the child and he had slipped in, tied himself with his brother, with the burn-scarred friend, other men whom he'd never seen, and it was only the money, and the thought that she might come, that kept him there waiting, long after he knew he should be gone.

Six

At six o'clock Joan was propped up on a pile of cushions in the displaced bed. The doctor had been and gone, speaking of night nurses and the need for Cyril to rest. The cushions supporting Joan's back laid bare the dark, angular corners of the armchairs. Cyril made no comment but his daughter saw him shift about. The uncushioned chairs would give him pain, aggravate the disc that had slipped when they were still children. She wondered if he ever thought of the cause, linked his sciatic twinge to those clumsy pirouettes with Simon on one arm and herself on the other, held aloft by the speed of the spin. How they had shrieked, she and her brother, delighted and terrified, how strong her daddy had seemed, how almighty.

She watched as he eased himself again, patting for the missing cushion. The pain might even be a comfort to him, she thought; as if the pain of the world were a finite thing, and by taking some upon himself he might somehow reduce the suffering of his wife.

Suzannah shivered. The cloud that had hazed the lunchtime sun had gone, along with the deacon, leaving the evening sky clear, the air warm and still. The chill was in the house, in the ticking of the clock, the clutter of furniture and the half-bare upstairs room. She found her mother's eyes, large and luminous in her shrinking face, shining on her.

'You'll be wanting to get back, darling,' she said, in the quiet, hoarse voice that even in the space of the weekend had become familiarly hers.

'I'll stay if you like.'

'No. You get on back. You've work to go to in the morning.'

Suzannah stood up. 'Is there anything I can get you, before I go?'

Joan's head waved slowly on the pillow. She wants me to go, thought Suzannah, she wants me to leave them alone. She crossed the room and took her mother's hand. Again there was nothing to say, nothing appropriate or far enough from the truth. What did Austin say, when he left? God bless you, probably – or something else, equally false. Suddenly, with a flutter of movement, Joan pulled her close. Her voice was no more than a whisper, barely audible, a shape of lips against her ears. 'Be wise, my darling. Don't try to take what cannot be yours.'

Suzannah pulled back. 'What?'

'This new man of yours. Nothing good can come of it.'

'I don't know what you mean.' Suzannah, too, was whispering. From behind came the sound of Cyril rising from his chair, crossing the room, leaving the door ajar.

'I know you, darling, I know this excitement in you. You think of him all the time.'

'I've said nothing . . . '

A finger rested, feather-light, on her lips. 'Hush now, I'm not criticising.'

Suzannah shook her head, trying to rise from the bed, and felt a tremor through the hand that held hers.

'What is it that makes you so guilty?' The hoarse whisper became a croak. 'Is he married?'

Suzannah looked away at the floor.

'Oh, my darling, try to be wise.'

She would not look, but sat with her face turned away until the feeble grip on her arm relaxed. The clock was chiming the quarter when at last she did look back. Her mother's eyes were closed, her mouth hanging open like an old woman's.

With pain in her throat, tears breaking on her cheeks, Suzannah packed her weekend bag. She heard her father in the hall, telephoning for a taxi.

Simon stood behind him on the porch, waving as the taxi pulled away.

She telephoned every evening, filling the time between coming home to the flat and the sound of Henry's car in the street, the grumble of the engine as he parked by the kerb. It was always Simon who answered, her little brother, sounding tired.

One evening he sounded less tired, a laugh in his voice as he picked up the phone.

'Is she better?'

A moment's silence.

'No, but Austin has been here, cheering her up.'

'Is she worse? If she is I'll come back but I can't take a lot of time off work.'

It wasn't true. She could take a week off, probably two. Henry could authorise it, a discreet note from the sixth floor. But she had not asked for leave, neither from the bank nor from Henry himself. It was Henry she could not leave. Their life together was a magical secret, of candlelight and romance, champagne and roses. She would not be the one to introduce sickness, death, the darkness outside the warm pod of his flat.

Their love was a dry-eyed, smiling thing, not to be smothered by talk of cancer, of priests and the ever-after.

I will only come if she is dying.

Shocking even herself with the unspoken thought, Suzannah hastened the conversation with Simon.

'Will she . . . is she . . . ?'

'We don't know, Suzannah, the doctor says you can't tell.

She went the next afternoon; a note to Personnel, seven days' compassionate leave; another note for Henry, left on the mantelpiece, below the gilt-edged bedroom mirror. No mention of death, or sickness. Three lines to say that she loved him dearly, and would soon be back in his arms. Easy words.

Simon looked thin, pale under his tan. Her father in the cushionless chair beside the displaced bed, grey-faced, stumble-speeched, drunk with sleeplessness. Simon sat in another chair, reading. There was nothing to do but wait. The clock in the hall rang out the quarters. Dimly, through the kitchen window, came the sounds of the neighbour's children, bubbles of laughter in the quiet air.

Word had got around that the patient would eat grapes, peeled and seeded; that she had, when still capable of speech, expressed a wish for them. Suzannah had never heard the wish, only learned of it, finding the fridge full of other people's dishes, tupperware boxes and favourite china bowls filled with black and green orbs, wet and fleshy without their skins, obscene, like gouged eyes.

We will never have grapes again, she thought, staring out at the darkening garden, when this is over.

When this is over. Once she is dead. The end of waiting. She thought how the clichés tripped off their tongues; there was nothing sensible to say, nothing that could not wound.

Joan's body had given way. Two stones lighter but she looked bigger somehow. They could see the full size of her head, the hair standing clear, and her eyes, wheeling round to Suzannah, staring with such intensity that her daughter was moved to look away.

The neighbour's children had a swing. She could see the tops of their heads bobbing up above the hedge as the swing lifted higher and higher. Noisy, gap-toothed, a question suddenly in her mind – were Henry's children like these?

Without thinking she put her wrist to her nose and sniffed. A drift of roses from the bottle of scent, breathtakingly expensive, left on the mantelpiece one night before he slipped away, back to his home in Cavanagh Road.

The scent clung sweetly; she let her hand rest against her cheek, feeling the softness of skin against skin, imagining his hand there, warm, manicured fingers touching her cheek. 'Suzannah,' whispering her name on his breath, 'you are all that I want for the rest of my life.'

The clock chimed once more. Seven-fifteen. He would be there now, coming in with his smile to find the flat dark and cold, her note on the mantelpiece where he had left her perfume of roses, absent for the very first time, without notice, without consent. She could see the pull of his brow, his brief sniff of discontent.

Looking back at the bed, at the piled cushions, at the mournful faces of her father and brother in the gloom, she felt impatient. Why could she not die sooner? Why keep me here in this dark house, making Henry annoyed?

In the morning the neighbour's children went swimming. Suzannah watched them through the window; carrier bags from the supermarket, stuffed with bright towels.

The doctor's coat was in the hall. As she walked down the stairs, Simon came to meet her. She turned away, unable to look at the distress on his face.

Someone had been outside, there was a trail of footsteps on the hall floor. Simon grabbed her arms.

'Mummy's dying!'

'Huh?' She had no word for it, only breath taken in surprise.

His face was fierce, her little brother again, arms flailing, hair as fine and wild as when he was a boy.

'But now, she is dying now!'

She thrust him aside. In the sitting room the doctor was looking at his watch; a death head on the sheet where her mother had been.

'It was very easy.'

Someone had left the french doors open, flooding the room with sunlight. It was her father who had gone outside. Through a lens of tears, Suzannah saw him clearly, wearing the same shirt he had worn the day before; standing on the grass, the trail of his footprints dark in the dew.

Seven

Crowds, like the chickens in Handel's yard; noisy, aimless. A crush of women, high heels and shopping baskets, pushing and pecking round the bus-stops outside the station.

Take the fast train to Victoria, the note had said, slipping out into his hand as he opened the familiar manilla envelope. The same typeface as the address label; the same typist then, the one he had always imagined, comfortable with spectacles, addressing the envelopes and counting the money.

He crossed the station concourse, weaving between heaps of rucksacks, multicoloured nylon, chattering foreigners lounging on the pavement. Outside, buses rumbled around the forecourt, there was a queue for taxis and another queue for pizzas. A photograph glared at him, a triangle of yellow dripping like melted plastic, he could smell the stall from as far as the traffic lights.

The streetnames were smeared black. Liam stopped a man with an umbrella. He knew nothing but asked Liam for a pound.

He walked in a circle, crossing dangerously against the lights. Why hadn't she sent him directions, for God's sake? Spared him a few typed words on the little square of paper that she folded so unobtrusively in the money? He saw a policeman on a corner and asked the way.

Speak to no one.

Mornington Court was a block of flats. Soot-dark bricks and dirty windows. A mangled pushchair lay wedged across the bottom of the stairs. He climbed over it. The stairwell stank of urine. There was litter in the corners and graffiti on the walls.

A radio played behind the door of Number Three. He

walked up another flight, and another. The door to Number Eight was ajar. He used his elbow to push it wide.

Faded floral wallpaper hung in torn strips from crumbling plaster. His shoes made prints on the dusty plank floor. A plastic washing line hung across the balcony, orange and yellow pegs dancing in the wind. The glass door to the balcony was broken. A pool of rain and soot had blown in. The floor in the bathroom was also wet, floorboards swollen like a sponge. In his mind was the planked window of the outhouse in Smithies' yard, the sunlight coming through the cracks, the spiders who watched patiently from the walls. He sat on the floor of the main room and waited.

An hour passed. A smell of frying drifted in from the landing. He had done as the message instructed. The last sentence read 'Burn this letter'. And so he had, taken it out into the yard and set it alight, watching the flames flap out in the breeze. There was nothing left to consult, to check if he had come to the right place.

He waited, squatting against the wall, blowing on his hands to keep them warm. Through the balcony railings he could see a café across the road, the windows all steamed over.

Another hour dragged past. The smell of frying faded, blunted as it sank into the stale air of the stairwell. Getting up, he spoke aloud. 'Bugger this, I want some food.'

He brushed plaster dust off his coat and walked cautiously down the stairs. There was no one about. In the café he ordered a toasted sandwich and sat on a high stool against a narrow shelf that served as a table. Hungrily he closed his teeth on the soft, buttered toast.

'You were told to speak to no one.'

The speaker was beside him. Short grey hair, a black raincoat with a collar of imitation fur.

Liam swallowed. 'I didn't know the way.'

'Two hours I've had to sit here. Waiting to see if you were followed.'

'I'm sorry.' Liam took another mouthful of sandwich. A slice of tomato had come adrift, hanging from the toast like a greasy tongue.

'Two hours! Do you know how many cups of tea it takes to fill two hours? Liver damage, that's what I'll get.'

'I've been waiting too.'

'Speak to no one, that's what you were told. No men with umbrellas. No policemen. That youngster couldn't take his eyes off you. Into his walkie-talkie the minute you turned your back. Are you thick or something?'

Liam looked around. The lunch bar was full.

'Why did you ask me to come?'

'It was a test.'

'A test?'

The man sipped his tea. 'You failed.'

An advertisement for milk had been stuck to the wall above the counter. It was torn, a corner of blue paper hung free. The sellotape was yellow, dimpled where the damp had come between its film and the gloss wall.

Liam ate the rest of the sandwich. 'Can I go then?' he asked, wiping his hands on a paper serviette.

'Not so fast.' The man held the sleeve of his coat. 'You haven't been paid for nothing.'

'I haven't been paid to come here,' said Liam.

The man ignored him. 'Listen to me carefully.' Liam could see a rash of spots on his chin. Little red pimples with yellow heads. 'I'm going to take my cup back to the counter and then I'm going to the bog.' His thumb gestured to the door at the back. 'While I'm gone I want you to leave.'

'Why don't I just walk out now?'

'Because I'm giving you instructions.' The man still had hold of his sleeve. 'Go back to the flat and look in the cupboard under the sink. You will find a blue box. One of those insulated picnic boxes. Pick it up. Don't look inside.' The man interrupted himself to squeeze Liam's arm. 'Don't look inside,' he repeated. 'Just pick it up, take it out into the street and go home with it.'

'Take it back to Smithies?'

The man nodded. 'Hide it. In a month or two someone will fetch it away.'

The box was heavy. He could barely lift it down the stairs, almost lost his balance heaving it over the pushchair. Outside it had begun to rain. There were few cabs in sight. By the time he saw a 'For Hire' sign the lid of the box was shiny with water.

Another policeman stood on the corner. Liam sat well back.

The box was like something alive on the floor beside his feet. The queue for taxis stepped forward as the cab swung into the station. He saw their eyes on the box and hurried away, afraid of how they would remember him. On the train he dried the lid with his coat and slid the box into the gap between the backs of the train seats so that only a corner of blue plastic was visible. Rain wooshed against the windows as they left the station, its loud clatter drowning the noise of the wheels.

He kept the box in the kitchen, under the sink as they had kept it in Mornington Court. He checked it twice a day, running his fingers around the lid, fighting the urge to slip the catch and look inside. He did not look. It could be another test, nothing but bricks or scrap metal. Or not a test, layers of plastic sticks, grey putty, whatever form it took now, their vengeance.

He had sold seven pictures by the time they took it away. Easter brought the tourists. He spread landscapes along the quay wall, put up his prices and they paid what he asked; lovely women in high shorts, Americans with fat wallets, hitch-hikers from Europe who paused at the figures, laughed at Handel's sheep and paid money for the sunsets, pink skies and pink water.

Enid Evans watched him through the shop window. Glyn had come along, meek-faced, and offered him ten pounds for the old sketch of Enid with her carrots.

'It's a likeness,' he said, chewing on his pipe. 'I know she's no beauty but it is a likeness.'

Enid chuckled as she wrapped his cheese. 'I saw you with the tourist girls!'

Liam set up his easel and offered twenty minute portraits for five pounds. Children were made to queue. He grew stiff from squatting, straining to copy the soft, unformed features.

The candle blossoms had fallen, Matilda's leaves were in full bloom once more. He met Mrs Handel in Smithies Lane. She had her apron on.

'Are they coming, then?'

'They are. Just for a weekend. Mr Alland sent a telegram. I've to go in and air the place.'

'Only a weekend?'

'Crying shame, I call it. This lovely house lying empty all this time.'

'Why don't they let it?'

Mrs Handel scowled. 'You never know what you'll get with tenants.'

'Weirdos you mean?'

She nodded darkly. 'Artists and all sorts.'

Liam threw back his head and laughed.

'You may laugh, Mr McGuinness. Landlord took a big chance with you.'

Liam held open the gate. 'This weekend, is it?'

Mrs Handel nodded. 'Shocking, I call it.' She put her key in the latch. 'Shocking.'

Liam went home, smiling.

The kitchen door was open, the cupboard door agape. An empty shelf where the box had been.

No note.

No message.

Only the absence of the box.

He put his coat back on and went down to The Swan for a pint.

Eight

The washing machine thrummed. She lay in bed and listened to the regular thump of the drum. Bright yellow light looked in around the curtains, showing through the flower pattern. It will be too much, her mother had warned. It's too strong a pattern. Suzannah had never admitted that she was right, that her bedroom was overpowering, a trap, flowers leaping from the walls and windows, even from the bed, a floral cave, ugly and stifling.

She swung her feet out of the bed. The machine had gone into spin, a high, rising whine. When it reached full speed the casing would start to shudder, make a noise like the chattering of giant teeth. Gassy had been predicting its breakdown for years, but still it thundered and whined and shuddered, spewing clean linen when the cycle was complete. Barefoot, Suzannah descended the stairs. The noise stopped just as she reached the bottom, the last creaking turn of the drum defiant in the silence that crept in after it.

The housekeeper was on her knees before the open door, hauling sheets into a plastic basket.

'Shall I put them out for you?'

'That would be a mercy.' Gassy groaned as she pulled herself upright. 'These are the last of your poor mother's sheets. All the others are done. I never thought the machine would survive the load it's had to bear.'

'Perhaps Dad will think about a new one soon,' Suzannah said, lifting the basket from the floor.

'Better late than never.'

'Where are the pegs?'

Gassy reached into the larder and handed her a bag. 'There should be enough in there.'

Suzannah opened the back door.

'He's said I can stay, you know. He wants me to stay on and look after him.'

'Of course he does,' said Suzannah. 'He'll need you more than ever now.'

'I was worried, I thought perhaps with you staying home and all . . . '

'Me, staying?' Suzannah hitched the basket against her hip.

'You are, aren't you? Staying to look after your father?'

Suzannah stared.

'It's none of my business, I know.' Gassy shook her head. 'I just assumed, with you having no husband to look after, and your poor mother gone, that you'd be stopping home to look after him.'

Suzannah turned the door handle. 'I think you're mistaken,' she said, stepping out into the sun.

There was a sponge on the washing line, a faded blue sponge with the line threaded through a hole in the centre. It was Gassy's invention, a relic of the dark back street in which she had been raised, where unwiped washing lines left black streaks on clean clothes. Suzannah pulled the sponge the length of the line. It collected only a remnant of dew but she could feel

Gassy's satisfied eyes on her back. It would give her something, thought Suzannah, show some softness in this hard girl who did not know her daughterly duty.

A breeze blew the sheet against her face, a damp caress of cotton. The last of your poor mother's sheets, Gassy had said. Suzannah let the cool cloth blow against her. Mother hadn't said look after your father. Nothing of that. Be wise. Those were her words.

And you with no husband to look after. As if that was all a woman could do, look after men.

I would look after Henry.

It is Henry who needs me.

If it weren't for Ruth we'd be married by now. There'd be no talk of coming home to look after my father.

Suzannah jammed a peg on to the corner of a pillow case. Damn Ruth!

The pillow case flapped out in the breeze.

'Damn mother!' The words blew out into the wind. 'Damn mother, for dying.'

Her father was wearing his dressing gown. She caught him in the sitting room, with a guilty face, pushing the stopper back into the decanter.

But Cyril, it's only half past ten.

She saw him start, as if he too had heard the words, her mother's voice filling the silence. With a gesture of defiance he raised his glass to Suzannah. 'Will you have one?'

Suzannah rubbed her arms. 'It is a bit early, Dad.'

Her father lowered himself into a chair. 'I won't hit the bottle.' His voice was weary. 'I won't become a drunk, if that's what you are thinking.'

'I hadn't thought it, Dad.' Suzannah moved towards the sideboard. 'Who makes the rules anyway?' She filled a sherry glass and sat in the chair facing him. The furniture had been restored, moved twice: the first time when her father and Simon had carried the empty bed back upstairs and then a second time, for the funeral, chairs and sofa pushed back to make room for the crowd who littered the carpet anew, with pastry crumbs and shards of potato crisps.

Only Gassy had cried at the service. Suzannah stood between

her father and Simon, supported by the close, dark suits, dry-eyed, watching Austin as he stepped up into the pulpit to read the lesson. Mother must have told him, she thought, someone must have told him what to read. She felt her brother stir beside her at the familiar tale of the lost sheep, the story they had liked best at bedtime, years ago.

At the end of the reading Austin closed the Bible with a soft thud. She looked up to find his eyes upon her, serious and sad. He turned away and left the pulpit as the priest at the altar resumed the service.

Suzannah stared at the coffin.

Be wise, darling.

It was hard to believe they burned the coffins. All that polished wood and plush silk going to waste. Surely there were men on the other side of the curtain, waiting to decant the body. Surely a van waited outside to take the coffin away for re-use. She wouldn't mind, not as much as she minded the beautiful polished wood, so briefly glimpsed, burning.

The engines began, a mechanical hum as the coffin moved slowly towards the curtain. Beside her in the pew Simon shuffled his feet, cleared his throat. Her father stood pale and still. At the end of the service she held his hand and led him to the car. It was Simon who lingered on the steps outside, playing the host, inviting people back for 'drinks'.

Cyril had sat in the same chair as now throughout the afternoon, facing the window and barely, it seemed, hearing the words of condolence, the murmurings and whisperings, felt his hand shaken or his shoulder squeezed. The guests hovered away from him, preferring to speak to Simon who had somehow managed to retain his tan, his glowing good health, in the silent house.

'When will you go back to Hong Kong, Simon?'

The same question a hundred times over, everybody wanting to think forwards, to remind him of life and the future.

'I shall have to go quite soon.' His answer was invariably polite. 'They won't keep my job for ever.'

'I expect Suzannah will stay on for a while?'

And again, Simon would smile. 'I expect she will.'

'It is easier for girls.'

'And she doesn't have a career.'

In the kitchen Suzannah helped Gassy warm the *vol au vents*, rinsed glasses and crumpled crisp packets into the bin. When finally she emerged, the crowd had gone. The pile of tupperware and china, emptied of peeled grapes, had been reclaimed. Only an aunt remained, her mother's sister, and a husband whose name she could not remember. They stood with Simon in the dining room, still shaking their heads and exclaiming at the suddenness of it all. 'I only saw her last Christmas, she looked fine then!'

Simon nodded loyally.

Seeing Suzannah alone, the aunt took her to one side.

'I know this isn't the time, but . . .' She paused, sucking her teeth. Suzannah looked at the bony fingers, burdened with rings. 'I would like a memento of your mother. When you're, you know, clearing up. I don't mind what it is. She always said I could have the little card-table from her sitting room. If she ever,' the aunt cleared her throat, 'you know. She said if she went first . . . But I wouldn't mind what it was. Just a memento – anything will do.'

Suzannah opened the door of the sitting room.

'There it is,' cried the aunt, 'in the corner over there.'

Beside the card-table, a man sat on the arm of her father's chair. The back of a dark suit. Austin. He had his hand on her father's shoulder. In the light from the windows she could see the wet streaks on her father's face, his lips pulled tight with the effort of weeping.

Austin's voice was low and smooth. '. . . Into thy hands we commend her spirit . . . '

The aunt backed away from the door. Suzannah shuddered. She wanted to run, but stood rooted, a terrible convulsion rising in her throat.

'Mummy!' she screamed at last. 'Mummy, Mummy, what have they done to you?'

Her father turned, hands flying up to wipe his cheeks. Austin, too, turned, frowning. The aunt ran into the hall, pulled her from behind; black crêpe and hard, bruising rings. Through the noise of her weeping she could hear their voices. Austin had turned away; even before they closed the door, turned back to her father, beginning again: 'Into thy hands . . . '

The aunt and her husband were leaving, edging out towards their car. Suzannah's outburst was over. She had washed her face, allowed her aunt to powder her nose. The aunt sniffed a good deal; the bangles on her arms rattled; it was a kind of penance to let the poor woman comb her hair.

'It's just like Joan's,' she said. 'Your mother had lovely hair when she was a girl.'

Outside, on the drive, Simon shook the husband's hand. The aunt dispensed bony hugs and proceeded into the car. 'You won't forget about the little table, my dear.'

Suzannah shook her head. The car moved slowly down the drive, past the fading blooms of the laburnum, and out into the road with a final wave of black crêpe.

Suzannah stood behind her brother on the porch. 'She wants the card-table.'

'The card-table?'

She nodded. 'As a memento. Apparently Mother promised it to her.'

'I don't believe that.' Simon sniffed. 'It was Ma's favourite piece of furniture. When did she ask you?'

'Just now. As she said goodbye.'

'I'm surprised she didn't want to take it right away. It'll be years before they come and visit Dad.'

'Perhaps she did.'

'And didn't have the guts to suggest it?' Simon kicked a polished black shoe against one of the big stones that marked the border of the drive.

'Would you like to go for a walk?' Suzannah asked, on an impulse.

'All right.'

'Ought we to tell Dad – in case he wonders?'

'No!' Her brother put out his hand. 'Leave him now. Austin is still talking to him.'

Suzannah remembered the little scene in the sitting room, the deacon's mellifluous voice reciting the psalm.

'I'm sorry I made a fuss.'

Simon shrugged. 'I wish I could have screamed, too. All those dreadful people drinking to her death.' Once more he kicked the stone. 'All of them like mother's sister, I suppose, eyeing the place for mementoes.'

Suzannah wanted to apologise again, for behaving like a child, for screaming. The scene remained in her mind's eye: Austin's back, her father's tears. Suzannah will stay behind. It's easier for girls.

'Come on.' Simon led the way along the drive, pausing to lift a wind-blown twig from the gravel. 'Dad'll have to get someone to do the garden. He can't manage it on his own.'

'Gassy's husband has been cutting the grass.'

'I know, but only as a temporary thing.' Simon smiled. 'It's hard to imagine Gassy having a husband.'

They walked out into the road. Austin's car was on the grass verge, displaced by the cars of visitors that had filled the drive before he arrived. They walked in silence. With surprise Suzannah remembered that it was a weekday. People were at work. Henry would be sitting in his office on the sixth floor, overlooking the river. Would he think of her, of the funeral? She had told him on the phone of Joan's death, the doctor's quiet pronouncement, her father standing on the lawn in yesterday's shirt.

A small sigh on the wire.

'It's over then, you can come back to me?'

'After the funeral, Henry.'

'When is the funeral?' Brusque; she had the impression that there was someone else in the room with him.

'Can't you come back in the meantime?'

'It's just for a few days, Henry. I must stay here and be with my father.'

'Don't stay too long, Suzannah.' She heard the impatience in his voice. 'I need you here with me in London. I'm lonely.'

The last words were whispered, full of intimacy. The annoyance she felt dribbled away. This was the way he had won from the beginning, by needing her, making her indispensable to himself.

They reached the main road, Simon's polished shoes clicking on the tarmac. Her own shoes pinched, new black courts and tights too warm for the day.

'I want to ask a favour of you,' said Simon as they turned onto the bridle path. 'I want you to come with Dad and see me off to Hong Kong.'

'When are you going?'

'On Thursday morning.'

'So soon?'

'I must. They want me back.'

'OK. I'll come down as far as London with you. You can drop me near the flat.'

'No. I want you to come to Heathrow and then come home with Dad afterwards.'

'I can't do that, Simon. I have to go back to work.'

'You must, you can't leave Dad alone so soon.'

'Why must I? Why should it be me who stays? I may not be a lawyer in Hong Kong, but I do have a life too, you know.'

Simon raised his voice. 'I'm not saying you don't. I'm just asking you this favour.' His hands fiddled at his collar, loosening the knotted black tie.

'Dad's got to be alone sooner or later. He's got to get used to it sometime,' cried Suzannah. 'I want to go back to London, Simon. I've had enough, just the same as you.'

They were shouting now, oblivious to the passing cars, other people on the path; brother and sister, quarrelling as they had done as children.

'It's not Dad I'm thinking of.'

'Who then? Yourself? You'd never forget yourself for a minute! You wouldn't be the one to stay behind. You've got a big important job in Hong Kong. The whole colony has come to a standstill without the great Simon Haig at the helm!'

Simon stabbed his forefinger in the air. 'Yes, I am thinking of me. I'm asking you to do something for me! But it's my mistake, I had forgotten how selfish and stubborn you are. You never did care whom you hurt, so long as Suzannah could do what she liked, everyone else could burn!' He stormed away from her, back in the direction of the house.

Suzannah ran after him, caught hold of his arm.

'Why does he have to go to the airport at all?'

'He wants to, to see me off.'

'Did he ask you if I would come?'

'No.' Simon shook his head. 'It is me who is asking you, for my sake.'

'Why?'

'Because . . .' Simon pulled his arm free and stuffed his hands in his pockets. 'Because I couldn't bear to see him waving goodbye with no Mum there.' His voice dropped and with the gesture of a small boy he wiped his nose on the sleeve of his shirt.

Suzannah moved closer to him. 'Why didn't you tell me that was the reason, Squirty?'

'I've been trying to.' Simon sniffed and then laughed. 'You haven't called me Squirty for years.'

Suzannah slipped her arm into his. 'I haven't seen you for years. It's still a good name for you, even if you have grown so big.'

They walked back along the road. In the hedgerow blackberries were beginning to show, little globular buds forcing out in the place where their flowers had been.

Austin's car was pulling out of the lane. He turned swiftly, taking advantage of a gap in the traffic. An arm waved to them through the open window.

'The deacon has taken a shine to you,' said Simon.

'Nonsense.'

'He has. It's obvious.'

'It's not obvious at all.'

'You admit it then?'

'I do not. For God's sake, can you see me going out with a deacon?'

Simon laughed. 'He'd be good for you.'

'I doubt it. In any case, you're imagining things.'

Simon poked her, less than gently, in the ribs. 'I believe you've taken a fancy yourself, Miss Haig.'

'I have not! In any case – ' she thrust her chin up in defiance – 'I'm already spoken for.'

'Spoken for?'

'Yes.'

'Anyone I know?'

'I doubt it.'

'May I know his name?'

Suzannah was silent.

'It is someone I know.'

'It's possible you know of him, he's in the City.'

'So, why the mystery?'

She stopped to ease the heel of her shoe.

'Is he married?' Simon's eyes were sharp. 'He is, isn't he?

Really, Suzannah!'

'Don't be so prim.'

'Is it serious, or is he just one of your throw-aways?'

She felt herself blushing. 'He is certainly no throw-away.'

'Does Father know?'

'I'd prefer it if he didn't.'

'Did Mother know?'

Suzannah looked away. 'I think she guessed.'

Simon took her arm, as if to steer her along the path. 'What is it with you, Suzannah, you have all those City wimps to choose from – why go for a married man?'

She shook her head. 'Perhaps he has something they don't.'

'Suzannah!' He pursed his lips. 'We'd better get you married right away. I can't have my sister behaving like a floozie.'

'It's not like that.'

'What is it like, then?'

'We're in love. I mean everything to him.'

'But you still give the eye to a passing priest.'

'I did not! And in any case, he's not a priest, he's a deacon.'

'Priestling, then, as in duckling-about-to-become-duck.' Simon chuckled. 'I can just see you in a vicarage – in a backless dress and fishnet tights.'

Suzannah giggled. 'I'd wear my tee shirt with the big armholes, where you can see everything sideways.'

'Perfect!'

Laughing, arm in arm, they turned into the drive, stopping abruptly at the sight of their father on the porch. His face was the colour of whey. In his hand was an armchair cushion. He held it vaguely towards Suzannah.

'Gassy doesn't sew,' he said, sounding faintly puzzled. 'She says her eyes aren't up to it.'

Suzannah took the cushion from his hand. A seam had come undone. Through the gap squeezed a lining of scarlet silk, latticed by the spreading stiches of the seam. All at once Suzannah could see her mother by the window, cutting a thread on her teeth, frowning as she held a needle up to the light.

'I can mend it, Daddy,' she said, hoarse-voiced.

Nine

The house was quiet, cool after the warm crushed air of the train. From the ground floor came the cry of a child. A thin, bored wail, muffled by carpets and heavy wooden doors that had graced the house long before it was converted into flats. On a table in the communal hall lay two letters. She put them in her mouth, looking for her keys as she climbed the stairs.

A brass key into the latch and the internal front door swung open. Henry had been; a dozen red roses in a vase by the door, a note beneath it: 'To my darling girl.'

I have seen enough flowers, she thought. Henry wouldn't think of it, the mountains of wreaths and bouquets, her father's bold white cross, laid out uselessly in the stone garden of the crematorium. Enough flowers for a lifetime.

She filled the kettle with water and opened the first envelope. A statement from the bank, a list of her cheques and in the credit column a Standing Order, five hundred pounds marked H. Alland.

The second envelope contained a brief letter; steady handwriting slanting across the page.

> Suzannah,
> Just a note to say that the invitation to lunch stands. You won't be poisoned and you might enjoy it.
>
> If you would like to telephone me I am usually here in the evening and early in the morning. Otherwise it is a matter of luck.
>
> Yours,
> Austin.

Lunch with a priest.

Priestling, priest-not-yet.

The kettle switched itself off.

What harm could it do?

But he will talk about God.

Suzannah shrugged, dismissing herself. He has never mentioned God.

Except at the funeral.

She looked at her watch. Quarter to seven. He might be there, if no one was actually dying.

A voice answered. Not Austin.

'Hello?'

'Is Austin there?'

'Is that Suzannah?'

She hesitated, it was a man's voice, but not Austin's.

'Yes – '

'He's down at St Luke's, but he'll be back before nine. They called him out just before tea. He said you might ring.'

'He said I might ring?'

'He did. I'm Brother Bernard, by the way.'

He sounded old, courteous. Suzannah smiled into the phone. 'How do you do.'

'I'll look forward to meeting you, my dear.'

'Is he so sure I'll come?'

'Oh, yes.' The old man laughed. 'I've promised to go out.'

'To go out?'

'He didn't ask me to, not in so many words, but I'll be going to the cricket anyway, as it's Saturday.'

'What Saturday?'

'The Saturday after next. That's when you're coming, isn't it?' His voice grew faint. 'He's written it on the calendar.' The voice returned. 'Here it is, Suzannah Haig, twelve thirty.'

'We haven't agreed the date,' said Suzannah. Nor even the event itself, she thought.

'Well, if you stay for the afternoon I might meet you at teatime. Goodbye, my dear. I'll tell him you rang.'

'Goodbye.' Suzannah put down the phone, kicked off her shoes.

The bloody nerve.

I shan't go.

Not on Saturday. I'll tell him I've got something arranged.

She thought of Henry. I'll tell him I've got a date with my lover.

But you haven't. Never on a Saturday. He spends Saturdays at Cavanagh Road.

Assuaging his guilt.

I'll tell him I have to keep Daddy company.

He would ask Daddy to lunch, too.

God forbid!

Why not?

It wouldn't be the same.

The same as . . . ?

Seeing Austin alone.

The phone shrilled under her hand.

'Austin?'

'Who is Austin?'

'Oh Henry, it's you.'

'Of course it's me. Who is Austin?' Spoken sharply.

'I'm sorry, I was half asleep.' A little lie.

'And dreaming of Austin?'

'He's a sort of priest.'

Henry laughed. 'A priest! Well then, I have nothing to fear.'

'Don't, Henry, don't mock.'

There was a silence at the other end of the phone. Then, as if he had changed gear, Henry began to speak in a cheerful voice.

'Suzie, my love. How are you?'

'I'm all right.'

She carried the phone towards the chair and rested it in her lap. 'I'm glad it's over.'

'Good. Now you can get back to normal. How about the Paradiso for lunch tomorrow? That should put the colour in your cheeks.'

She felt herself smiling into the phone. 'Henry, that would be lovely.'

'And I've got a surprise for you.'

'What is it?'

'I'll tell you tomorrow.'

A noise came down the receiver, the sound of a mouthpiece being kissed, then he was gone.

Late in the evening she sat by the kitchen window and opened a pot of yoghurt. A shower of rain had left the cars parked below looking new-washed, tinged with pink by the evening sun. The sky was also pink, dappled by clouds like pink puffs of dough waiting for the oven. In the distance, under a wider layer of cloud, like a pool of spilled milk, lay the rooftops of Cavanagh Road. She had been there once, early in the spring, counted the houses until she faced his imposing facade of red bricks and tall windows. The lawn was a flat rectangle, surrounded by dark, treated soil in which stood uniform rose bushes, cut back to their stumps. She waited on the pavement, staring up at the carved front door, a brass knocker, the head of a snarling tiger. A light came on in the window downstairs. She had a glimpse of high ceilings, tall bookcases, then a figure came to the window. It was Henry, closing the curtains.

Using a teaspoon to eat the yoghurt, she turned the pages of the Sunday paper. Henry had ordered it for her, to help fill the hours when he could not be with her. She read it dutifully, every weekend, so that she would know what he had read and be of interest to him. Lately she had realised that he was not interested in what she had read, or even what she thought, if it was of other than him.

The front page of the paper reported the discovery of a terrorist cell; a cache of arms, plans to plant a string of bombs around England. Two men had been caught. They were looking for a girl.

The report made much of the bomber's inventiveness, the skill of their designs.

She turned to the inside pages. Foreign News. Terror was in vogue. There had been bombs in Paris, a hijack in the Far East. In Africa a petrol-filled tyre set alight around the neck was called a necklace.

Staring out of the window, she tried to imagine it. The bombing would be abstract; a strategy, a plan, planted months in advance; activities far removed from fatal wounds and showering glass. But the petrol necklace would be immediate; a certain frenzy required to tie the victim down, fit the tyre and set the match, a degree of hysteria. Yet perhaps this too was planned, a supply of tyres kept handy, the heroes popping down to the filling station with a jerry can.

Suzannah shuddered, folding the newspaper to one side. There was nothing in it to talk about. Henry would declare such dark topics unsuitable on the lips of his Suzie, inappropriate for a lunch in the Paradiso arranged for the purpose of making her happy, erasing the death of her mother from their conversational menu.

Nevertheless she mentioned the necklaces, the bombings,

even her mother in an oblique way, between the lobster bisque and chef's special chicken which was no more than a breast stuffed with frozen spinach.

'Suzannah! You've got to put all that behind you!' Henry put down his fork and took her hand in his across the crisp white cloth.

'I keep thinking of her, Henry. I keep thinking of my mother. It's such a little time ago that she was telling me to be happy, that life is so short.'

'She was right.' He squeezed her hand. 'Life is here to enjoy. Not to spend worrying about dying.'

'But she was gone so quickly.' Suzannah felt a prickling of tears. 'She was fine at Christmas. She wanted to know who gave me those earrings. I lied to her, Henry, I didn't tell her about you. Now she's dead.' Feebly she clicked her fingers. 'Stuffed into an expensive box and flung on the fire.'

'Suzannah . . .' His smooth voice followed the movement of his fingers, stroking her arm. 'My darling girl, you mustn't think like this. Those priests have made you morbid.' Raising himself he pulled his chair closer to hers.

She rested her head on his shoulder, feeling the grain of the suitcloth against her cheek.

'Will you come over this evening, Henry? Will you come to the flat?'

'Of course I will, darling.' He sat up. 'But on one condition.'

'What is that?'

'That we have no more tears spoiling your pretty face.'

'I promise,' she said, meekly. 'No more tears.'

Ten

She put on a dress of scarlet silk. One that he liked because it clung to her hips and swung as she walked and had cost more than she might have paid for a good winter coat.

And perfume, and high shoes, and fine denier stockings that slithered on her legs.

'Henry!'

His cheeks were cold.

'Come inside into the warm.'

He looked her up and down, smiling.

'You are a beautiful woman, Suzannah.' He held her close, nuzzled her ear. 'I could eat you.'

She laughed, pulled away.

Tall candles flickered as she opened the door of the kitchen. 'I've made a special supper for us, to make up for being so unhappy at lunchtime.'

She felt him hesitate beside her and ran on before he could speak. 'Oh, please say you'll stay. I've made it all specially for you.'

He shook his head. 'I can't stay tonight, Suzannah.'

'Just for supper?'

He pulled her close. 'Darling girl, what can I do? Nothing would please me more than to stay the whole night, every night, with you.' He moved up behind her. She felt a soft kiss, like the stroke of a feather on her neck. 'But just because I can't stay doesn't mean we can't celebrate.'

'What is there to celebrate?'

'I told you last night on the telephone, I have a surprise for you. I would have told you at lunchtime if you hadn't been so miserable.' He was pulling a bottle from his briefcase.

'Champagne! Why?'

'Because I'm attending a special weekend seminar.'

'A seminar?'

'With you!'

She clung to his arm. 'A whole weekend!'

'A whole weekend.' He was easing the top off with his thumbs. 'We're going up to my cottage. We'll leave on Friday night and stay until Sunday.'

'What about Ruth?'

He faltered, just a fraction, a crack of a second between her question and the smooth, soothing reply. 'I've told her about the seminar.'

'Does she believe you?'

'Of course.'

'But she must suspect something, you've never had a weekend seminar before.'

'She knows there are changes going on at the bank. We're all going on courses to keep up with the new technology.'

There was a small pop and the liquid bubbled into their glasses.

'To us, darling.'

She raised her glass. 'To our first whole weekend.' Together they drank champagne and kissed over the bubbles.

Though he could not stay for supper, they had time to make love before he hurried away.

'Can't you ring and say you've been delayed?'

Henry shook his head, pulling on his trousers. 'I'm late as it is. We're going to Michael's school concert. He's playing percussion.'

Suzannah suppressed her answer, the memory of her own school concerts, all the tone-deaf children sent to play triangles.

Eleven

The journey took more than two hours; fighting clear of the city and then the motorway, clogged with traffic for the ferries. Suzannah sat back, cradled in soft leather. The car was a cocoon, muffling the world. She remembered the first time she had sat in it. The voice in her ear: This is a married man.

He had singled her out. From a circle of people, a reception at the merchant bank where she had been one of the junior staff chatting uneasily with the people from the sixth floor. He had singled her out. Smiling, working his way around the group, eliminating as he went, until he stood to one side of her, a little behind, so that to answer his question she had to turn away from the rest and give him her exclusive attention.

She could no longer remember what the question had been,

or how he had made her turn to look at him; only his smile, and the fresh glass of champagne that he put in her hand.

Later in the evening he rested his hand on her arm, it felt cool, soothing. 'You look a bit pale,' he said, and the smile on his lips was warm. She remembered looking at his mouth, the way the smooth-shaven skin showed laugh lines on either side, a hint of maturity and experience. 'Let me get you another glass of champagne.'

'No, really . . . '

But he was already reaching for a glass. He kept his other hand on her arm, resting against the table, camouflaged by a display of flowers.

'I think you need some supper, Suzannah. I know just the place.'

'But – ' She was about to say, what about your wife? The champagne moistened her tongue. Perhaps he meant to bring his wife too?

He squeezed her arm, very gently.

'I'll be back in a moment.'

She waited by the flowers. The pressure of his hand remained. For an instant she saw him again. He was helping a woman into her coat, holding out the sleeves and settling the collar. The woman smiled and Suzannah saw him smile back, and saw how mechanical his smile could be. This was not the way he had looked at her. She watched as he guided the woman through the door.

Had anyone noticed? She looked at the people around her. The loud voices were false, as fragile as the glasses dancing in their fingers; no one was looking at her.

'I know just the place.' He was back again, his hand once more discreetly touching her arm.

'And your wife?'

'She wanted to go home,' he smiled. 'I've put her in a taxi.'

Suzannah paused. A waiter re-filled her glass.

He is a married man.

'My car is in the basement. I'll bring it up and collect you from the door.'

She combed her hair in the cloakroom and put on her coat.

Perhaps I could just go. If I jumped into a taxi he might not see me. He wouldn't wait for long. He would come out of the car park, find me gone, and go home.

She tucked her bag under her arm and hurried down the steps. There were no taxis. From an underground gate came the flash of headlights, a long, shiny car nosing up to the road. He pulled up by the kerb and got out to open the door for her. She sat on soft leather, saw a child's seat strapped into the back. He is married. He has children. She felt the clutch of gravity as the car accelerated away down the night-empty street.

He looked the same now, driving to his cottage, as he had done that first night; in the dim light of the oncoming cars his face was stern, determined, rather than happy.

'Did Ruth say anything?'

He shook his head.

'What will she do this weekend?'

He shrugged. 'Much the same as usual, I expect. The boys keep her busy.'

She reached towards the steering-wheel and touched his hand. 'Does it make you feel guilty?'

A little smile softened his frown. 'Nothing about you could make me feel guilty.'

'Even if she suspects?'

He glanced away from the road. 'Suzannah, don't worry about things that don't concern you.'

She stared out at the traffic. On the left they passed a blur of lights against the sky, Canterbury, the cathedral welling up out of the darkness.

'Look, Henry, isn't it beautiful?'

He barely glanced across. She remembered that he would have seen the cathedral before, many times; that this journey was familiar, just as their destination was familiar, part of the fabric of his life.

'It must have been an astonishing sight for the pilgrims,' she said.

'It wasn't floodlit then.'

'No, but even in daylight it must have been impressive.'

She looked back at him but his head was turned, looking over his shoulder as the car swung into the outside lane, streaking past lorries and tankers. The needle registered ninety miles an hour. There was no need to hurry. They had the whole weekend. But Henry drove as he seemed to live, always at a pace, as if he were afraid of being left behind.

She remembered the first roses he had sent her, a dozen long-stemmed roses, and a note tied with ribbon: 'I don't want to wait to love you. I love you now. You are the woman I have been looking for all my life.'

They left the motorway behind. She peered out into the countryside, at darkened fields, a line of hills, softly rounded. The roadsign said Dover. A ribbon of lights marked the approach road. Henry took another turning, bypassing the town, the castle looming on the cliff. The road was quiet and dark, villages flashed by, like a series of film stills, then he was turning right, down between the cliffs. Another village, flat-fronted houses, the lights of a pub spilling over the pavement, and then the car turned into the dark, a steep ascent, phosphorescence on the sea and a line of trees.

'Here we are.'

He parked the car behind the trees; leaf-laden branches overhanging a lawn. An overgrown hydrangea, purple in the car lights, almost blocked the path to the door.

The cottage was large; hardly a cottage at all. A steep tiled roof hanging low over white-squared windows, a front door of solid oak. Henry carried their bags upstairs. Suzannah waited in the hall. She could see a sitting room, an open fire-place flanked by cavernous armchairs of brown leather, cracking a little around the buttons. The storage heaters were on, the floor in the hall glossy with wax. Through the french windows of the dining room she caught a glimpse of grass, a glimmer of light on the sea beyond. There was no sign of a telephone. The bookcase in the hall was crammed with paperbacks.

'They're all detective stories,' said Henry, tumbling down the staircase, two steps at a time. 'They were Aunt Matilda's. Almost everything here was hers.'

She followed him into the kitchen. Dark oak beams and an old-fashioned dresser. Propped against the dresser was a note. 'Eggs and bacon in the fridge. Evans will keep a loaf for you.'

'Who is Evans?'

'She runs the village shop. She sells just about everything, even postage stamps.

'That's useful.'

'Yes, if you can stand her curiosity. Her husband owns the garage next door, between them they know everything about everyone.'

He held her hand as they went upstairs. The main bedroom had a wide bay window with an upholstered seat beneath. There were two smaller rooms, the third with a painted cot tucked under the slope of the roof.

Henry's suitcase was neatly packed; his leather shaving bag matched the suitcase and bore his initials in gold. In the bottom were two pairs of shoes, each with its tree in place. She put them in the wardrobe and hung his clothes above them. On a shelf above the rack was a photograph album.

She took it down and sat on the bed. Squares of coloured paper, carefully mounted; a woman in a bottle-green dress, smiling; Henry smiling, a boy in school uniform scowling; older pictures, a young woman holding a baby, curly hair tied into a bow.

Henry came out of the bathroom wearing a heavy silk dressing gown and black backless slippers. His wet hair was carefully combed, exposing a shiny expanse of forehead.

'Is this Ruth?'

He looked down at the album in her lap.

'Where did you find that?'

'It was on the shelf in the wardrobe.' Suzannah repeated her question, pointing to the girl holding the baby. 'Is this Ruth?'

He looked over her shoulder. 'That was just after Michael was born.'

The young face stared back at Suzannah, open and happy.

She looked at the more recent pictures. 'She has changed, Henry.'

He was looking at his face in the dressing-table mirror. 'Yes,' he said, 'she has.'

Suzannah looked again. It was hard to imagine that the smiling girl with the baby had become the woman in the bottle-green dress. The blonde hair had faded to grey, more crushed than curled. The knitted dress showed the spread of her hips.

She turned a page of the album. Here were pictures of Cavanagh Road. A baby lying in an armchair. She peered at the upholstery, drinking in the details, the square of wallpaper visible in the corner, a drape of velvet, an impression of great luxury and comfort, the fine weave of his life.

His dressing gown rustled as he sat beside her on the bed. He put his arm round her waist.

'It's marvellous up here at this time of year.' She smelt toothpaste on his breath. 'Tomorrow you'll see the beach.'

He turned to the back of the album. 'This is where we are.' He pointed. 'This is the view of the bay from the garden.' He turned to the next page. 'Here's another one. This one is taken from the beach.'

The cottage was at the edge of a cliff, above a long flight of steps cut into the chalk.

'It's beautiful, Henry. But why do you come so seldom – you haven't been here once in all the time I've known you.'

He shook his head. 'Ruth refuses.'

'But why?'

He pushed the album aside. 'We haven't come all this way to talk about Ruth.' His hand slipped between the buttons of her blouse; his lips covered hers, greedily sucking them into his own.

She woke early, roused by the gulls, crying and calling over the cliff. The sky hung grey over a sea the colour of steel. Seated under the bedroom window she looked down at the bay. The beach was empty, a string of seaweed marked the progress of the tide. On the other side of the bay was a tumbledown house, semi-derelict, part of its chimney fallen away, a heap of rubble on the grass; but the house was still inhabited, it seemed, for the door was open and she could make out a figure moving about in a glass lean-to at the side.

Henry was sleeping with his mouth open, his handsome face blotched pink like a child's. She drank a cup of coffee in the kitchen. Henry did not stir. There was a boy's anorak in the cupboard under the stairs. She put it on and set off for the village.

The road was steep. On one side the cliff curved out over the water. On the other sheep grazed, close up to the fence. They ignored her, cropping noisily as she passed.

The village was a ribbon of houses, a main street that opened out by a quay with Evans' Village Shop on the corner, a square of concrete in front, and next door, a pair of petrol pumps. A sign in the shop window said 'Open', but there was no one about. Suzannah peered in. A light was on in a glass-fronted refrigerator. She could see sides of ham and beef; sacks of potatoes slumped in front of the counter and on the shelves behind everything imaginable, rows of tins and jars, lengths of rope, garden forks, scouring powders.

'What d'you want?'

A woman leaned out of the window above the door.

'Are you Mrs Evans?'

'I am.'

'I've come from the cottage. I think you're keeping a loaf for us.'

'From Matilda's Cottage?' The woman stared down at her.

'Mr Alland's cottage,' said Suzannah.

'Who are you, then?'

Suzannah swallowed. 'I'm a friend . . . '

The woman eyed her suspiciously. 'Mrs Alland's friend?'

'No, Mrs Alland isn't here.'

The window closed with a bang. After a few minutes the woman appeared around the side of the shop wearing a blue pinafore and carrying a loaf of sliced bread in each hand.

'Brown or white?'

'Oh, brown if you have it, please,' said Suzannah. 'It's very kind of you.'

'I'm not giving it you,' the woman said sharply.

'No, of course not.' Hastily Suzannah pulled a handful of change out of her pocket. 'Shall I take them both, as you've saved two for us?'

'I thought it was just the weekend you've come for.'

'That's right,' Suzannah smiled.

'What do you want two for, then?'

Suzannah scratched her head. 'Look, I just thought, as you've saved them for us – I mean, you won't be able to sell them on Monday . . . '

The woman glared at her.

Suzannah held out the money.

'Are you having two or what?'

'Yes,' she said, decisively. 'I'll take them both.'

The woman took the money and handed her the bread.

'Thank you,' said Suzannah. She turned to go.

'Are the babbies with you?' said the woman.

'The babbies? You mean Michael and Sammy? No. No, they're not with us.' Once more she started to go.

'Not so nice, now.'

Suzannah turned back. 'I'm sorry?'

'Not so nice for a weekend,' said the woman.

'Oh, the weather.' As if to demonstrate her agreement Suzannah pulled up the zip of her anorak. 'No, it's not so nice.'

She hurried back to the cottage. The sheep had moved away from the fence. A wooden sign marked the road to Matilda's Cottage: 'Smithies Lane'. A man stood beside it. He had been coming towards her as she climbed the hill but stopped by the sign. A big man, with a dark beard, staring at her. Keeping to the other side of the road, she hurried on.

Henry was in the garden, his tailored trousers tucked into a pair of wellingtons. He smiled as she approached. 'Good morning, my darling.' He held out his arms and she walked into his embrace. His hands went inside the anorak, pushing down inside the waistband of her jeans.

Suzannah pulled back. 'Let me put the bread away.'

He followed her into the house.

'Do we need two loaves?'

She shook her head. 'I felt I had to buy them both. That Mrs Evans is very strange.'

'What did she say?'

'Nothing, really, just stared at me.'

Henry lifted the lid off the bread crock and Suzannah pushed the loaves inside. 'She was probably expecting Ruth.'

The lid slipped back into place. He leaned forward, kissing her ears, her cheeks, her lips. She felt the silver-flick of his tongue in her mouth, his hand on her hip, pulling her against himself.

In the afternoon the sky cleared. Henry helped her down the cliff steps and they walked arm in arm around the bay. The upper part of the beach was shingle but as it dropped towards the sea, the shingle gave way to soft, greyish sand.

Far out to sea, a ferry ploughed diagonally towards the horizon. Pieces of rubbish, plastic cups and aluminium cans were caught in a line of seaweed half way up the beach.

Henry sighed. 'I used to come here when I was a kid. The beach was cleaner then. Nowadays the ferry people just throw their stuff overboard, they never think of where it will land.'

The cliffs towered around them, closing the bay against the sea.

'Is there no other way down?' asked Suzannah.

Henry shook his head. 'Only the steps, but they're not exclusive to the cottage.' He pointed upwards. 'You see the sort of landing half way down – it stretches round that jut of cliff that's called the Head. There's a path that leads down to it.'

'Does anybody use the path?'

'Sometimes the tourists find their way up here from the village. And there's an artist living in Smithies.'

'Smithies?'

'That's the place you can see from the cottage.' He pointed to the opposite side of the bay. 'It is semi-derelict, but I don't suppose he pays much rent. The path from Smithies joins up with the steps from the cottage. It's the only way he can get to the beach.'

Suzannah stared upwards. The artist's house was obscured by overhanging rock, but she had seen it from the cottage, a tumbledown, perched on the cliff edge.

'Suzannah.' Henry had taken both her hands. She heard the pebbles grind together as he settled his stance in front of her. 'You're very beautiful.'

She had the impression he meant to say something else but had changed his mind or could not find the words.

He started again, looking down at her, his chest so close to her face that she had to raise her chin to see his expression. He looked stern, as he had in the car, determined.

'You're everything I want.' He folded her close against him, so that she could no longer see his face but only hear his voice. 'Ruth is no use to me anymore. I have tried, I have really tried to want her again, but I cannot. She has become so . . .' He paused. '. . . so unattractive to me. Every time I see her I compare her with you.'

*

'You could have knocked me down with a feather!' cried Enid Evans.

'Who was she?'

'Some bit of stuff.' The potatoes tumbled into Liam's bag. 'Came down here as cool as a cucumber. "I've come from the cottage," she says, "I think you've got a loaf for us." '

'It's a wonder you sold it to her, Enid,' Mrs Handel joined in. 'I'd have sent her packing.'

'You're not running a business,' said Mrs Evans, slamming the drawer of the till. 'Her money is the same as yours.'

'She was a pretty lady,' said Liam, 'from what I saw.'

'Oh yes, Mr McGuinness. I'd expect you to notice that.'

'You'll be asking her to pose for you next,' said Mrs Handel.

'I might just do that, if she comes back.' Liam put his change in his pocket and went out.

Not Ruth. The shock of it had taken his breath away. He had watched from Smithies as she came out of the cottage, the boy's anorak disguising her shape. He had walked to the top of the lane, waited as she came back up the cliff with the two loaves in her arms. A girl, barely a woman; a bright scarf, daffodil-coloured. Not Ruth.

Twelve

'Daddy?' She moved the telephone receiver from one ear to the other, continuing to brush her hair as she spoke. 'I'm coming for the weekend, is that OK?'

'Suzannah! That will be marvellous.'

'Is everything all right?' Remembering that everything could not be all right, she ran on, 'Is Gassy looking after you? Are you eating enough?'

'Yes, yes.' Her father was laughing. 'It's her weekend off. It's a good thing she doesn't know you're coming or she'd get into a terrible flap.'

'I'll be there about seven.'
'Tonight?'
'Yes, tonight.'
It was noon on Friday. A week since they had been to Matilda's Cottage, since he had told her, lying beside her in the bed, continuing the statement that he had begun on the beach, that Ruth was no longer attractive to him, his marriage was no longer valid; that she, his darling Suzannah, held the key to his happiness.
'But you'll go back to Cavanagh Road,' said Suzannah, 'won't you?'
'For now,' Henry nodded. 'For another week or two. I must spend time with Michael. He must know that I love him before I go.'
'When will you tell him about us?'
There had been a small pause.
'When I have told Ruth.'
'But she knows, doesn't she?'
'There is a difference between knowing and being told.'
'We must be quite sure, Henry, sure of ourselves. Perhaps it's too soon, perhaps we should wait for a bit.'
'No, Suzannah, I don't want to wait. I have waited long enough. I would have told her weeks ago – if it wasn't for your mother and everything.'
'What had Mummy to do with it?'
'You weren't here, darling. I couldn't very well leave home for you if you weren't here.'
Suzannah sighed. How strange the connections were; the footsteps in the dew, her father in yesterday's shirt winning a reprieve for Ruth.
'I didn't know you were waiting for her to die.'
'I wasn't, darling! Not like that.' Henry's voice was smooth with reassurance. 'I was only waiting for you to be there for me to come to.'
Under the cover of the sheets Suzannah had folded her arms, taking in each hand the soft flesh of the other forearm. 'And how will Ruth react? How will the children take your going away?'
There was a brief silence and then Henry's voice came back, flowing and confident. 'Children are resilient. Sammy is too

young to notice and Michael will get used to it in time. When he gets to know you he will understand completely.'

'But boys need a father.' The little cliché tripped off her tongue, a snake's wriggle, an excuse.

'They will still have a father. And I will be a better father, for being happy.'

The argument did not last. Hers was only a feeble resistance. How could she argue, say it could not be, or might not be? He was so sure of their happiness. He wanted her completely, loved her completely. Surely that meant everything she could wish for?

Except . . . She sniffed the air, as if what she missed could be identified, like a smell, a memory: the dust-dry smell of garden gloves, magnolia and myrtle, laburnum and vibernum, names like prayers and the tall certainty of wellington boots.

The Friday evening train was crowded. A hot smell of bodies, men in rolled sleeves, suit jackets bundled on to laps, crumpled newspapers and windows jammed open.

Her father opened the door before the taxi had turned round.

'Suzannah!' He beamed, hugged her against his chest.

'You feel thin, Daddy. Is Gassy not feeding you?'

'She's doing a wonderful job. It's my appetite that is to blame.' He took her bag from her hand and led her upstairs. Her bed had been made up, even an old nightie folded on the pillow. Suzannah threw down her jacket. The silence of the house was like a physical constraint, enfolding them, dividing their sentences. She shrugged her shoulders, as if to shake herself free.

'What's for supper, Daddy?'

'Gassy's left us a casserole,' said her father. 'And there are still some beans in the freezer.' He followed her down the stairs. 'It won't take a minute. We've got one of these micro cookers.'

'A microwave?'

He nodded, his smile uncertain. 'Gassy thought it would be a good thing.'

'Gassy did?' Suzannah laughed. 'I'll bet she's persuaded you about the washing machine too.'

'Well, as a matter of fact . . . '

'Daddy, she's making mincemeat of you!'

Her father sighed. 'I knew you'd say as much.' He rested against the door frame. 'There didn't seem any harm in it.'

In the harsh light of the kitchen Suzannah saw how pale he was, pale and gaunt.

'I don't want Gassy to leave, Suzannah. I must have some continuity.' His voice wavered. She put out her arm and with a lurching gesture he came towards her. 'Without your mother here, I must have someone who knows me.'

Awkwardly she hugged him, wanting to stop the words.

'What you need is a drink,' she said. 'How about a drop of sherry?'

The cupboard was well stocked. She noticed that his glass of sherry went down in one swallow and he went straight to the bottle for a refill.

'Here's to you, Suzannah.'

'And you.'

Suddenly he smiled. 'I've got a good bottle of Burgundy to have with our supper.'

Suzannah smiled back. 'Let's hope Gassy's casserole lives up to it.'

He raised his glass again. 'Here's to Gassy's casserole.'

It was just as the meal was ready that the call came. Her father started for the phone.

'I'll go. It'll be for me.'

He hesitated in the hall until Suzannah reached the phone, waited for her to lift the receiver and only on seeing her wait, took himself off to the kitchen.

'Hello?'

'Suzannah? How was the trip home?'

'Oh . . . crowded, you know, Friday night commuters.'

'But you're there now.'

'Yes, we're just about to have supper.' The sherry had made her tongue slow.

'Are you all fixed for tomorrow? Bernard said you rang.'

She paused. 'Yes.'

'Can you drive over? I'd pick you up but I'll be working until half past twelve.'

'That's OK but you'll have to tell me where you are.'

He gave her time to scribble the directions on a pad.

'That's easy to find.'
'Good.'
Silence.
'I'll have to go – the supper.'
'Yes, of course.'
With a smile on her lips she helped her father dish out the casserole.
'The trouble with microwaves is that they give you no time to let the wine breathe,' said her father.
Suzannah took a sip. 'Tastes all right to me.'
'These are the last of the beans.'
'From the garden?'
He nodded. 'Your mother had a huge crop last year.' He paused.
Suzannah looked at her plate. The last of her crop. It would go on like this for years. The last of this, the last of that, until all her presence had seeped away.
'Did you find a man?'
Her father hadn't heard the question, turning away to blow his nose.
'To do the garden – did you find someone?' Suzannah pursued her question doggedly, it would be all right if they could keep a conversation going.
He drank some wine. 'Yes – through the office. My secretary's grandfather, actually.'
'Her grandfather? He must be ancient.'
Cyril emptied his wine glass and wiped his mouth with his napkin.
A thought flashed into her mind. Does Austin do it like that? Suddenly she saw the deacon at the altar, in coloured robes, drinking wine from a silver cup.
'He's about sixty-seven. What they call an active pensioner.'
'How old is your secretary?'
'I don't know.' Her father looked up. 'Younger than you, I should think. Probably about twenty.'
'What is her name?'
He thought for a moment. 'Tracy. She reminds me of you in a way – she has the same colouring. She's getting married next month.'
Suzannah ate some casserole. It tasted of onions and stock

cubes. The runner beans were good, squeaky firm against her teeth.

'What will you buy her for a wedding present?'

He sighed. 'I've no idea. I've always relied on your mother for that sort of thing.' He re-filled his glass and took a long swallow of wine. 'Gassy suggested a cake stand.'

Suzannah giggled. 'Gassy would suggest a cake stand.'

'No good?'

'No, Daddy.'

'Will you help me find something, Suzannah?' He looked anxiously across the table. 'I mean, if you're not busy tomorrow.'

Suzannah cleared her throat. 'We could go shopping in the morning, if we set off early.'

'That would be splendid. We'll go after breakfast and I'll take you to lunch when we've finished.'

'I can't have lunch, Daddy. I've got a date.'

'Oh . . . well, that's all right then.' He spoke too quickly, needlessly straightening the knife and fork on his plate. 'I can have something here.'

Suzannah took a deep breath. 'Shall I put it off, Daddy? I could go to lunch another day.'

He shook his head and picked up the wine bottle. 'I think there's another glass each in here.' He filled her glass and then emptied the bottle into his own. 'Is it someone special?'

'It's Austin.'

Her father looked puzzled for a moment. Then he remembered, surprise replacing the puzzlement on his face. 'The young deacon?'

Suzannah nodded.

'He's invited you to lunch?'

Suzannah nodded again.

'Well, I never.'

She stood up and began to put the plates on a tray. Her father stood also, more out of courtesy than to help her. 'Are you sure?'

Suzannah laughed. 'I'm sure I'm going to lunch, yes. Why, I don't know. Shall we use the dishwasher?'

'I hardly bother with it now.' He followed her as she carried the plates into the kitchen.

'What will you have yourself, tomorrow?'

Her father consulted a list on the wall. 'Gassy's left a steak and kidney pie – look, here.'

Suzannah stared at the list. The whole weekend was mapped out, a campaign of meals to be conquered.

'Never mind the pie, Daddy. Have something in town.'

'I couldn't do that,' he said immediately.

'Why not?'

'Not without,' he paused, 'not on my own.'

'But Daddy, you mustn't think like that. You've got to start living again.'

He shook his head and turned back to Gassy's list.

She could read his face.

'Gassy won't mind, Daddy. You could eat the pie another day.'

Cyril waved his hands. 'It might offend her.'

'We can eat the pie tomorrow night, if we must.'

He pointed to the list. 'But she's got chops for Saturday.'

'We'll eat pie and chops, then! We could even be really wicked and throw the pie away.'

Her father looked stern. 'We couldn't do that, it would be a waste.' Then he caught Suzannah's grin. 'I could tell her it was off?'

'Tell her the freezer broke down.'

'God no!' He slapped his forehead in mock horror. 'She'd be out ordering a new one.'

Suzannah looked round, 'That reminds me . . .' Her eyes lighted on the washing machine. 'She didn't stint herself, did she?'

'It is supposed to be a very good one.'

'It's about the most expensive washing machine available. Look, even a tumble dryer built in.'

Her father shrugged. 'It didn't seem very important – and it pleased her no end.'

Suzannah hugged him. 'I'll do this washing up and then I'm off to bed. Tomorrow we'll go and find your Tracy a wedding present.'

Thirteen

He was boiling potatoes, watching the flicker of the bottled gas under the pan, when a red van drew up by the gate. The flap in the door slapped open and an envelope fluttered down, a small square of brown manilla, seeming too small, too light to have been the object of a special journey. Liam waved through the window as the post van backed round and drove away.

Another note. A small white paper folded inside the paper money. As before there was no name, no instruction, just another London address and a date.

And an extra twenty pounds for the fare.

Liam opened the kitchen drawer. The postmark on the envelope was the same as the others, the same typewriter had been used, the same little woman, he imagined, typing for a few pounds a week, sending out messages, and money, and never asking the reason.

He put the fold of money into his pocket and went out to the studio. Handel's sheep had their heads between the fence-wires, noisily cropping his vegetable patch. Liam's shout barely disturbed them. He ran across and manhandled their heads back through the fence.

'Between you and the rabbits I shall starve!' he shouted.

The sheep took a step back, blank eyes never leaving his face.

Speaking to himself, he added. 'If I'm not caught first.'

He squatted down to pull a weed, feeling the rolled notes hard in his back pocket. One of the sheep leaned through the fence again, a stain of green clinging around its mouth.

'Good are they?' Liam whispered. 'My carrot tops nicer than plain old grass, eh?'

The sheep blinked.

'You'll be having the rest while I'm gone, I suppose? While I'm down in London behaving like a bloody fool.'

He brushed the dust from his hands and stood up.

'I should give this up,' he said, still addressing the unmoved sheep. 'Even you wouldn't be tempted by one hundred pounds a month for God knows what. I don't even know what it is I do.'

He stared gloomily down into the bay. The day was still new, the sun a glow of silver, like a bright moon over the sea. He watched the dark speck of a gull, diving. 'I love this place,' he shouted. 'The sea, the Head, the people in the village – even you bloody sheep are my friends here. I should not be risking it all; I should not have let Brendan talk me into it.' He hugged his arms about himself. 'I shall give it up. When the season is over I shall tell them where they can put their money.'

There was a direct train to Cannon Street. He sat alone in a corner seat, watching the country sliding past; the green slopes of the Weald, folded as though a spoon had been stirred through when the mixture was soft. Then the suburbs, the city. Here, the train seemed to lose its momentum, as if the mixture had become stiff, dense with brick and fume, rooftops like the spines of broken books, rack upon rack into the distance; flat squares of park, youths and dogs.

Henry Alland's house would not be one of these. Liam had a picture of the Alland house in his mind. A drive filled with glossy motorcars, an iron gate painted black, Samuel David peeping out at the world from a warm room. His hands turned, a twirl of empty fingers, yearning to bring the child's body close against himself, to touch hair that was the colour of the sun on a pale morning; Ruth's colour, as it might have been.

Through the smeared carriage window he watched the roofs and factories, littered streets and small, brave gardens. Not from one such as these would the boy look out upon the world. Samuel would be a grown man before he would look open-eyed at these. Samuel David, my son.

This time he had kept the note. Ignored the instruction to burn it. The address was a door in a street wall, painted pale blue, between a coin-op and an all-night grocery store. Three bells. He touched the first by mistake. A woman came out screaming, a language from Europe, her voice followed him up the stairs drowning in a thunder of synthesised guitars. A door at the top, wide open, two boys in a sleeping bag on the floor, waving a greeting. Liam opened the curtains and turned down the volume.

Cries of alarm. Pale faces screwed up against ordinary daylight, voices that whined in the silence.

This was Brendan's army.

'You have something for me?'

White legs below an unbuttoned shirt. 'We expected you to come later, tonight.'

'There are no trains at night.'

The cardboard lid of the suitcase was dented from being used as a seat.

'Sean'll be here later,' said the one who had remained in the sleeping bag.

'Who's Sean?'

The boy shrugged. 'The guy who lets us stay here.'

'Is it this I'm to take?' Liam pointed to the case.

The boy sniffed. 'That's what he said.'

'Home,' said the other, sniffing too, as if to punctuate his speech. 'You're to take it home.'

Liam carried the case down the stairs. The thunder began again, and the foreign woman came out to scream.

Trains to Dover were delayed. Someone had reported a bomb in a high glass-faced tower by the river. Commuters like refugees massed on the pavement outside Cannon Street, sitting on their briefcases, grumbling. Liam waited in the street with the suitcase, smiling at the irony. Was this another test? A trap to test his nerves? Would they take so much trouble to test a courier?

Not a test, then, the contents of this suitcase only a coincidental addition to the madness of brick and flying glass that threatened the street. He could go down to Victoria or Charing Cross, catch a train from there. But the note had said 'Travel from Cannon Street'. So he waited, stood in the doorway of a sandwich bar that was closed for the day, keeping the suitcase close against his legs, conscious of his size, of his beard, his big coat, obtrusive among the bank clerks. They might be looking for someone like him, one who did not fit, could not mingle among the young ferrets with their narrow ties and sharp eyes and rolled newspapers like batons. He waited in the doorway with the suitcase, sweating inside his coat. He had no newspaper, nothing to defend himself from a hand upon his shoulder, a quiet voice in his ear.

No one spoke to him. The empty, scurrying eyes of the commuters looked right through him. After an hour a babble of announcements sent them hurrying into the station. He hurried with them, and fought like them for a seat on the train, hemmed in by coats and newspapers, with the suitcase on the parcel shelf above his head.

'What've you got there, Liam?' The barman stood in the doorway of The Swan, a polishing rag poised against the brass plate of the pub door.

'Oh . . . some bits and pieces.'

'Been staying in London?'

'No – just a day trip.' Liam shifted the suitcase from one hand to the other. He saw the barman's eyes on it, waiting for him to explain why he had come back from London with a dented suitcase. 'Some canvas and things.'

The barman nodded, losing interest. 'See you later, then?'

'Sure.'

The suitcase fitted snug inside the Smithies' coalbunker. Standing in the corner of the yard, the old bunker was a relic of days when the tumbledown was a farmhouse, with warm coals in the fireplace where now there were only boards blocking the draught. Liam padlocked the lid, comforted by the thick concrete walls. Whatever it was in the suitcase, it was safe in there.

Turning back to the house, he passed the studio, caught sight of his own work through the glass. Large on the easel was the portrait he had started, the child, drawn from memory. His lip curled at the sight of it. 'Desperate,' he whispered, 'desperately bad.' He turned to the sheep, raising his voice. 'How will I get it right if she does not bring him back?'

Less than a week had passed when an old Ford drew up in the lane. The man he had seen first in The Swan. Liam unlocked the bunker and brought out the suitcase. It was black with dust.

The man checked the locks, scarred hands bent like claws.

'I didn't open it,' said Liam.

The man smiled. 'No, McGuinness. I know you didn't open it.'

Liam fingered his mouth.

'How is my brother?'

The man looked up. 'Brendan?' He stared at Liam's face. 'You're not much like him, are you?'

Liam shrugged. Before he could reply the man said, 'It would be good for your brother to be more like you.' He smiled. 'He'd be more use to us if he had your nerve.'

'Nerve?'

The man smiled and put the suitcase carefully into the boot. 'You'll be having a visitor soon,' he said, walking round to the driver's seat. Liam noticed that he stooped, as if his body, too, were clawed, burned skin causing him to bend.

'What visitor? Brendan?'

'No. It'll be a woman. You're to keep her for a week or two.' He put the key into the ignition.

'Wait!' Liam held the door. 'Why is she coming here?'

'To stay with you.' The man smiled again. The tightening of his jaw pulled the scarred skin of his neck into cords.

'What has she done?'

The man laughed. 'You needn't worry. It's not what she has done – it's what she is going to do.' He pulled the door closed and Liam watched him drive away.

Fourteen

Suzannah sat at a gateleg table that was covered by a cloth of checked linen. Tiny crumbs of toast had settled in the weave. As she ran her nail across the cloth the crumbs lifted, bouncing up like a sprinkling of spores before falling to rest again, invisible on the big checks.

She had left her father in the shopping centre, waiting for Tracy's cutlery to be gift-wrapped.

'I knew you'd help me find something nice, Suzannah.' He turned and squeezed her hand. 'It's so wonderful to have you with me.'

She smiled, feeling herself flush at the emotion in his face.

'If you should ever grow tired of London, you know there will always be a home for you here.'

He had cut himself shaving, she could see a nick in the skin above the tweed cloth of his coat.

Seeing that she had no answer, he went on. 'I wouldn't restrict your freedom, my dear. I know that you're quite grown up, now. But I am sure . . .' Behind him a salesgirl held out a credit slip for him to sign. He scribbled on it briefly and turned back to Suzannah. 'I'm sure we could get along well together. And with you not being married . . . '

Suzannah looked at her watch. 'I'm sorry, Daddy, I'll have to go or I shall be late.'

'Yes, of course.' The tweed collar was suddenly close, her cheek against his. She glanced back as she hurried away. The shop assistant had put the credit card in his hand. He was waving the card, like a small flag.

'Bye, Daddy,' she called. 'I'll see you later on.'

Once more she ran her nail across the cloth, lifting the crumbs out of the weave.

'Why don't you ever speak about God?'

'Would you like me to?'

Austin's back was turned. He opened a can of sweetcorn and poured the contents into a saucepan.

'I think it's odd that you don't,' said Suzannah. 'Shouldn't you at least make an effort to convert me?'

'Perhaps I am.'

'You're not. You've never mentioned religion.'

'I talk about my work.'

'But religion isn't a job.'

'What is it then?' He took a wrapped quiche out of the fridge.

'That looks nice.' Deliberately she changed the subject, to see if he would change it back.

'From the supermarket, I'm afraid.' He took a large bottle of Worcestershire sauce from the cupboard. 'The economy size we can't afford.' He grinned.

'My father used to say that. I never understood the joke.' Austin nodded. 'I think the words have changed their meaning. Economy used to mean sparing. Now it seems to mean something large and unmanageable.' He held down the lid of the bottle with his thumb, shook the sauce until it swirled freely against the glass, then sprinkled it over the quiche. 'This'll give it some flavour.'

She watched him turn on the oven and put in the quiche.

'Do you do a lot of cooking?'

'When I get time. We have a kind of rota but it's difficult to stick to.'

'How many of you live here?'

'Three of us at the moment. Father Bernard, me and another chap, but he's only a temporary guest.

'No women?'

Austin smiled. 'They're not forbidden.'

While the quiche was warming he showed her round the flat. It was unmodernised, occupying the ground floor of an old house. In each room was a tiled fireplace, brown dado rails, and in the bathroom, that had been built on to the kitchen, an old geyser shuddered into life each time the hot tap was turned on.

'Which is your room?'

He showed her the room which would have been a dining room before the house was converted. It was sparsely furnished. At the end of one bed was a suitcase, lying open to reveal a small collection of clothes.

'Those belong to the other chap.'

'Where is he?'

'At the hospice.' Putting out his hand, Austin guided her from the room.

'His mother is there. He has come from abroad to see her so we have let him stay here.'

'But you live here all the time?'

He nodded.

'And you go to the hospice every day?'

'Yes.'

'Do you preach to them there?'

'No. They're very short of staff, they don't need preachers as such, just people who have time to talk to the patients.'

'Like my mother?'

'That's right – except that she was lucky enough to be able to remain at home.' He led her back into the kitchen and she settled at the table while he heated the sweetcorn and took the hot quiche out of the oven.

The Worcestershire sauce gave the egg a strong, salty flavour.

'It's good, Austin.'

He smiled. 'It's very ordinary. I'd have made you something special if I'd had the time.'

'What can you cook?'

'You'd be surprised.'

'Where did you learn?'

'Here and there.'

Suzannah put a dab of margarine on the hot sweetcorn. 'I think Gassy prefers it without my mother. Daddy doesn't try to tell her what to do.'

'How is your father?'

She shrugged. 'He wants me to come home and live with him.'

Austin's eyebrows rose. 'He's asked you, has he?'

'This morning, in the middle of a department store. He reminded me that I'm not married.'

Austin shook his head. 'It must be lonely for him. I've been meaning to come over and see him.'

'There's no need. No one is dying there now.'

He looked up, eyes bright with hurt. 'It's not just the dying I care for.'

'Sorry,' said Suzannah. 'I didn't mean it that way. It's just that everyone seems to be relying on me to make him happy. Simon's gone back to Hong Kong. No one visits any more. They seem to expect me to look after him.'

The meal was finished. Austin put their empty plates in the sink.

'And you don't want to look after him.'

'No. I love him dearly, and I miss my mother, but no, I don't want to look after him.'

'Would you be willing to come home if it wasn't for your affair?'

'My affair?' Her voice rose. 'It isn't an affair. You make it sound like something smutty.'

Austin turned on the hot tap and began to scrub the plates with a brush.

'I don't think it's smutty. I couldn't think that of you.'

'Then why do you call it an affair?'

'Because there isn't another name I can think of.'

'It isn't an affair. We just love one another. It's as simple as that.' Avoiding his eyes, she looked around the kitchen. 'Where do you keep your tea-towels?'

His hands came out of the water, curls of wet hair lying flat on his skin. 'In that drawer over there.'

She opened the drawer and took out a striped towel. It was neatly ironed and folded.

'I like you, Austin,' she said, on an impulse.

He turned to her, smiling broadly. 'I hoped you would. I hoped – '

'You're so wholesome,' she interrupted. 'You make me think of brown bread – and lettuce.'

'Brown bread and lettuce?' He grabbed the free end of the tea-towel. 'Brown bread and lettuce!'

Keeping hold of her end of the towel she danced away. The towel jerked him towards her. For a second his hand was on her hair, her head almost on his chest. 'Suzannah . . . '

She heard the tremor as he breathed and moved away from him, out of reach. 'I am – ' she hesitated – 'taken.'

'Taken?'

'Spoken for.'

'But he has a wife and children.'

'He is leaving them.' She took a plate from the draining board and began to dry it. 'He is coming to live with me in the flat.'

Austin stared out at the garden. After a silence he asked, 'How old are they?'

'Who?'

'His children.'

'Michael is about fourteen, but Sammy is only little.'

'And what do they think of you?'

'We haven't met, not yet.' She put the plate down on the table. 'Henry is waiting for the right moment.'

'And you? What are you waiting for?'

'What do you mean?'

'Will you be satisfied when he has left his home? Will you want him to marry you?'

As he spoke Austin took the corners of the tablecloth and shook it through the kitchen door.

How should she answer? How to explain the fearful complications of Henry? His need for her; the fierce importance to him of having her on his arm, of her being his? She had never been so wanted, it was impossible to resist. She did not want to resist. He was handsome and rich; he loved her; living with him would fill all the silences, the dark places that her mother's death had exposed.

Austin broke into her thoughts, asking another question before she could answer the first.

'And what of the children?'

She raised her shoulders. 'Children are very resilient. Henry will be a better father if he is happy.' She took the tablecloth from his hands and began to fold it.

'Don't fold it.' Taking the cloth back he spread it out over the gateleg table. 'Bernard likes a tablecloth. He says it reminds him of his granny.'

Suzannah smiled, relieved to think of something else.

'You cannot live with blinkers, Suzannah.' Austin's face remained solemn. He put his hands on her shoulders, his pale, serious eyes were close to hers. 'Whatever you do, you must know it, acknowledge your action and all its results.' He pointed to the squared cloth on the table. 'People spend their lives moving from one situation to another, without pause. They behave like prisoners, clinging to the walls of their cells, eyes on the floor, keeping to the small square of the world that they can see.'

He led her slowly into the hall. 'That is how the damage is done – by people not looking out to see how what they do affects others.' He pointed to the newspaper on the hall table, the headlines declared a life sentence for the bombers. 'Those men are not fundamentally different from you and me; they are just keeping their eyes down, looking at their own little square; they justify what they do by shutting everything else out, convincing themselves that the hurt they cause cannot be prevented.'

Suzannah shrank away from him. 'I don't see what IRA bombers have to do with me.'

'They're still looking for a girl,' said Austin. 'She's your age, she was at school when you were, growing up at the same time as you, in the same country.'

'Hardly the same country!'

'But it is not Ireland that has made her a monster. It is the things she wants – or imagines she wants. Her desire for them has made her blind. How does the proverb go?' He paused, screwing up his eyes as he tried to think of the words. 'All men are blind in their own cause – something like that. Have you heard that one before?'

Suzannah shook her head.

'Think of it, Suzannah. Think of all the people in history who have caused pain. None of them really intended to do evil. They set out to do something else. Pain and evil were just the by-products.'

Suzannah nodded, tired of his insistence.

Austin held out her jacket.

'Am I being dismissed?'

He shook his head. 'I don't want you to go, but I have work to do.'

'This doesn't count as work, then – preaching to me?'

'I'm not preaching to you, Suzannah. I'm just trying to show you that what you do matters. You are not just a pawn, you cannot make the breaking of that family someone else's business.'

'But it isn't my fault. Henry says their marriage was dead long before I came on the scene. I am just the catalyst.'

'But he still loves his wife.'

Suzannah looked up. 'How can you say that? You don't know either of them.'

'He must love her, after so many years of marriage, and a new child so recently.'

Suzannah shook her head. 'They have been unhappy for years, more so since Sammy was born. Henry says that the birth of the child has left her empty, she has time for no one but Sammy. He can't live with her any more, he needs a woman who has time for him. With me he is happier than he has ever been in his life.'

Austin stopped by the door. 'It is your happiness, too, that is at stake.'

She put her hands in the pockets of her coat. 'Thank you for lunch.'

With a sad smile, he opened the door. 'It hasn't been quite as I imagined it would be.'

'No.' She looked up at him. 'And you did go on about God after all.'

'Did I?'

'That is what it was all about, wasn't it? You think I shall be damned if I live with Henry.'

'I think you will be unhappy. If not now, then later. You are not hard enough for what is to come.'

'You make it sound like a nightmare.'

He shook his head. 'It isn't just Henry, it's the whole family you are taking on.'

'The only problem is Ruth. But there's no reason why I should ever have to see her. The children are sweet, there won't be any difficulty with them.'

'I hope you're right.'

The open door filled the hall with daylight. Suzannah reached up and planted a kiss on his cheek. 'Don't look so sad.'

'Be good, Suzannah.'

He called after her as she opened the garden gate. 'Remember, there's always brown bread and lettuce, if you get tired of it all.'

She looked back, surprised. But he had gone inside and shut the door.

Fifteen

Henry's belongings filled the flat to overflowing. He went back to Cavanagh Road more times than she cared to count and each time he returned his car was laden, the back seats folded down to make room for his possessions: trunks full of clothes, a desk, a bookcase, crates of books, a table lamp, all things that he said he could not be without.

Ruth allowed him to see his sons once a week. There was no formal arrangement, only her agreement that he should take them out on Sunday afternoons. He took them to the park, to the cinema, for a row on the Serpentine. Suzannah suggested he bring them back to the flat for tea.

Henry shook his head. 'Not yet, Suzannah.'
'Why not?'
'They're not ready.'
'Do they know I exist?'
'Oh yes,' said Henry. 'I've told them all about you.'
'Well then, why not bring them over here?'
'I've told you, they're not ready.'
It's you who isn't ready, Suzannah thought, watching the relief on his face as she let the matter drop.

Their affair had become a kind of marriage. Every morning Henry took the train into the City, but now Suzannah remained behind.

'It will be more discreet,' Henry had said. 'You don't need a job, and I don't want people to talk about you.'
'But how will I live?'
'Darling girl, I will give you everything you need.'

And so he had; new clothes, a credit card, a new chequebook for an account in her own name. She spent his money easily, quickly learning how to choose the things that pleased him; the food he liked, the clothes that he admired. With great care and patience he taught her how to make love, to please him and to please herself. She learned the lessons well, delighting in the quiet confidence of his body. This was experience. This was knowing what you wanted.

She learned, too, how to look after him; to be ready with a clean shirt, one of the many that hung in the long shared wardrobe with mirrored doors that he liked to keep open while they made love, so that he could watch himself. The shirts were white, monogrammed, or subtle shades of grey and blue that set off his eyes and the cut of his dark, expensive suits.

At weekends he wore cashmere sweaters, carefully tailored slacks, a leather jacket, soft as a glove. He declared his love in the street, kissed her indiscreetly in the supermarket, a different man from the weekday Henry, for whom the delicately shaded shirts, the polished shoes and glossy leather briefcase were an armour. In those clothes, when he smiled, one saw more of his straight, white teeth.

He never spoke of his visits to Cavanagh Road, never reported what was said or how Ruth had behaved. One Sunday afternoon she went to the park near his house. They were already there, on the far side of the lake, a man and two boys. Michael, almost as tall as Henry, hanging back, looking bad-tempered, while his brother hurled bread at the ducks. Henry did not recognise his true love sitting, wearing a headscarf and an old coat, across the lake. His own coat trailed in the mud as he showed Sammy how to break the bread into small pieces. The little boy ignored him, his face wide with delight as whole crusts hurtled across the water, sending the ducks quacking for cover.

'There is mud on your coat, Henry,' she said when he returned, hours after she had seen him leave the park.

'Is there?' He slipped off the coat and held it up against the light. 'I don't see any.'

Suzannah stared at the coat.

'I thought I saw mud, I must have been mistaken.'

'There was mud on it from the park. We were feeding the ducks. But Ruth sponged it for me while we had tea.'

'You had tea?'

He looked up. 'Yes, it's Sammy's birthday on Tuesday. She'd baked a cake.'

Suzannah sank down into a chair. 'You sat in Cavanagh Road eating birthday cake?'

'Ruth made it specially, I couldn't hurt Sammy's feelings.'

He pulled her up and put his arms about her shoulders. 'What is it, Suzannah?'

'You never explain anything.' She struggled to keep the whine from her voice. 'You never tell me what happens when you go there. Suddenly I hear that you sit having tea with her.'

'I don't want to talk about Cavanagh Road with you, Suzannah.'

'But how does she behave, Henry? Does she ask you to come back?'

He stroked her cheek and kissed her lips, as if to wipe away the question. 'I won't go back. That is all that matters.'

'But do you quarrel? Do you have fights?'

He looked surprised, as if the idea of a quarrel had not occurred to him. 'Of course not.'

'Have you never quarrelled with her?'

He thought for a moment. 'No. Not in the way you mean.'

'Not even about me?'

'No. Not even about you.' Again he stroked her cheek.

'You never tell me anything!' she cried, exasperated by his calm. 'You go back there week after week, but you never tell me what happens, you never tell me if she makes a scene. Suddenly I hear that she bakes you cakes!'

'It doesn't concern you, Suzannah.'

She brushed his hand away.

'Of course it concerns me. I am the cause, am I not? You wouldn't have left if it were not for me.'

'That's not entirely true.'

No, thought Suzannah bitterly. Another girl would have done as well. As long as she was pretty enough to be seen with you.

She did not voice the thought. He put his hand on her cheek once more and she allowed it to remain, calmed by the strong fingers gliding smoothly over her skin.

'Suzannah, darling,' he whispered. 'You mustn't be jealous. It is you that I love.'

'I'm not jealous, Henry. I just need to be sure.'

'But you mustn't wish me to quarrel with Ruth.'

'I don't, but I do need some sign, something to show me that she won't drag you back there.'

His expression became stern. 'My marriage is over, Suzannah.' He held her close against his chest. 'The future is for us.'

His sweater was soft against her face.

A month passed before he gave her the sign she wanted. One evening he came home with tickets for a Sunday matinée .

'Four?'

'Yes. You and I and Michael and Sammy.'

'Henry!' She kissed him. 'Shall we bring them here for tea afterwards?'

His smile faltered. 'Not here, darling. Not yet.'

'Why not? We could give them a lovely sticky tea before you take them home.' She jumped up, full of ideas. 'We can use those coloured glasses – the ones with the built-in straws, they'd love those. I'll make pancakes and gingerbread men!'

He held up his hand. 'Slow down, Suzannah.'

'Why?'

'We can't bring them here.'

'Why not? It's your home.'

'They're not ready. These things must be done gradually.'

'Will I do?'

She had chosen her clothes with care. Wanting to look young and yet old enough, right for the theatre but not overdressed, she had settled for black trousers and a blouse of bright pink silk with a ribbon of the same colour in her hair.

He looked her up and down.

'They won't notice what you wear.'

'They might,' said Suzannah brightly.

Henry took hold of her hand. 'You mustn't expect too much of this meeting, Suzannah.'

'I'm not expecting anything.'

He shook his head. 'It just might be more difficult than you think.'

'Why? They know who I am, surely?'

'Yes, but they might not know what to say to you.'

Suzannah frowned. 'Why should that be a problem? I'll be perfectly friendly.'

After a moment, Henry said, 'I don't know what she has told them about you.' He hesitated. 'They may have the wrong impression.'

'That I'm a tart with a short skirt and dyed hair?' she cried.

Henry looked at her and put his hand against her cheek. 'I just don't know.'

He drove to Cavanagh Road while Suzannah made her own way to the theatre. 'The Second Great Year!' blazed the posters. 'Winnie the Pooh – the musical!'

The meeting was to take place in the foyer. She had chosen this venue herself, believing that it would be right to meet Henry's children in a warm, bright place, with just time to smile at one another before going in to enjoy the show.

She watched them come up the steps, Henry holding the hand of a small boy, a crown of white-blond hair, looking shyly up from behind his father's arm. Michael stayed in the background and made no reply when, in a voice that sounded loud and artificial, she said, 'Hello, Michael. How nice to meet you.'

Inside the theatre the boys scrambled to sit beside Henry. Suzannah waited, embarrassed, while he ordered Michael to sit beside her. Throughout the first act the boy remained motionless, his elbows frozen against his sides to avoid the shared armrest. During the interval she bought Sammy a marzipan mouse and for Michael, because he seemed too old to want a marzipan mouse, a bag of toffees. Sammy ate the mouse immediately, tail first. Michael watched every mouthful.

When the performance was over, Henry ran through the rain to fetch the car. She waited with the boys by the door. Sammy's hand had slipped into hers as they came out of the darkened cinema; she hardly dared look down at him, fearful that he would see she was a stranger and take it away.

Conscious of Michael standing silently behind her, she twisted round to speak to him. 'Did you enjoy the show?'

He looked at his feet. 'Bit stupid.'

She realised, with surprise, that he was quite ugly, pale and skinny with large protruding teeth.

'Did you enjoy it, Sammy?'

The little boy grinned. 'I liked Pooh!'

Suzannah smiled. She tried to think of something else to say, but her mouth had gone dry.

Michael suddenly pulled open the foyer door and began to walk down the steps to the pavement. Sammy's hand was gone, reaching out for his brother.

'Michael,' she called. 'Where are you going?'

He stopped and pointed wordlessly across the road. Henry's car was waiting at the kerb. She hadn't seen it, she'd been expecting him to come from the other direction.

'I'm sorry,' said Henry as they climbed in. 'I got caught in the one-way system. Was I a very long time?'

'It's all right.' She smiled and automatically leaned across for a kiss. None came. Henry cleared his throat. 'I'll drop you at the flat, Suzannah.'

'Oh?'

He looked at her hard and she realised what he meant. He would drop her off first, so that Ruth wouldn't see her with the boys.

When they reached the flat, Henry turned round to the children. 'Say goodbye to Suzannah.'

Before they could reply she turned in her seat, leaning round the padded head restraint to smile. 'I've got a bottle of lemonade and chocolate biscuits. Would you boys like to come in and have some?'

Henry frowned but Sammy was already clapping his hands. 'Yes pleee. . .se!'

They waited on the steps while she fiddled with her keys. Sammy pushed past her as she opened the door, only to halt at the sight of the unfamiliar hall. 'Straight up the stairs,' said Suzannah. 'My door is first on the right.'

Henry and Michael trooped up after her.

'What a funny sort of house,' said Michael, loudly.

'It's a flat,' said Henry. 'Just part of a house.'

Suzannah left them in the sitting room and poured lemonade into the coloured glasses with the built-in straws. She had no pancakes or gingerbread to offer, but she put chocolate biscuits on a plate and returned to the sitting room. Sammy had settled on to the sofa but Michael stood in the middle of the room pointing to a table lamp.

'That's ours!'

Suzannah put down the tray. Michael spun around, pointed to the bookcase, the pictures. 'These are our things!' He turned to her, his voice loud with accusation. 'What are they doing here?'

Henry fiddled with something on the mantelpiece. 'They are my things, Michael,' he said quietly. 'I've brought them because I live here now.'

The boy turned back to Suzannah. 'You can't take our things away!' he shouted, stabbing his finger into the air in front of her. 'They're ours!'

She picked up a glass and put it carefully into Sammy's hands. Then she turned to Michael. 'This is your Daddy's home now, Michael.' With the gentlest smile she could manage, she held out a glass.

'I'm not drinking YOUR lemonade,' he screamed.

Henry put his elbows on the mantelpiece, his head in his hands.

Michael's feet thundered on the stairs. The house shook with the slam of the front door.

'You must let me be the judge of things, Suzannah. You

knew I didn't want to bring them here.'

'I couldn't see what harm it could do.'

Sammy sat on the sofa and sucked noisily through his straw.

'You must always follow my lead where the boys are concerned. Michael will come round to you in time.'

'He won't,' said Suzannah. 'He hates me already.'

'Nothing of the sort,' said Henry. 'He's just not ready yet.'

Suzannah nodded, pretending to be reassured, wondering what Henry thought the boy should be ready for.

Sixteen

The girl arrived on a Tuesday. No more than nineteen, a narrow face and straight, thin hair. She carried a cylindrical bag with green web handles.

Liam showed her the little room over the kitchen, the bare bed and a wooden chair.

'Where's the bedding?' Her accent was hard, from the north.

'Have you no sleeping bag?'

'No.'

'Don't you know I have nothing?' Liam asked, looking at her lips, an almost invisible line above a protruding, bony chin.

She shrugged. 'I thought you were equipped. I was told it was a safe house.'

Liam wondered if she had another meaning for the word. Safe meaning soft blankets, the safety of comfort.

They returned to the kitchen. He filled the kettle and put it on the stove. 'I'll borrow some blankets from the village.'

'You'll do nothing of the sort!'

'Why not?'

'My being here is a secret.'

Liam ignored the shrill tone. 'You can't sleep with no blankets. You'll freeze.'

'I won't freeze. I can put on the electric fire.'

'I can't afford electric fires.' Liam warmed the teapot with water from the kettle. 'Do you want milk in your tea?'

'And sugar.'

She watched him spoon tea from the caddy. 'I forbid you to ask for blankets in the village. My presence here is not for advertisement.'

Liam laughed. 'You forbid me?'

She put her hands on her hips, thrust her fingers into a wide belt that held men's jeans around her narrow, boyish hips.

'You're to do as I say. I'm an officer, I outrank you.'

'I was hoping for a woman,' said Liam quietly.

Her mouth twitched. 'That is a very unprofessional remark.'

Liam laughed again.

'You're to leave me alone!' shouted the girl.

Chuckling, Liam stirred sugar into her cup and placed it before her. 'You have nothing to fear from me. I shall be quite as professional as you.'

She took the tea and started up the stairs. Liam carried his mug out to the studio.

Pegged on a line, as in a photographer's darkroom, were pastel sketches he had made of the quay, tourist pictures of fishing nets and seagulls, rubber tyres bumping together between the boats. Mrs Evans had promised to take a dozen for the shop; she would charge eight pounds each and give him five pounds for every one she sold.

He was busy with the frames when the girl appeared in the doorway.

'What is there to eat?'

Liam spoke with a pin between his teeth. 'What will you make for us?'

The girl's chin came up. 'I'm no skivvy. Do you think I've come here to cook for you?'

'No, but I expect you take food, like other mortals.' He positioned a pin and tapped it rapidly into the frame. 'There are potatoes in the larder.'

'What about meat?'

'There's no meat here. I don't eat it.'

'You're vegetarian!' she cried, incredulous. 'I'm starving to death and all you've got is potatoes?'

'Evans's might still be open. She'll sell you meat if you want it.'

The girl shook her head. 'I mustn't be seen.'

Liam shrugged. 'It's up to you.'

She leaned against the door, silent for a while, watching him work.

'Have you no television?'

'No.' He cut a square out of the mounting card, and placed it over the picture.

'Radio?'

He shook his head.

'No television, no radio? How do you know what is going on?'

'I know all that I need to know. I like to keep a clear head.'

A smile played on the thin line of her lips. 'No newspapers either?'

He shook his head.

'You don't know who I am then?'

'I don't,' said Liam softly. 'I have no wish to know.'

She shifted against the door. Handel's sheep were a few yards from the fence, facing inland, a cluster of shabby behinds, threads of wool straggling in the breeze.

'Sure, you're probably wise not to listen to all that fascist crap,' said the girl. 'But what do you do all day?'

'I work,' said Liam.

She smiled. 'You call this work?'

Liam said nothing but turned away from her.

'What's that?' She pointed to a gold fibre-tipped pen.

'That's for the mount,' said Liam. 'They like a bit of gold round the picture.'

'Who is they?'

'The people who pay money for them.' With the aid of a rule he drew a double band of gold around the mount.

'This art business, it's a good cover.'

He looked up. Her face was in shadow, the outline a sharp silhouette against the light from the bay. 'It's no cover.'

'Sure it is.'

'It is not. I was painting long before I was mixed up with you folk.'

She lingered by the door, wincing at the noise of the hammer.

'Just potatoes?'

Liam nodded. 'You could roast them. There's also some cheese, if you're that hungry.'

'Cheese? Well, that's better. I was thinking we'd eat nothing but potatoes.'

Liam put down the hammer. 'You can get all the food you need without killing things.'

'Food perhaps.' She turned her face out towards the bay. 'But there are some things you have to be ready to kill for.'

He moved towards the door and she went ahead of him into the yard. 'What would you be killing for, then?'

'Freedom.'

'Freedom from what?'

'To live as we want to live. Freedom from oppression.'

He pulled the studio door closed. 'I'm free enough. It's only you people who oppress me.'

'We oppress you?' she echoed. 'How is that?'

He paused in the yard to pull up a weed. 'With your money.'

'But it's for our freedom that we are fighting. Not for money. You're not paid for what you do, McGuinness. You're paid so that you can continue.'

'Sure,' said Liam, pushing her gently ahead of him into the kitchen.

When the meal was over he went upstairs, took two blankets off his own bed and put then on the Vono.

'Will you be cold yourself?' The meal had softened her a little. He saw a glimpse of the Belfast girl she was; overcrowded Catholics, sharing blankets and social security.

He shook his head. 'I'll be all right.'

She was holding her mug, full of hot milk, close to her unformed breasts. 'Make sure you wake me in the morning. I don't want to sleep late.'

Liam turned his back and started down the stairs. 'I rise at dawn,' he said without looking up. 'I'll be in the studio.'

He heard her coughing in the night, a sharp, hoarse bark, like a frightened puppy. In the morning he could smell the hot, burning smell of the electric wall heater that hung above the door of her room. She was washing her hair in the kitchen sink, thin arms sticking out of her tee shirt.

'That's a bad cough you have,' he said. 'You should take something.'

She turned a small towel around her hair. 'It's nothing.'

'Are you coughing, Mr McGuinness?' asked Mrs Evans.

'Not me.'

The beak-nosed face came up, quick as a bird. 'Is the corned beef for her, too?'

'It is.'

'You can't win a girl's heart with corned beef!'

'No.' He put the beef and cough mixture in the pockets of his coat. A bell rang at the back of the shop.

'That'll be Glyn with the milk.'

'Does he want a hand?'

Liam followed her into the back, where the Evanses's home was, a few rooms between the shop and the yard. A sideboard with a bowl of fruit. A mirror over the frigidaire. Her husband was hefting milk crates.

'Here, Glyn. Mr McGuinness will give you a hand with those.'

Glyn smiled at him, red-faced and breathless. 'Taking time off from the girlfriend, eh?'

Liam picked up a crate. 'You don't miss much.'

Glyn laughed. 'They've been laying bets in The Swan. Two to one you'll be married before Christmas.'

'Married!' Liam stopped, feeling the wire edge of the crate against his fingers. 'I'll not marry that girl.'

'But she writes regular,' said Enid Evans. 'All those letters.'

Liam eased the crate against his hips. 'You want this inside the shop, Mrs Evans?'

The shopkeeper cackled after him. 'You're a dark horse, Liam McGuinness. But you can't fool me!'

He gave her the cough mixture in a glass, mixed with whisky. She drank it in silence.

'They know about you in the village.'

She was sitting at the kitchen table, already drowsy with the medicine.

'How do they know?' The drowsiness lifted for a moment, showing her face full of alarm.

Liam shrugged. 'They saw you arrive, I suppose.'

'What was said to you?'

Liam smiled. 'They said I can't win your heart with corned beef.'

Her scornful snort was lost in a yawn.

'Do you want coffee?'

He turned to find her head on the table, eyes flicking as she slipped into sleep.

He poured a capful of whisky into his own mug of coffee and, with his eyes on the sleeping girl, settled back to drink it. Who would she be, he wondered? This slip of a thing from Brendan's army. Had she no home that she must strut about in places such as these, calling herself an officer?

Without thinking he reached for his pad and started to draw. She was a study of bones, angular and lifeless. An hour passed. He had completed four sketches, hard, ungiving lines upon the page, when she woke and opened her mouth in a wide yawn that was cut short as she saw his pad and lunged forward to grab it from his hands.

'Do you want me to be caught?'

Liam laughed. 'They're not portraits, nobody would recognise you from these.'

'It's an unnecessary risk!' She ripped up the pages, scattering small pieces on the stone floor.

'I can't take you seriously,' said Liam. 'You and my brother, you're just children.'

'I don't know your brother.'

'Brendan? Why, he's just a boy. Those people are using him.' He looked up. 'They're using you, too.'

The thin lips sneered. 'If anyone is being used, it is you.'

Liam put the paper in the bin. 'You may be right there.' He turned to her and smiled. 'They're laying bets in The Swan that you'll marry me.'

'Marry you!' Her eyes flashed. 'A man like you? I'd rather be dead than tied to a lump like you, sponging off the cause, betraying us all.'

The next morning her bag was by the door. She wore a wig and a full-skirted dress. The bodice of the dress was shaped for breasts, flaps of material hanging loose against her bony chest. She looked like a child playing in her mother's frock.

'I want you to take me to the station.'

'What station?'

'Dover, I'm going back to London. You're to take me to the station by car.'

'I don't have a car.'

'Then hire one.'

'Hire one?' said Liam, astonished. 'Why don't you get the bus?'

She would not take the bus, nor hitch-hike. They would go by car, she insisted. Finally it was Liam who walked across the field and paid Handel ten pounds for the loan of his battered pickup. He had to coax her out of the house and all the way into Dover she trembled like a sparrow.

'Are you really on the run?' he asked, looking at the thin fingers, twisting and wittling on her lap.

She made no answer. When they reached the station she stayed in the pickup while he bought her ticket. Once on the platform she grabbed his arm and made him kiss her like a sweetheart. The little mouth contained sharp teeth that got in the way of his lips.

He pushed her away. 'For God's sake!'

She dragged his face back to her. 'No one will look at us kissing.'

'I don't want to kiss you.' A strand of her own hair came from under the wig and became entangled in his hands.

With an impatient gesture she pulled it away from him and stepped up on to the train. Once her case was inside she leaned out and began to kiss him again through the open window.

'Think of it as part of your job.'

Liam wiped his lip. 'Tell me one thing, what is it that you have done?'

A whistle blew and the train began to move. Her eyes were full of pride. 'I killed a pig. I set a trap and killed a pig.'

The train gathered speed.

'Why?'

She called back but the words were lost. The last he saw of

her was the strand of long hair like a piece of thread, caught in the wind.

Seventeen

'You don't have to come, Suzannah. Only if you want to.'

She did not want to. She never wanted to see his children again. She wished they had never been born. Without Michael and Sammy his leaving Ruth would have been a single act, simply a matter of packing his case; no excuse for visits and agreements and afternoons in the Science Museum.

'No,' she said. 'I want to come. I must get to know your children.'

The exhibition halls were crowded. Suzannah looked around, there were few women about, mothers, or women pretending to be mothers; just single men and children, fathers in search of something to share, spending their day of access in the free shelter of the Science Museum. Michael and Sammy stayed close to Henry and Suzannah trailed behind, unwilling to impose herself between them. All around her she saw children looking bored and fathers, hopeless. Henry was smiling, the same smile he used to encourage Suzannah. 'We are going to be happy. This is what we want.'

By four o'clock Sammy had begun to whine. Suzannah suggested tea in McDonald's and for the first time Michael looked enthusiastic.

'What would you like, Michael?' she asked as they stood before the crowded counter.

'Are you paying?'

Taken aback, she nodded. 'I'm treating you, yes.' She looked to Henry for support but he was showing Sammy the brightly coloured menu above the counter.

'I want a strawberry thick shake,' Michael answered.

'And what would you like to eat?'

'A cheeseburger, a Big Mac and double large fries.' Michael curled his lips as he spoke, as if the words were abusive.

He led them to a table in the corner and began to eat before anyone else sat down. Suzannah watched in horror as he drank the milkshake and ate the burgers and chips simultaneously. She had imagined that Henry's children would be like him, neat and well-mannered. Michael was ugly and rude, and Henry did nothing to discourage him. She tried to catch Henry's eye but he seemed preoccupied, helping Sammy eat a finger of pastry.

Michael finished his food and sat back, panting.

'I feel sick,' he said.

Henry looked up. 'It's your own fault. You shouldn't have eaten so much at once.'

The boy pulled a face. A moment later he jumped up and ran towards the cloakrooms. Henry remained in his seat.

'Shouldn't you go with him?' said Suzannah. 'I think he's ill.'

Henry shook his head, an expression of fastidious distaste had settled on his face.

Sammy sucked on the wide straw of his milkshake. It rattled as he drew in wind. Henry turned to him. 'Don't do that!'

Minutes passed before Michael returned to the table. His face was white, tear-stained. 'I've been sick,' he said in a weak voice.

Henry folded his arms. 'It's entirely your own fault, Michael.'

Tears rolled down the boy's cheeks. A child at the next table laughed loudly.

'Don't be upset,' Suzannah whispered. Michael glared at her, freckles showing like a rash on his tear-streaked face.

Sammy, too, began to cry. Henry turned to comfort him. With a rush of sympathy for the older child, Suzannah tried to dab Michael's cheeks with her handkerchief. He made a noise with his mouth and pushed the handkerchief away. She looked at her hand, he had spat into her palm, a trace of vomit in the spittle. She started to cry out, wanting to push her fist into the boy's ugly face, but she caught the look in Michael's eyes. Bright with tears they stared at her, a ring of wet lashes filled with unhappiness.

Henry took her back to Matilda's Cottage. Fast and dangerously, they sped through the Friday night traffic, the lights of the cathedral passing unremarked, to awake with the sun spilling into the bedroom; to make love with great passion. Suzannah cried out endearments, for she did love this man; his love was all that she needed. He could banish her fears, shut out the white silence of the displaced bed, the trail of dew in the hall, the old, sour smell of death.

When his moment came Henry closed his eyes, concentrating on his pleasure, keeping every fraction for himself; even this she could love. His self-centredness had a kind of innocence, there was childlike simplicity in the way he always left her body almost immediately and stared at his face in the mirror, making a pretence of combing his hair. She wanted to ask what he was looking for, and a question slipped in, unwelcomed, did he do that when he made love to Ruth?

She got up and pulled the curtains open, letting in a warm square of sunlight. Down in the bay, the tide had retreated, exposing long needles of rock at the foot of the Head. She could see the tumbledown house on the other side; a man was working in the garden, his coat draped over the gate.

She showered in the old-fashioned bathroom, bare feet on a tiled floor. When she was dry Henry brought her a glass of orange juice.

'It's too late to have breakfast, shall we have a brunch?'

She prepared the meal with the food they had brought from London.

'I'm not going down to the village shop again,' she said. 'That woman in there gives me the shudders.'

Henry laughed. 'She'll be so disappointed if you don't – you're probably the best gossip of the season.'

He dragged a set of white iron furniture from the garage. Suzannah scrubbed away the dust and cobwebs and he helped her pull them into the shade. Working on the old-fashioned cooker in the kitchen, Suzannah prepared prawn and mushroom pancakes for them to eat outside, followed by bowls of yoghurt, sweetened with honey.

When the meal was over she pushed her chair to one side and stretched out her legs to the sun. A gentle wind fluttered the hem of her skirt. In the raised bed beside the patio a rose bush was flowering, brilliant yellow heads smiling with sunshine; on the far side of the lawn sparrows scuffled under an old cherry tree.

'Are you happy, Henry?'

He smiled at her, showing his even, polished teeth. 'Of course I am happy. With a girl as pretty as you, how could I be anything else?'

'I wish it could always be like this. It's so peaceful. I wish we could live here instead of London.'

Henry reached across the table to take her hand. 'I've been thinking – would you like to come here in the summer?'

'To stay, you mean?'

'We could stay as long as you like. A month, six weeks?'

'But can you be away from work for so long?'

He sat back. 'The bank is pretty quiet in August. I'd have to go back for the odd meeting, but otherwise they could manage without me.'

He sat up and took hold of her other hand, so that she had to stretch out to him across the table. 'We could bring the boys.'

Suzannah looked up. 'Here?'

'Yes, why not?'

'What about Ruth?'

'She'll be glad of the break.' He breezed the question away. 'School holidays always exhaust her.'

'She won't agree to your bringing them up here. I thought you said she has a thing about this place?'

'I can persuade her.'

Suzannah paused, gently freeing her hands from his own. How could he persuade her? How could he persuade Ruth of anything when he was no longer with her? Could there be so little difference between them, even now?

And how would she manage with Michael, with his unhappiness? The boy had spat into her palm, there could be no clearer message than that.

She went inside and brought out the album of photographs. Ignoring the pictures of Ruth, she stared at the children. Most of the pictures were of Sammy: a little boy in the bath with a plastic duck, a toddler on the beach grasping the legs of his mother. The pictures of Michael were all old and faded, as if the younger child had taken his place and Michael was forgotten.

'Henry, why are there no pictures of Michael?'

'There are, lots of them.'

'There's nothing recent.'

Henry looked over her shoulder. 'It was Ruth who liked to take photographs. I used to let her get on with it. Perhaps Michael refuses to pose these days.' He turned a page of the album. 'But here's one. I took it in the garden last year.'

Michael was sitting on a swing. It was too small for him and the camera had distorted his bent legs. He looked cross, in absolute contrast to Sammy who stood in the foreground, holding something out to the camera with a broad, confident smile.

'Was Michael jealous when Sammy was born?'

Henry thought for a moment. 'I don't remember him being jealous. If he was, he's over it now.'

Would you have known, Suzannah wondered?

She looked again at the photograph, at the boy scowling from the outgrown swing. For no reason she could recognise, Austin's words came into her mind, his warning against living with your eyes down, watching only your own square.

'If we did come down for the whole summer, I should have to go back to visit my father at least once.'

'But you've been up there so often.'

'Nevertheless– ' she took his plate and stacked it on top of her own – 'I can't leave him alone all summer.'

'You mustn't let him rely on you, Suzannah. I need you here, with me.'

'He needs me, too,' she said, softly, conscious of her own contradictions.

'Why?' Henry looked up. 'He has a housekeeper, doesn't he?'

She went up to look at the two small bedrooms at the top of the stairs. Each had a narrow dormer window, one with a single bed beneath it, a bare calico cover on an old-fashioned, blue-striped mattress.

She called down the stairs to Henry. 'We'd have to bring lots of things with us.'

He came up, two steps at a time, smiling. 'What sort of things?'

'Duvets, sheets, towels – there's only the bare furniture.'

Henry looked in the airing cupboard. 'There used to be loads of stuff. Ruth must have taken it all back to London.'

'So she had decided that she wasn't coming back?'

Henry shrugged. 'I remember her packing. She said something about the place being spoiled. I didn't realise she was taking so much away.' He shrugged and put on the smile that she had come to know; determination rather than happiness. 'Make a list, Suzannah. Write down everything we'll need to make a perfect holiday.'

Suzannah looked at the cot. 'Will Sammy still sleep in that?'

Henry continued to smile. 'We'll buy him a bed of his own. A small one, that'll fit under the eaves.' He was suddenly gay, light-hearted. 'You wait Suzannah, it will be marvellous. We'll be a family, just the four of us.' He patted her bottom.

'But Henry, they don't like me. They'll never accept me.'

'Of course they will, before you know it, they'll love you.' He turned and hugged her. 'How could they fail to love someone so pretty?' He lifted up her hair and kissed her neck. 'You make a list of what we'll need, I'm going down to the village.'

'What for?'

'To The Swan, to buy champagne, if they have any. We're going to celebrate, my darling.'

He ran, whistling, down the stairs.

Suzannah leaned against the door. And Ruth? What would Ruth think of his plan? How would she be persuaded? He spoke of her with such impatience, flicking his fingers, as if he could physically dismiss her. But she could not be so dismissed. She was here in the house, in every room, even the absence of the bedding bespoke her presence. She was present in all their lives, in the books that he had brought from Cavanagh Road; an inscription on a flysheet, a bookmark poking from the novel beside his bed. Whenever he spoke of the boys, whenever any portion of his other life intruded, there was Ruth, just as present as the shrill voice on the telephone.

'But she is all right?' Suzannah asked him once when he had taken the phone into another room. 'She is coping?'

'Of course she's coping. Women always cope better when they don't have a man's neck to hang themselves around.'

It wasn't what Suzannah meant. She used the word 'coping' to avoid a more emotive word. What she wanted to ask was, 'Is she grieving?' But 'grief' was disallowed, not a word for the lips of his darling girl, not for the death of her mother nor the abandonment of Ruth.

It came to Suzannah that he could not bear to think of either death or grief. She had heard Ruth's voice on the telephone, trilling like a bird, and watched his face going blank, like a machine shutting down, retracting its parts to present a cool white facade. I am not listening.

It had been thus on the day she returned from lunch with Austin, found Henry waiting in the flat to bundle her back into her coat for the journey to Cavanagh Road.

'Stay in the car, Suzannah. I haven't told her yet. She'll only believe I'm going if she sees you here, waiting for me.'

She had waited in his car for hours, watching the rain, thinking of Austin's words – wondering what he would have to say to her now. What words would he use to describe her waiting there in the car, watching the house?

The front door opened and a woman appeared. Henry came out, walked past the woman and down the steps. The woman slumped against the door, her hand across her mouth. Henry put a bag on the back seat of the car. He showed no emotion, no pity, there was nothing but the shake of his hand on the steering wheel, the squeal of tyres as they pulled out into the road.

Shrugging away the memory, she found a notepad and pencil and began to make a list of what they would need: sheets and pillowslips, bath towels and beach towels. With a flicker of curiosity she opened the cupboards in the kitchen, counted cutlery and crockery. It was strange to think that Ruth had done the same. The oven door was faulty and would not close without a special turn of the handle. Had Ruth fretted over it too? There were enamel storage tins in the pantry, with faded, handwritten labels. She studied the handwriting, wondering whose it was, Matilda's or Ruth's?'

The holiday approached. If Ruth raised objections, Suzannah did not hear of them.

Anxiously she telephoned Gassy to ask her for recipes, for the cakes and sticky puddings that had delighted her brother as a child.

'What do you want them for?' the housekeeper grumbled.

'I'm cooking for a family, Gassy. I need to know how to make your wonderful cookies.'

'For a family?' The housekeeper made a little noise, a polite cough. 'I'm sure your father would like you to cook for him.'

'But he has you, Gassy,' answered Suzannah.

Henry was exultant. 'Delicious,' he cried, stealing from the wire tray of cookies left cooling on the counter. 'The boys will love these.'

'Do you really think they will?' she asked, her face puckered with anxiety.

Henry laughed. 'Just you wait and see.'

'But will they really?' She clutched his arm.

'Suzannah, relax.' His fingers stroked her hand. 'You don't look pretty when you're anxious.'

A van delivered Sammy's new bed. A wooden base, a blue-painted headboard with a row of ducks at the foot. Suzannah vacuumed the rooms, scrubbed the kitchen floor, removed the spiky-written labels from the tins in the larder; baked and cleaned and worried until at last, it was Saturday and the day had come. Suzannah stayed behind, alone in the cottage like a nervous bride, while Henry went to collect his sons from Cavanagh Road.

With infinite care she made up the beds, put blankets under the bottom sheets and tucked them in the duvets, so that restless feet would not break free and grow cold in the night. Laying fresh paper in the drawers she hummed a tune from a half-forgotten film; a woman in a pinafore had hummed as she rolled out gingerbread dough, still humming as the first little men went into the oven. Suzannah hummed, smoothing down the paper and laying out the linen. On the top of the wardrobe in Michael's room she found a poster of a racing car. She pinned it to the wall. All boys liked racing cars. She would give them extra pocket money, sweets when they went shopping, so that they would love her more quickly . . .

The doorbell shrilled in the hall. Could Henry be back so soon? She took off her apron and went downstairs.

A man leaned against the porch. A long coat, dark, curly hair, a dense beard. He stood upright as she opened the door.

'Yes?'

The man stared. 'It's you again, then.'

'I beg your pardon?'

'I saw you the last time. I thought . . . ' His voice trailed away. A lilt of Irish, soft as the breeze.

'Did you want to speak to Henry?'

'No, it was Ruth, I . . . '

'Ruth isn't here.'

'You've come in her place, have you?'

She looked at him sharply but there was no insolence in his look, no ulterior meaning to his words. His face was open, bright eyes that flicked from her face to her body, like darting insects.

'I'm from Smithies,' he said.

'Oh, the artist.'

He smiled. 'That's right.'

Suzannah held the door, unsure whether to invite him in.

'I've lived there a while.' He smiled again, settling comfortably, one foot up against the porch wall behind him. 'It was in a mess when I moved in, but it's all right now.'

Suzannah nodded. 'Good.'

'Are you staying long?'

'For a few weeks.'

'It's nice in the summer.'

'Yes,' said Suzannah.

The artist raised his eyebrows. 'Would you be having the children?'

'Yes. They're coming today.'

'Today is it?' He grinned broadly and took his foot off the wall. 'You'll be busy then, cooking and all.'

Suzannah smiled. 'I am, actually.'

He held out his hand. 'Perhaps another time?'

Suzannah smiled politely. 'Perhaps.'

He whistled as he walked away down the drive.

The sun had faded, shadows gathered thick on the lawn, when she heard the car in the lane. Michael was out before Henry had parked. He ran straight past her, up the stairs.

'It's just the same!' he cried. 'Nothing has changed.'
Henry followed with a suitcase, smiling.
'Can we go to the beach tomorrow?' Michael had run down again, expecting to see his father on the stairs. Finding Suzannah there instead, he blushed, looked awkwardly away.
'I expect we shall,' she said, wishing she could make her voice sound normal.
Sammy was behind her, climbing the stairs one at a time. Unselfconsciously he held out his arms and she lifted him on to her hip and carried him into his bedroom.
Henry carried in a suitcase. 'Sammy's things are in here. Ruth packed separate cases for them.'
He released the locks and opened the lid: the case was as neatly packed as his own had been – little shorts and tee shirts, pyjamas and sandals, a cardboard box of toys. Sammy reached in and plucked out an ancient teddy bear.
'What's his name?' asked Suzannah.
Silently the child wrapped the bear's arms about his neck.
'What do you call him, Sammy?'
'It's my bear.' Michael stood in the doorway. 'Sammy stole it.'
Unable to think of a reply, Suzannah smiled. 'Oh dear,' she said eventually. 'But I'm sure you didn't mind Sammy having him?'
The older boy shrugged. 'No choice.' Abruptly he turned and left.
Suzannah finished unpacking and put the empty case on top of the wardrobe.
'Barrow,' said Sammy suddenly.
'What is barrow, Sammy?'
'Barrow,' he said again, hugging the bear against his chest.
'Is that the bear's name, Barrow?'
He nodded. 'Barrow Bear.'
'Would Barrow Bear and Sammy like some supper?'
She held out her hand. The little boy took it and, with the bear under his free arm, accompanied her down the stairs.
Michael emerged from the sitting room, staggering under the weight of a small television.
'Where are you going with that?' Half way through the

sentence Suzannah tried to soften her tone, to sound less like a schoolteacher.

Michael ignored her, pushing past with the flex caught between his teeth.

'I said he could.' Henry followed his son. 'There's some programme he wants to see – nothing you'd want to watch.'

The television was to stay in Michael's bedroom for the whole holiday: an unspoken excuse for them not to have to sit uncomfortably together downstairs.

Late in the evening Henry opened a bottle of wine.

'To a successful holiday,' he said, raising his glass.

Suzannah raised her own.

'Don't look so worried!' He patted her knee. 'Everything will be fine.'

'I wish you didn't have to go to London,' said Suzannah.

'It's unavoidable, my love. But only for a few odd days.'

'What shall I do with the boys when you're not here?'

'Why, the same as we shall do tomorrow. Take them to the beach. Or to the village. They can watch the boats, talk to the fishermen. There's plenty for them to do.'

Suzannah sipped her wine.

'Take each day as it comes,' said Henry. 'You've got a whole month to get to know them. Just relax.'

The first few days were easy. Henry marshalled them all down the cliff steps, he carried deckchairs and a parasol, sandwiches and cookies packed into a green canvas bag. The sun shone and the water was calm.

Michael loved the sea. Henry could hardly persuade him to come out to eat his lunch. His declared aim was to swim to a small rock in the middle of the bay. Suzannah watched from the sand, the rock wasn't far but he swam awkwardly, thrashing the water and making little progress.

Eighteen

A thick mist accompanied the dawn of the fifth day; a damp grey wall that hung over the bay, hiding the view of the sea and the beach.

Suzannah woke to find the other part of the bed already empty. She could hear Henry in the bathroom, the splash of the overhead shower competing with an unearthly booming sound that had disturbed her dreams. She went downstairs and put on the kettle. The sound filled the house; when she opened the door it was outside too, swirling in with the mist.

Henry came down behind her, carrying his briefcase.

'What's that noise, Henry?'

He leaned forward and kissed her. 'Did it frighten you? It's only the fog warning, telling the ferries that they are close in.'

Suzannah listened again; the sound was flat, like the cry of one who has wept too long, so that the feeling is lost, and only the crying itself remains.

Henry ate breakfast with her in the kitchen, thickly buttered toast with honey. He was dressed for work, she caught a whiff of aftershave and toothpaste.

He looked at his watch. 'I'll have to go soon.'

Trying not to sound plaintive, she asked, 'Will you think of me while you're there?'

He patted her shoulder. 'Of course I'll think of you. Is there any more coffee?'

She filled his cup and stood close by, staring through the window while he drank it.

'God, look at the weather. What will I do with the boys if we can't go to the beach?'

'It'll be all right,' Henry put his arm around her hips. 'The sun will shine. You'll have a lovely day. Look, its clearing even now.'

He pointed towards the east, where weak, orange light was striking blindly into the mist, picking out the bulky shadows of the garden.

Henry buttered a second slice of toast.

'What are you going to do today?' she asked.

He smiled. 'I'm going to the bank.'

'I know where,' she said, suddenly irritable, 'but what will you do?'

'I have a meeting to attend at eleven-thirty, then lunch in the Boardroom. After lunch, provided the discussions have gone well, and all the work earlier this year has been right, we'll clinch the deal.'

'And why can't they do that without Henry Alland?'

'Suzannah!' he cried. 'It's my deal. I've worked on it for months. I have to be there. I'm sorry, my love, but I must go.' He held her close for a moment and then his face lit up as if he had thought of a solution. 'Would you like to keep the car? You could take me to the station and have the use of the car while I'm gone.'

She shook her head. 'We can do without the use of the car for a day.' She put her head on his chest. 'It's you we can't do without.'

He picked up his briefcase. 'I must go.' His kiss was firmer than usual, the strong, smiling lips of the banker covered her own, tasting of sweet coffee.

She followed him outside. The rising sun had split the mist into ribbons, stabbing the corners of the garden with its harsh, early light. The windscreen-wipers swished as the car turned out into the lane. As the sound of it retreated, she realised that the fog horn, too, had ceased, leaving only the sound of birds and leaves dripping on to the mist-sodden grass. Returning to the kitchen, she cleared the plates, sliding uneaten corners of toast into the bin. It was almost full. She lifted out the white liner, twisted it once, and secured the opening with a wire from the drawer. Outside, her slippers slapped loudly on the wet path. The roses had dropped their petals, a shower of yellow on the grass, as though the mist had been too much for them, the pinhead droplets of water too great a weight to endure.

The dustbin stood in a recess by the gate, where the chestnut trees had made a roof against the drizzle. The lid parted from the bin with a thud, releasing a puff of sour air. She laid the new rubbish over the old and pushed back the lid. Under the trees the ground was almost dry, the air very still. She stood for a moment, enjoying the silence, looking back at the cottage. A trail of creeper clung to the side wall, framing the windows in a dark, shivering green. Above it the rooftiles were glossy with water and on the far hip of the roof, a seagull perched, looking silently out to sea.

Michael was watching her. His solemn white face seemed to hang in the glass of his bedroom window.

She waved. For a while he remained still, as if he had not seen her, and then a hand came up, like a limp white flag. She smiled at him and hurried back up the path.

He was in the kitchen before her, standing by the table as she wiped her feet.

'Good morning, Michael, would you like a cup of coffee? It's still hot.'

He looked at Henry's empty cup. 'Has Dad gone?'

'Yes, he went a little while ago. He did look in on you but you were still asleep.'

'When's he coming back?'

Suzannah put her head on one side. 'Don't you remember, he told you last night? He'll be back at about half past six.'

Michael shrugged. 'I didn't realise he would be away all day.'

'Yes,' said Suzannah, brightly. 'It'll be just the three of us.'

Michael looked out at the garden, as if something there had caught his interest.

'Will you have the coffee? Or would you prefer milk?'

'Milk,' he grunted, not looking at her.

It was Michael who led the way down the cliff steps after breakfast. The mist had cleared completely, leaving a blue, transparent sky, a pale echo of the colour of the sea. Sammy scrambled down behind his brother. They had devised a game of counting the steps. Sammy would shout out the numbers, frequently out of order, and Michael would make him go back a few steps and come down again, until the order was right. Below them stretched the beach, a small arc of pebbles and sand. Weighed down by the canvas bag full of lunch and swimming gear, and a tall bottle of lemonade, Suzannah followed as quickly as she could. Michael had consented only to carry her sunbathing mat, rolled under his arm. She climbed down awkwardly, the breeze caught the brim of her sunhat and she tried to hold on to that too, using her elbows against the rocks to keep her balance.

On the flat landing of rock that linked the steps with the path that led around the cliff, the artist had set up his easel. He had his back to them, hunched over his work. At his feet was a large case and beside him, on a camping stool, an open box of tubes and jars.

As the boys reached the landing he paused to raise a flat, paint-laden knife in greeting.

Suzannah quickened her pace, conscious that the painter had turned to watch her descent.

'Don't disturb the gentleman, boys,' she called.

The artist looked up. 'I'm no gentleman, ma'am.'

Michael looked at the canvas. 'Will it be a picture of the beach?'

The painter put down his palate, an old china plate dappled with bright pools of colour. He wiped his hands on a rag. 'It might be.'

'Are you the man who was here before?'

He smiled. 'I have been here all the time. It is you who was here before.'

Michael frowned as he thought about this, his lips curled back to show his teeth.

The artist was looking at Sammy. Suzannah noticed an intense interest in his expression.

The strain of the picnic bag dug into her shoulder. 'Come on. Let's get down to the beach.'

Sammy took her hand and she pulled him against her, like a woman gathering her skirt. They were half way down the next flight of steps when something made her look back; the artist stood in front of his easel, once more wiping his hands, staring down at her.

Michael dumped her mat on the bottom step and ran off among the rocks. She carried it to the middle of the beach.

'Why didn't you bring the deckchair?' Sammy asked.

'It's too big to carry,' said Suzannah. 'Only your Daddy can manage a big chair on those steep steps.'

'My Daddy's very big and strong,' said Sammy proudly.

'Yes he is, very strong indeed.'

Sammy giggled and together they spread out the mat and dug a small hollow in the sand for the bag.

'That'll help to keep the sandwiches cool,' said Suzannah.

'Can we have lemonade now, please?'

She put two paper cups on the mat and unscrewed the cap of the bottle. It was made of flexible plastic that collapsed as she pulled off the cap. Lemonade spouted out over the mat.

Sammy chuckled.

'It is a messy bottle, isn't it?' said Suzannah.

'It's a messy mess,' he shouted.

Michael was just visible. He had climbed on to one of the tall rocks that clustered at the foot of the cliff. She waved her cup and pointed to the lemonade. He was facing her but gave no sign of having understood. She replaced the bottle top and let Sammy dig another hollow to keep the lemonade cool in the sand.

Her bikini was under her clothes. The breeze chilled her midriff as she pulled off the dress, but the sun was warm on the mat. She rubbed oil into her body until it gleamed and lay back.

The sun grew brighter. She could hear the swish and flush of the sea, and Sammy chattering to himself, playing in the sand nearby. High above, the white square of the painter's canvas marked his place on the cliff. She pulled down the brim of her hat to shield her eyes. The air under the hat was warm, full of the dry smell of the straw.

Nineteen

'Sammy!'

Suzannah shot up, blinded for a moment by the glare. It was Michael who had screamed. He was high on a rock, pointing to the water. She saw him jumping down, crumpling on to the sand, and then up again, pounding across the beach.

Sammy was in the sea, his short, plump legs striding

fearlessly in the shallows. She was on her feet, running, her bare feet thumping on the hard packed sand, then tossing the water high into the air. The cold made her gasp. Michael reached Sammy ahead of her, just as the first large breaker rolled towards him.

Sammy began to scream, clinging to Michael who tried to hold him out to her across the water. She grabbed the little boy's legs, shrieking, 'Sammy! Never do that again, never!'

Squirming in her arms like smooth wet jelly, the little body almost broke free as she struggled for her footing. Michael put out his hands not, as she first thought, to take Sammy back, but to pin the child about her, pressing his legs to her hips. Sammy continued to scream as she struggled up the beach and did not cease until she put him down on the sand near the mat. As he tried to run off, Michael reached out and gave him a single sharp slap with the palm of his hand. Bleating, Sammy sank on to the sand.

'That's what children need,' said Michael.

Suzannah was too breathless to speak. She rubbed Sammy with a towel. The little boy submitted, letting out small noises, as if trying to gather momentum for another long scream.

'Look, he's going back.'

'What?'

Michael pointed up the cliff.

Suzannah looked up. The artist was near the bottom of the steps, wearily climbing upwards.

'Didn't you see him?' said Michael.

Suzannah paused. 'He was coming down for Sammy?'

'Yes.' Michael nodded. 'He must have seen him go into the water. He came running down the cliff steps, so fast I thought he'd fall.'

As the painter regained the platform he looked back at her and raised his hand. Tentatively she waved back, and then quickly turned away.

'It's time for lunch,' she said.

Michael helped her unpack the sandwiches and cake. She said nothing when he opened the bottle of lemonade and drank with long, noisy gulps.

At the sight of the food Sammy moved closer to his brother.

She put the box of sandwiches on to the mat. The older boy helped himself to three and handed one to Sammy. The little boy ate in silence, his face dirty with tears.

When the sandwiches were finished she gave them a wedge of cherry cake and stood up to shake the crumbs off the mat. She was packing away the box when Sammy approached her, holding something in his fist.

'What is it, Sammy?'

'Present,' said the little boy. He opened his hand. Lying stickily between his fingers was a whole pink cherry.

'I saved it,' he said. Plucking the cherry from his hand he pushed it into her mouth.

'Why, thank you, Sammy!' said Suzannah, laughing as she chewed the cherry. It was hot and sweet.

Falling backwards on to the sand, Sammy clapped his hands with delight. 'Castle!' he shouted.

'You want to build a castle?'

Sammy nodded energetically. 'A big castle!'

'Will you help us, Michael?'

The older boy pulled a face.

'I know it's childish,' she said, when he did not answer, 'but we'd build a much better one if you'd help us.'

They moved to the edge of the water and began excavating the wet sand. Sammy scooped up a handful and held it out to her, dark grains clinging to his fingers.

'Dirty!' he cried, with delight. 'Dirty! Dirty! Dirty!'

Michael filled the bucket and turned out a perfect mould.

'This'll be the keep,' he said. 'And we've got to have a moat.' Abruptly he stood up and dusted the sand from his knees. 'You stay here, I'm going to find something for the bridge.'

Suzannah smiled. 'All right then, Sammy can stay and help me dig the moat.'

She used Sammy's spade to dig a trench in the sand. The little boy worked beside her, singing to himself and chattering. The sun was warm on her back.

'Michael's coming back.' Sammy pointed behind her. His brother was returning, loping across the sand with a piece of driftwood under his arm.

'That's going to be some bridge,' said Suzannah.

Michael laid the wood across the trench.

'Do you think it's too big?' His voice was full of concern. 'I could try and split it.'

'It's fine,' said Suzannah.

Using Sammy's bucket Michael turned out a series of towers and set them in a square within the area bounded by the moat. His face was full of concentration, the lower lip tucked in behind his protruding teeth. With more care than she would have expected from him, he built up the sand and squeezed out a wall between the towers, using his fingers to shape the battlements.

'There,' he said, when it was finished. 'I wish we could show it to Dad.' He smiled at Suzannah, looking straight into her eyes. 'It's better than the ones he builds.'

Suzannah smiled back, full of warmth.

'Bang!' shouted Sammy.

Suzannah looked round. The little boy was pointing at one of the towers. Set too close to the moat, it had split in two and collapsed.

'Michael, you've had an earthquake!' she cried. 'You'll have to start all over again.'

It was the wrong thing to say. He withdrew from her, visibly, folding his arms and drawing up his legs, reminding her of a colourless insect disturbed by the light.

Helplessly she sat in the sand, trying to think of the right words.

Without warning his foot shot out and demolished the rest of the castle wall. For a second Sammy looked as though he would start to scream but then he stood up and began to stamp, gleefully kicking the castle to bits. Suzannah watched in silence as Michael joined in, shouting and stamping until the castle was no more than a heap of disturbed sand. Sammy picked up the plank and, barely keeping his balance, attempted to run away with it. Michael went after him, pretending to run but checking himself to let the little boy stay ahead. Before long Sammy dropped the plank and simply ran.

Suzannah sat on the sand and watched. Sammy was giggling, weaving easily around the rocks and shingle at the base of the cliff. Above them the painter had come round in front of his easel, one of his brushes poised in his hand. Michael stumbled on a rock and got up again, running in earnest now, diving for his brother in a low gully at the bottom of the cliff. Eventually the little boy was caught and tossed, squealing with delight, into the air.

Suzannah smiled as they ran back to her. She held out her arms and Sammy ran straight into them. Her heart lifted. Somehow, without knowing how it was done, she had found a way to be with them.

Michael collapsed, breathless, on to the mat.

'Is there any more lemonade?'

She handed him the bottle.

They ate the rest of the cake and then she shook the sand from her dress and pulled it back over her costume. Sammy had taken his bucket to the shingle patch to fill it with pebbles. He chose, not for colour or shape, but indiscriminately, for the joy of the noise the pebbles made falling together into the bucket.

Michael came to help roll up her mat and fold the wet towels into the green bag. He let Sammy put his pebbles in the front pocket of the bag, and, despite the weight of them, slung it over his shoulder. They waited while she tied her sun hat under her chin and then Michael led the way, with Sammy behind him and Suzannah at the rear.

The climb up the steps was slow. Her legs felt stiff, heavy-kneed. The artist was a dark shape against the flat rock of the landing. She did not look up, but could feel him watching their ascent.

There was no other way. He had moved his easel right into their path. She kept her eyes on the steps disappearing beneath them; on the back of Michael's legs, at an old scar, the shape of a harp.

They had almost reached the landing. 'Good afternoon.' Soft words in the still air.

Sammy looked at his brother.

'Hello,' said Michael, two-tone, a sudden break in his voice like the host of a cracked horn.

The painter was looking at her. 'Has it been a good day for the beach?'

'Yes.' Suzannah smiled.

'Home now, is it?'

Michael moved round the easel. 'What have you painted?'

'What is it to you?' There was no harshness in the words, not, what do you care, but, what do you see?

Michael gazed solemnly at the board.

'It's a picture of Suzannah.'

'Of me?' Her head spun.

'So that's your name.'

She walked back to the easel, circling to avoid his open box of paints. A woman in a red costume. From the back, sitting with her knees up and buttocks like a small pear in the sand.

'You wouldn't keep still. I had to be quick.'

She stepped away from it, unsure of how to react.

'If I'd have asked you'd have said no,' said the Irishman.

'You should take it home to show Dad.' Michael's voice was high again, the momentary adult gone.

Sammy picked a pebble from the path and held it out to the painter.

He smiled. 'Is that my payment?'

Sammy pointed to the bag. 'I've got lots.'

The painter took the pebble from Sammy's hand. 'Thank you, little man.' He squatted down, until his face was almost level with the boy's. 'Are you going to be a fine man, like your Da'?'

Suzannah frowned, not quite knowing why she did. 'We must go, it's getting late.'

The artist put the pebble in his pocket and raised his hand. 'Until next time, then.'

She took Sammy's hand.

'Goodbye.'

Twenty

Round and smooth, the pebble fitted neatly into Liam's fist. He sat outside The Swan waiting for opening time. The boy had grown well. He had listened to them counting the steps, the childish voices coming closer, lifting his heart.

Glyn Evans shouted across the street. 'You're starting early.'

'I've got a thirst to quench.'

The shopkeeper crossed the street and sat beside him on the low wall of the pub garden. 'You been painting?'

Liam nodded. 'It's thirsty work in the sun.'

'You brought some pictures down with you?' Glyn indicated Liam's bag.

'I have. You never know when someone will buy.'

Glyn put a pipe in his mouth and a lighted match in the bowl. 'Is there a living in it?'

Liam shrugged. 'I get by.'

'My wife worries about you.' Glyn sucked on the pipe.

'Mrs Evans?'

'She thinks you ought to get a wife.'

Liam chuckled. 'Does she now?'

'But not just anyone, mind; she didn't like the one you had a while back.'

'Which one?'

'The skinny one – with the cough. Very concerned, Mrs Evans was.'

'She didn't say anything to me,' said Liam.

'Ah, now, she wouldn't. But you'd think you were her own son, the way she prattles on.'

Liam smiled.

'She says it's unhealthy for a man to live alone – especially you being a vegetarian. It winds her up no end. She thinks you don't eat.' Glyn turned to blow his pipe smoke away from Liam's face. 'And she likes to know what's going on.' He took the pipe out of his mouth. 'You take that lot up in Matilda's place. She can't stop talking about them neither – it's not the morals, it's the fact no one told her.'

Liam laughed. 'I can imagine.'

He thought of his own surprise, the first time they came, the shock that had caught his breath, that it was not Ruth.

'It gave me a turn, myself,' said Glyn.

The fluid in his pipe gave a gurgling noise as he drew in the smoke. 'I was all ready to say "Hello, Mrs Alland," and suddenly it's a stranger. I looked into the car when he came for petrol, and there she was. I hardly knew what to say.'

'She has striking looks,' said Liam.

'She has that.' Glyn took the pipe out of his mouth and gave Liam a nudge. 'And not just her face, neither.'

Behind them Liam could hear the barman sliding the bolts. It was opening time. He stood up. 'Not just her face,' he agreed.

'I'd best be getting back,' said Glyn.

Liam nodded. 'Give my regards to your Mrs.'

Inside the bar smelled of stale beer and smoke. Liam sat on a stool and ordered a bottle of stout.

'Will you have a pasty today, Liam?' the barman asked as he opened the bottle.

'I'll have two,' said Liam. 'Cheese and onion.'

Briefly, as the plate was put before him, his mind swung back to the stranger with burned hands, his brother, Brendan, raising his glass to their mother. What would they ask of him next? Pushing the plate to one side, he lifted the bottle to his lips and drank deeply.

'What are you making?'

'Soup.'

'What sort of soup?'

'Tomato soup – you like that, don't you?'

He looked suspiciously into the saucepan. 'It doesn't look like that when Mum makes it.'

Suzannah stirred the mixture. 'How does your Mum make it?'

'In a tin.'

'I see.'

She tasted the soup and reached for the salt. It was Gassy's recipe: tinned tomatoes with potato stock and onions. But it didn't taste quite like hers.

'Will Dad be home soon?'

'In a little while. Will you lay the table for me, please?' He went into the dining room and she heard him struggling with the drawer of the sideboard.

'It's stiff,' she called. 'Pull it to one side.'

She waited, stirring the soup, and eventually heard the sound of cutlery dropping on to the table.

Michael came back to the kitchen. 'What are we having with it?'

'There's some nice bread, and cheese.'

Michael's eyes widened. 'Can we put the cheese in the soup?'

'In the soup?'

'Yes, you know, let it melt.'

Suzannah hesitated. 'Well, I suppose so, if you like it that way.'

She handed him sideplates and napkins. 'Ask Sammy to wash his hands, it's almost ready.'

She served the soup and waited anxiously for Michael to taste it.

The squares of cheese dropped into the bowl with a splash.

Michael took some bread and chewed it, unbuttered, while blowing on the hot soup. They ate in silence. From time to time she used her napkin to wipe a smudge of soup from Sammy's chin. Michael tipped his bowl as it emptied, and ladled the soup into his mouth, pausing only to bite off the long strings of melted cheese.

'How did you like it?' she asked, at last.

'It was all right.'

'Do you always eat it with cheese?'

He grinned. 'Mum doesn't let us.'

Suzannah laughed. 'Better not let your father see you!'

The granary loaf was almost finished. She was slicing the crust when they heard the car in the drive.

Michael leapt for the door. 'Dad's home!' Sammy was close behind, skipping on the rug.

As if a switch had been thrown, the house came alive. She could hear Henry's voice in the hall, his laugh, and then they tumbled together through the door, all talking at once, Sammy on Henry's shoulder and Michael close behind, thin arms stretched by the weight of his father's briefcase.

'Did you have a good day?'

A bubble-burst of stories, the quiet day on the beach was transformed, as if every hour had been magical.

'I swam nearly all the way to the rock!'

'I got a jelly fish!'

'We built a castle with a moat and everything.'

'Suzannah made a drawbridge . . . '

'And how are you, Suzannah?' Kissing her on the lips. He smelt of cigar smoke, and brandy.

'A painting man was there!' Sammy cried. 'He did a picture of Suzannah.'

'Of Suzannah?' Henry turned to her. 'Did he ask your permission?'

She shook her head. 'It was quite good though, just the back of me, sitting in the sand.'

Henry's smile was weak, the corners of his mouth let him down.

'Was he a nuisance?'

'No.'

'He should have asked.'

'I'd have been embarrassed.'

'He should have asked though.'

Sammy pulled his arm. 'Come and see my pebbles!'

Henry let himself be dragged away.

Suzannah cleared the plates. Michael had turned on the television in his bedroom, she could hear the drone of a news reporter.

'Sammy ought to have a bath,' she said when Henry finally returned. 'He didn't have one yesterday.'

Henry poured himself a beer from the fridge.

'I'll go and do it in a minute,' he said. 'When I've had this.'

Suzannah felt cheated. She had looked forward to the bath-time, to holding Sammy's little body again, perhaps not resisting her this time, as he had done on the beach.

'I'll do it if you like.'

'No, you get ready to go out.'

'Where are we going?'

'I thought we could go out for a drink.'

'To the pub?'

'Yes, it's quite nice in there.'

'What about the boys?'

'They'll be all right for an hour or so. I'm not hungry yet, I had a very good lunch. You can make me a light supper when we come back.'

The sun was still shining as they set off in the car, long sloping rays along the cliff road. They left Michael watching television in his room. Sammy was already asleep in the blue-painted bed, with Barrow Bear beside him on the pillow.

The village was quiet. A man with an unlit pipe in his mouth was sweeping the garage forecourt. Outside the pub the picture of the swan creaked in a breeze that carried the smell of fish and seaweed, and diesel oil from the quay.

The bar was almost empty. Suzannah recognised the postman and smiled at him and then at the Irishman who was sitting at the bar, his large flat bag propped aganst his stool. He raised his hand to Suzannah. 'Hello there, Suzannah. Nice to see you again.' Henry walked towards the bar.

'I think we met before,' said the artist. 'Liam McGuinness.'

Henry shook hands without smiling.

'What'll it be – a beer or are you a cocktails man?' said the Irishman.

Henry let the Irishman buy him a beer and a glass of cider for Suzannah.

She watched them drink. The Irishman's glass was empty first, a circle of foam around the brim. Even in front of Henry, she noticed his eyes – looking her over.

'I hear you did some painting this afternoon,' said Henry.

'I paint every day,' said the Irishman.

Henry swallowed a mouthful of beer. He hadn't changed since he'd come home. His suit looked out of place in the gloom of the bar. Liam wore a soft-collared shirt, the rolled sleeves exposing tanned, muscular forearms that flexed as he raised his glass.

Henry's movements were mechanical. Suzannah watched the little bobble going up and down in his throat. Michael had one, just the same, it bobbed in and out of his collar when he was annoyed.

After two more bottles of beer, Henry said, 'I want you to show me the picture you painted of Suzannah.'

'It's not finished,' said the Irishman.

'Nevertheless, I should like to see it.'

'It's only a quick sketch. I did several this afternoon.'

'I should like to see the one of Suzannah.' Henry spoke stiffly.

Suzannah realised that this was why they had come. Not for a quiet drink together in The Swan, but so that Henry could see the picture.

The painter sighed. 'If it's important to you.' He bent down and lifted the flat bag on to his knees.

It was deeper than it looked. His dismantled easel lay wedged across the top with the box of paints that Suzannah had seen on the beach. The picture lay beneath it, protected by a square frame of wood. Details had been added, the castle turrets, a broken corner of Sammy's spade in the sand, a coil of hair that had come loose, curling down between her shoulder blades.

Henry cleared a space on the next table. The artist lifted out the easel.

'You paint on that thing?' asked Henry, scornful.

'When I'm out. I've a smarter one at home but it's too big to carry with me.' The Irishman smiled. 'You and Suzannah should come and have tea with me, I'd show you my studio.'

Henry's face was grim. He was silent as the picture was laid out on the table.

'You could bring the boys with you.' The Irishman grinned.

'How much do you want?'

'For what? Sure now, I wouldn't charge you for tea.'

'For the picture.'

The Irishman drained his glass. 'It's not finished.'

Henry signalled for more beer. Two men had come in from the public bar, farm labourers. They looked at the picture and wet their lips. Henry's face set.

'I'd like to buy it.'

'I don't want to sell it. This is only a preliminary sketch.'

Henry began counting notes from his wallet.

'I'll give you twenty pounds.'

The Irishman laughed, turning to her. 'Is it worth that much, Suzannah?'

Henry's eyes burned. He thrust the notes out. 'Take the money.'

The painter took a swallow from the new bottle. Without taking his eyes off Henry he emptied it and wiped the foam from his mouth with the back of his hand. 'One more pint and you can have it for nothing.'

Henry signalled the barman and put the notes back in his wallet.

The Irishman began to chuckle, cheeks turning, pink above the beard. 'So it was worth nothing after all?'

Henry put his hands on the picture.

'Do you want to ruin it?' The painter pushed his hands away. 'I'll be changing my mind in a minute.'

Henry waited in silence while the barman fetched newspaper and sellotape and the picture and protecting frame were turned into a parcel. The Irishman carried it to the car and laid it across the back seat. 'Shall I get someone to frame it properly for you?'

Henry looked at Suzannah. His face was red. 'Do you want it framed?'

'Later, perhaps.'

The Irishman grinned at her. 'One day you'll be glad you did.'

'When you're famous?' Suzannah asked.

'I already am!' He clapped his hands as he went back into the bar.

'Did you have to be so rude to him?'

'How did he know your name?'

'One of the boys told him.'

'Were you with him then? On the beach?'

'No, of course we weren't with him.' Suzannah slammed the car door. 'Sammy stopped to look at the picture and we got talking.'

'He didn't sit with you on the beach?'

'No!' She raised her voice, as if the denial would push it away, the little hidden wish that he had sat with them, painted front and not back, her face instead of the anonymous red buttocks in the sand.

Henry was looking away, watching the road.

When they reached the cliff he patted her hand. 'I'm sorry if I was rude.' His voice seemed to come from a long way off. 'There has always been something about that man that makes me uneasy.' He glanced at her, eyes bright in the twilight. 'Ruth was strange about him. When he first came she was kind. I remember her giving him daffodils from the garden, trying to cheer up that dreadful house of his. Then she changed, suddenly she wouldn't go near him any more, she wouldn't even let Michael go down the cliff by himself in case he met him.'

'Did she have a reason?'

He shrugged. 'Not that she told me. One day she said the place was spoiled.'

'Spoiled?'

'She began to talk like that. It started when Sammy was born. She would say odd things and then fail to explain herself.'

With an easy movement he swung the big car into Smithies Lane. 'Post-natal something or other, I expect.'

'Did you suggest a doctor?'

An awkward look came over his face. 'I think Wilson saw her.'

'Who is Wilson?'

'The family doctor, I've known him for years.'

'What did he say?'

Henry shrugged again. 'There was nothing to diagnose. She was just too old to be having a child. Anybody could have told her that.'

As they reached the cottage he changed the subject.

'You and Michael are going to be friends, aren't you?'

Suzannah smiled. 'I'm trying to be. I think he is trying, too, in his own way.'

'We must all try to be happy,' he said, decisively, and turned the car through Matilda's gate.

Suzannah struggled for the words that would describe how she felt. 'Sometimes he seems so . . . so . . . uncomfortable,' she said at last. 'As if he's wearing the wrong pair of shoes.'

Henry patted her hand. 'He is, in a way. The wrong shoes, the wrong mother. He's afraid to like you, afraid of being disloyal to Ruth.'

Suzannah sighed.

'Give him time,' said Henry.

Suzannah pointed to the cottage. Michael's face had appeared in the window of their bedroom.

'Why is he in our room?'

'Looking for us, I expect.'

'But why our room?'

Henry glanced sharply at her. 'Don't be so suspicious of him.'

'He does it all the time. I look up and find him watching me. It's creepy.'

'What do you mean, creepy? He's just a boy. Are you surprised that he needs to watch us?'

As Henry got out of the car Michael waved. Henry waved back, smiling. Suzannah opened the car door and lifted the painting carefully off the seat.

'I don't want that in the house.' Henry spoke without turning round, still smiling at Michael. 'You can leave it in the garage just as it is.'

Twenty-one

The sun was slipping away as Liam walked up the cliff road. He peered between Matilda's trees; Henry Alland's car was in the drive. The upstairs windows were open, a corner of curtain lazily flapping.

The new woman would go well with the car, he thought, with her hair the colour of dark gold, her bright-coloured clothes and her face that of a privileged child; like a butterfly beside him in the bar, she would be a treat for Henry Alland.

A belch of beer rose to his lips as he reached the end of the lane. He had drunk too much English beer.

'I should have told him I wanted stout.'

No one heard his words. Handel's sheep were on the far side, standing in a huddle facing out to sea. 'What's upset the sheep?'

He paused by the vegetables. Seedling weeds were showing between the tomato plants. He hurried into the studio, put down his bag and picked up a trowel from where he had left it the day before, on the dusty lid of the coal box.

The earth turned easily, surrendering minute scraps of green to the trowel's sharp point. Crouched over the plants in the last rays of sun, he could smell the tomatoes, a pungent, bitter smell, a poor echo of the flavour on the tongue. Remaining on his haunches he moved along to the potatoes, scraping up tiny weeds, the trowel scratching like a mole on the dry earth.

'Liam McGuinness?'

A man at the gate. A red woollen hat hiding his ears.

'Who are you?'

The man smiled, showing his teeth. 'Your welcome guest.'

An Australian, a nasal whine, sharp as vinegar.

Liam put down his trowel. Another one, like the greasy-haired girl, come to disturb his peace. 'None of you people are welcome.'

The man smiled again. A face without hair, pale eyes, almost lashless.

'There wasn't time to get a message to you.' He pushed the gate. Liam saw the big shoes, the careful step around the patch of mud where the ground dropped in front of the gate. The big soles would have left a fine print. The man went through the open kitchen door and put his backpack on the table. 'I'll be here for two weeks, maybe three.'

Liam followed him. 'I've heard nothing. Nobody warned me.'

'Like I said, there wasn't time.'

A pale hand thrust towards him. 'My name is Gouseman, you can call me Gouse.'

It rhymed with goose.

'That's not Irish.'

'Why should I be Irish?'

'I don't know who you are!' Liam raised his voice. 'I've had no warning. You come here with this.' He jabbed at the backpack. It didn't give; hard as a lump of lead. 'This . . . whatever it is. Why should I take you in?'

'Just relax, McGuinness. Go and get on with your weeding while I make myself a cup of tea.' Gouseman took a box of tobacco from one of the many pockets of his jacket and began to roll a cigarette.

'You can't do that!'

Gouse continued rolling, a precise, delicate action between finger and thumb. 'It's only tobacco.'

'I don't care if it's opium, you can't smoke it in my house.'

The box hit the table. 'I'll do as I choose. You are paid a salary, McGuinness. This is your job.' A yellow-stained finger pointed round the kitchen. 'To live here and do as you are told.' He took a match from a pocket in his sleeve and struck it against the table. The cigarette paper withered as he dragged in the smoke.

His face gathered in a scowl, Liam went back out to the yard. Mechanically he picked up his small collection of weeds and took them to the compost heap. He knocked the dirt off the trowel by banging it on the side wall of the bunker. He could hear the Australian in the kitchen, whistling, the sound of water filling the kettle. He walked to the gate and leaned against it, thrusting his hands in the pockets of his coat. It was low tide. The sea gleamed, yellowed by the downing sun. Along the Head the first light had come on in Matilda's Cottage. It would be the girl, making their supper, or perhaps bent over the bath as he had once drawn Ruth, with her breasts falling forward, her face red with the steam.

Sammy's pebble found its way between his fingers. He recalled the small hand holding the pebble out to him, his own hand coming forward, unbidden, to ruffle the white-blond hair.

Behind him the Australian put his head out of the kitchen door. 'Is there a room ready?'

Liam shrugged. 'There's a bed.'

Gouse waited in the kitchen.

'Will you show me?'

Liam took his time taking off his boots and stepped into the kitchen in his socks. 'I'd be glad if you'd leave your boots down here.' He opened the door to the passage. 'The girl slept in the room up the stairs on your left. The bog is out the back.'

'Thank you.' Gouse spoke with the home-made cigarette between his lips. 'Shall I call you McGuinness or shall we be friendly and use your first name?'

There was a pause. The Irishman drummed his fingers on the table. 'Liam will do.'

Gouse went upstairs, still wearing his boots. Liam heard the creak of the iron bed and two loud thuds as the boots hit the floor.

He was already up, drinking tea, when Liam came down in the morning.

'You'll have to do some shopping. There's no coffee and you've run out of bread.'

'There was half a loaf.'

Gouse shrugged. 'I had to eat something.' He held out a piece of paper. 'Look, I've made you a list.'

Liam looked at the large handwriting.

'Why can't you go?'

Gouse drained his mug. 'Because I am not here. Officially I don't exist.'

Liam filled the kettle from the tap. 'They'll have seen you arrive.'

Gouse shook his head.

'Sure they will,' said Liam. 'These village folk see everything.'

'Nosy, like the Irish, eh?'

'I'm not nosy.'

'But your women are.'

'I don't know any Irish women.'

'What is she then, English?'

Liam put the kettle on the stove. 'Will you give me a match?'

Gouse pushed a box across the table.

Liam lit the stove, the bottled gas burned silently; a blue light flickering round the ring.

'Well?'

'I have no women.'

'Not even a piece in the village?'

Liam ignored the question. He drank a mug of tea and took down the net shopping bag that hung on the back door. He was through the gate, ten yards along the lane, when a shrill whistle stopped him. Gouse waved from the window, a sheet of white paper in his hand. Liam went back.

'You forgot this.'

'I don't need your list.'

'Take it. You don't want to have to go twice.'

Mrs Evans had another customer. Liam took a wire basket and walked among the shelves, peering at the list.

Eggs.

Ham.

Coffee granules, large jar.

Butter.

He put a tub of margarine into the basket.

Cod steaks, six.
Ten pounds of potatoes.
The string bag wouldn't be enough.
'How long will your visitor be staying, Mr McGuinness?' Her fingers trilled over the adding machine.
'My visitor?'
'Coffee granules, Mr McGuinness. You've never bothered with granules before.' Her nose seemed to curve downwards as she smiled, like a beak. 'And I saw you looking at the butter. Someone special is it?'
Liam stuffed the list back into his pocket.
'It's just a friend.'
Mrs Evans put the cod steaks in a polythene bag. 'Will that be all?'
'And ten pounds of potatoes.'
'Ten pounds! Your guest is a big eater then? Or is it a family?'
'No. Just the one.'
'That's nice. I can give you a carrier for the potatoes.'
The plastic handles hurt his fingers.
Henry Alland's car was still there, wide tyres squatting on the gravel of Matilda's drive. Liam looked through the trees. The house had a closed look, locked and bolted, the way that townsfolk leave their houses. They would all be down on the beach, a family party on the sand.
Gouse was sitting on the Smithies' doorstep, smoking.
'It's a nice view you have here, Liam.'
'They all know you're here.'
Gouse stood up to watch him unpack, frowned at the margarine. 'I put butter on the list.'
Liam ignored him. 'They all know you're here,' he repeated.
'Yes, I heard you the first time.'
'I said you were a friend.'
Gouse smiled. A little, wily smle. His mouth was small, like the girl's had been. The one Mrs Evans hadn't approved.
Holding the cigarette between his lips, he began to peel the potatoes. 'We'll have to think of something better than that.'

Twenty-two

'You're not going away again?' Michael was barefoot, the striped pyjamas hanging off him like a prisoner's uniform. He stepped gingerly on to the gravel.

Henry was by the car. 'Just for the day, Michael. I'll be back before suppertime.'

Michael stared at the ground.

'Do you have to go?'

'Yes.' Henry's voice was patient. 'I did tell you that I was going, Michael. I told both you and Sammy yesterday.'

Michael looked up, his voice suddenly loud. 'Will you see Mum?'

Suzannah heard Henry's breath, a quick gasp before he answered. 'No, Michael, I've explained that to you already.'

'She'd be ever so pleased to see you.'

Henry looked at Suzannah, appealing to her.

She stepped forward. 'You mustn't make him late, Michael.'

The boy dodged away from her hand, and ran past into the house.

Henry shook his head and looked at his watch. 'I must go, I'm going to miss my train.'

Suzannah walked nearer to the car. The gravel was sharp through the soles of her slippers. 'Will you, Henry?'

'What?'

'Will you see Ruth?'

'Why should I?'

'Perhaps you will go, just to see if she's coping all right?'

Henry unlocked the car. 'I don't understand you, Suzannah. Why should you want me to see her?'

Her answer came without warning. 'I don't want you to see her. But if you do, I want you to be honest. I don't want you to hide it from me.' When the words were out she wondered where they had come from, expressing a fear so vague she had never voiced it before, even to herself.

Henry looked at his watch. 'I'll have to go or I'll miss the train.'

She stood in the porch while Henry climbed into the car. He

wore a dark suit, a dazzling white shirt and a tie of blue silk. He looked back at her and smiled, as a stranger would, like an advert for aftershave or expensive private dentistry.

Involuntarily, as she waved back, her mind produced an image of Liam: of his large, comfortable coat, his eyes that seemed to laugh even when his face was still. Henry's merely gleamed, like his teeth, and his smooth-shaved cheeks with their gloss of suntan. What was it that had prompted her question? Did she want him to see Ruth? Was that it? Did she need him to want to see Ruth – because that would be more natural, less monstrous than his cold, 'Why should I?'

The big wheels scattered gravel as the car spun out of the drive. Michael was in the kitchen. She heard the fridge door go, and running water, and then, a moment later, the slam of the back door. She stepped inside. A glass stood on the draining board, a skin of milk almost rinsed away. She watched from the hall as he descended the cliff steps. Ruth had forbidden him to go down alone; something to do with the Irishman. Suzannah frowned, watching as he climbed down, crabwise, until the steps twisted round the rocks out of sight.

Sammy was awake. She could hear small feet overhead, back and forth to the cupboard. The bed would be a pile of toys, the duvet obscured by furry animals and picture books and building bricks. In a moment she would go upstairs and say, 'Oh Sammy, what a lot of toys for such a little boy!' And he would show them to her, one by one, saving until last the button-eyed bear that slept with him far down under the quilt.

'Has Barrow Bear been in his burrow?' she would ask, and Sammy would tunnel down, upsetting the furry animals, picture books, building bricks clattering to the floor until Barrow Bear was found and thrust into Suzannah's arms. 'And how is Mr Bear this morning?' She would turn the bear over, fat, balding legs in the air, and then upright again to hear its long, mechanical growl.

'It's my bear.' Michael had said, standing in the doorway on that first day. 'Sammy stole it.'

She remembered her own inadequate reply and, later that first day, Henry telling her that Ruth had never liked the bear.

'We found it in the attic here when Michael was little. Somehow it travelled back with us to London. Ruth wanted to throw it away, she kept thinking of all the children who had sucked it while they went through their measles and chicken-pox.' Henry chuckled. 'It became Michael's favourite toy – until last summer when Sammy claimed it for himself.'

'Did Michael mind Sammy having it?'

'He didn't have any choice. Anyway, he's far too old to have a teddy.'

Suzannah's heart turned, imagining herself at thirteen, bereft of a favourite bear. Hers was still in her father's house, propped up on a windowsill with one arm raised, permanently waving.

Michael was coming back across the beach. He had been to the water's edge, the trail of his footprints visible in the sand. He started to climb the steps. She moved away from the window and began to dust. After ten minutes he hadn't appeared. She continued dusting, lifting paperbacks out of the bookcase in blocks to wipe the shelves behind them. She dusted the mantelpiece, moved the cloth carefully between rows of small shells that they'd brought up from the beach: ordinary, dull-coloured shells, brought because Sammy insisted, his little face pink with delight at the sound they made when he held them to his ear. She went back to the window and dusted the sill, still expecting, at any moment, to see Michael's head coming up over the steps.

Sammy appeared on the stairs. He had dressed himself in red shorts, a tee shirt, back to front, and red plastic sandals.

'Who's a smart boy in red this morning,' cried Suzannah.

'Smart Sammy!' said the little boy, sticking out his chest.

He stood still while she pulled off the tee shirt and put it back over his head the right way round. Then he let her take his hand as they hurried across the grass.

'Come on, we're going to look for Michael.'

They started down the steps, one at a time, Sammy putting his feet sideways.

'Has Michael gone away?'

'No, he's just gone for a walk.'

He held her hand tightly. 'Daddy went away.'

They reached the first landing where the steps spread out into a triangle and changed course, following the indentation of the cliff face.

'Daddy went away and Mummy threw a cup at the wall. She made a big red smudge.'

Suzannah peered over the edge, straining to see the rest of the steps. There was no sign of Michael. They hurried downwards, to the landing where the path from the Head merged with the steps. From there, despite the dazzle of sunlight on the sea, she could see clearly, all the way to the bottom. 'He must have gone up to the Head.'

They left the steps and took the path. Sammy ran ahead, glad of the flatness of the rock. The path followed a fault in the cliff, rising slowly round towards the top. Sammy reached a bend, she called to him to keep away from the edge, but already he was pausing, in the act of taking a step, showing the white chalk dust on the sole of his sandal. He looked back at her, a hand stretched out, pointing further up around the bend in the path where she could not see.

'Michael's there,' he shouted.

She hurried to catch up. The sun was warm, a ring of sweat formed under her hair.

Michael was sitting on an outcrop of rock, with his back to the path. Beside him was the Irishman. She could see the canvas as he moved to and fro with his brush, spreading an expanse of silver-blue, almost the colour of the sky. Michael was gazing at the painter, smiling, utterly absorbed.

Sammy walked ahead again, more slowly, as if even his childish eye sensed the delicacy of the scene. Frequently he turned to see if she was following. She was, slowly, feeling a desire, as they neared the artist, to smooth her skirt, the wish that it was long enough to gather in against her legs. He was looking back at the bay, pointing at something with the tip of his brush. At the sight of Suzannah he raised the brush in salute. Michael's face, open as it followed the painter's brush, closed at the sight of them. Sammy fell back into step with Suzannah so that they crossed the last few yards together, under the spell of the upraised brush and Michael's angry stare.

'Another fine morning, then,' called the painter.

Suzannah nodded. 'It is.' She looked down. 'Hello, Michael.'

'Why are you spying on me?'

'We didn't come to spy on you. I just wondered where you'd gone.'

He turned away to stare at the easel. With an agitated motion, he swung his legs back and forth. His heels hit the underhanging rock. Thuck, thuck. Each hit released a small shower of white dust on to the path.

'Your boy here wanted to know how to paint – '

Michael interrupted savagely. 'I'm not "her boy"!'

The Irishman's voice was mild. 'Well, I know that, Michael,' he said, dropping the end of his brush into a jar.

Michael stuck out his jaw. 'She's not my mother!' He covered his mouth as he spoke, as if to hide a smirk behind his fingers. 'She's just a bit of stuff. Because my father's having his Changing Life!'

'Sure, that's no way to talk.' The painter's voice remained mild but he selected another brush and turned his back square in Michael's face. The boy's smirk disappeared. His brows gathered in a frown, his bottom lip sucked in under his teeth.

Suzannah attempted a smile. 'Sammy and I were just about to have some toast and honey for breakfast. Why don't you come and have some too, Michael?'

She took the little boy's hand and shaded her eyes to look at the painter. 'Goodbye.'

He raised his free hand.

'Do you like tomatoes, Suzannah?'

She paused. 'Yes.'

'I'll bring you some, I've a good crop.'

She lifted Sammy up and sat him on her hip. Michael followed them along the path, keeping his distance. As he walked he kicked his feet into the chalk so that little showers of dust and stones hit the back of her calves.

After breakfast they walked down to the village.

Sammy skipped ahead, pausing now and then to point – at a wild flower in the hedgerow, a seagull sitting in the field, or the sheep who cropped the grass close to the fence.

'Baas,' shouted Sammy.

'Sheep, Sammy,' said Suzannah. 'Those are sheep.'

'Baa-sheep,' shouted Sammy, beginning to chant out a nursery rhyme. His high, childish voice carried clear over the cliff.

Michael maintained his distance, eyes down, hands stuffed in his pockets. She wondered what had caused such a change.

Only yesterday they had swum together, reached the rock together for the first time, Michael gasping like a stranded fish but getting up to pull her out of the water.

Holding Sammy by the hand, she waited until Michael overtook them and then matched her step to his, with Sammy running along to keep pace.

'Have you known the painter for long, Michael?'

He continued to walk, never lifting his eyes from the ground.

'I'm going to be like him one day,' he said suddenly, looking up with fierce eyes. 'I'm going to live for myself and care for no one.'

They reached the bottom of the cliff road.

'Ice cream!' shouted Sammy, pointing to the sign outside Evans' shop. Suzannah let him pull her inside. The shopkeeper bustled out from behind her counter, clucking as Sammy peered into the fridge. 'Is it a strawberry one for Sammy?' she cried as he pointed. 'That one comes in chocolate and banana flavour as well!'

Sammy put his hands in his mouth and looked at Suzannah.

'I think he'd like a chocolate one,' she said.

'Chocolate it is then.' The woman reached into the fridge and handed the ice to Sammy without a glance at Suzannah.

Michael helped himself to a choc-ice and immediately began to unwrap it.

'You'd better wait until I've paid for it, Michael.'

'That's all right,' said the shopkeeper. 'I've known Michael since he was a baby.' She tapped the keys of the till. As the cash drawer sprang out she stopped it with her broad stomach. 'And Sammy, too, though he was just a wee thing last time.'

Suzannah held out a pound note. Without thinking she held it just short of the woman's arm, forcing her to look up into her face. The woman's eyes were bright, meeting Suzannah's and then darting to Michael.

'Your Dad's gone off to London then, Michael?'

Michael nodded. There was chocolate on his teeth. He licked it with a tongue already smeared with ice cream.

'He's coming back tonight,' said Suzannah hastily. 'He's only gone for a meeting.'

The shopkeeper continued to smile at Michael, as if Suzannah had not spoken.

Suzannah took Sammy's hand. 'Shall we go and look at the boats?'

'Fishes,' cried Sammy. 'Can we see the fishes?' He dragged her impatiently into the sunlight.

Outside the store, Michael grunted a 'thank you' for the choc-ice. Suzannah made an equal effort to smile pleasantly in response.

They sat on a bench by the water and she unwrapped Sammy's ice cream. The air was still, magnifying the quiet sounds of the quay, the gulls squealing overhead, the shouts of the fishermen cleaning their boats. Sammy ran to peer into the great tubs of fish, sparkling with colour in the sun.

Twenty-three

There was no note. No need for a note. He had left them by the kitchen door. Fifteen tomatoes, small, like bright plums in a white polythene bag from the Evans' Village Shop with a price daubed in black marking ink: ninety-eight pence. But the tomatoes were not from the shop. They were a gift from his garden. Small round skins, plump with juice. She picked up the bag and looked across the bay to the square of beaten earth around his house. There was green at the side. A neat row of canes, and panes of glass that might have formed a cold frame against the wall in the spring.

Michael poured a lake of salad cream on to his plate. The smothered tomatoes looked like a pudding, red plums and custard. When he lifted a tomato on to his fork, a small patch of plate was left behind, an island of white with the yellow sea closing in.

'You shouldn't waste the salad cream, Michael.'

The tomato was poised before his mouth, dripping. 'I prefer mayonnaise.'

'I'll get some next time we go shopping.'

'Except on these. I like mayonnaise on ordinary tomatoes, but I prefer salad cream on these.'

'You've taken far more than you can eat.'

'You haven't eaten any.'

Sammy had copied Michael. The yellow cream lay in a puddle on his plate, on his chin and in a ring around his mouth.

'I'll have some later with your father.'

'Mum always gives us mayonnaise,' said Michael when he had finished. 'It's more nutritious.' He dragged the fork across his plate, ploughing a neat furrow in the salad cream that remained on his plate. The tines squealed.

'Don't do that, Michael.'

'Why not?'

'Because it's unpleasant.'

The squealing continued, back and forth across the plate, faster and faster.

'Michael, please!'

Sammy did the same, cackling with delight. Little gobbets of cream sprayed on to the table.

Suzannah jumped to her feet, her hand raised to slap the younger child.

'You're not allowed to hit Sammy,' shouted Michael.

The squealing stopped.

'I wasn't going to hit him,' Suzannah lied.

'I'm going to tell Dad.'

'You tell him, I'll tell him what you've been doing.'

'We can do what we like. You're not our mother.'

Suzannah began to stack the plates on a tray. 'Let's not quarrel, Michael.' Her voice wavered. 'Let's try to be friends.'

Sammy climbed down from his chair and offered a sticky yellow finger. 'Make up, make up, never never break up! If you do you'll get the shooo!!'

Suzannah smiled and wrapped his little finger round her own.

Michael pushed his chair from the table and walked out on to the patio. He stared down at the grass, arms folded, legs apart, Henry's stance echoed in the skinny shape of the boy.

She carried the plates into the kitchen and ran hot water into the bowl. Michael was gone. She could see his back disappearing down the cliff steps, just as she had seen it this morning. Did he go looking for the artist? The house was suddenly quiet, as if the noise of the quarrel had had an echo, a clatter of sound that died away with his leaving.

She made a cup of coffee and went into the sitting room. Sammy came to curl up beside her in the big leather armchair. She sipped the coffee. Sammy's eyes fluttered, he edged into her lap and his left thumb crept into his mouth.

She closed her eyes. The small body was warm against her thighs. The fridge hummed faintly through the wall. After a while it stopped and there were only the sounds of the house itself, the intermittent creak of wood, expanding and cooling as the sun moved round. She dozed, dreaming of Sammy on the beach, his legs coated with thick sand like marzipan; Henry had grown a beard: black, covering half his face; his smooth brown hair turned dark before her eyes, curling like something alive into a thick black mat.

The crack of the door shook her out of sleep. Michael was there, wide-eyed at the sight of her with Sammy in the armchair.

'Michael! You gave me a start.' She yawned. 'I was dozing. Did you have a nice walk?'

He held out a paper bag.

'What's in there?'

'Barley sugar.'

Suzannah took a piece. 'Thank you. Did you go down to the shop?'

He nodded, crunching. 'Mrs Evans gave them to me.'

'That was kind.'

'I did buy something though.'

'What was that?'

'I bought a postcard for Mum, and a stamp.'

Suzannah swallowed. 'What a good idea.'

Michael put another barley sugar into his mouth. 'Mrs Evans helped me write it.'

'Good,' was all Suzannah could think of to say.

'Are you coming to the beach?'

She looked down at Sammy, sleeping peacefully in her lap.

'It seems a shame to wake him, now. I'll tell you what, let's put Sammy on his bed and then have a cold drink together in the garden.'

Michael pouted. 'I want to go down to the beach.'

'I know, but we can't, so let's enjoy what we can do.'

Carefully she gathered Sammy into her arms and carried him up the stairs. He stirred as she sat on the bed. A small fist pushed her breast more comfortably against his cheek.

Michael watched from the doorway. 'He used to do that to Mum.'

'Did he?' said Suzannah, not wishing to think of Ruth. She could hardly bear to put the little boy down.

Michael put his hands in his pockets. 'I'll see you in the garden,' he said, turning to go.

With infinite care Suzannah laid Sammy on his bed and tucked Barrow Bear in beside him.

When she came down the stairs there was no sign of Michael. The sun was a white blur behind the clouds, the air cool, carrying the first flickers of wind. Far across the bay she could see a figure moving around the garden of Smithies. She sat for a moment, watching. It didn't look like Liam, the figure was small and pale; dungarees and a red woollen hat, pulled well down. The idea of Liam having a woman had not occurred to her. She watched a while longer and decided with relief that it wasn't a woman at all, but a small man.

It was half an hour later, when she had given up waiting and was standing on a chair in the larder, reaching for a bag of sugar, that she heard Michael behind her. She leaned around the larder door.

'Would you like that drink now?'

He nodded.

'Help yourself. There's a can in the fridge.'

He held the can over the sink to pull the ring. The lump in his neck bobbed up and down as he swallowed.

'Did you go for another walk?'

He shrugged. Something had changed his mood.

'Did you go down to the beach after all?'

'No.' He gulped at the can. 'It's all covered with weed.'

'What sort of weed?'

He stopped drinking to look at her with contempt. 'Seaweed,

of course. It's all over the beach.'

'It was clear this morning.' She remembered watching him cross the beach, his shadow sharp against the sand.

'The tide was in then. It's out now and there are heaps of weed everywhere.'

'So you didn't go down there?'

'No.'

'Where did you go, then?'

'I went round the Head.'

'Did you see anyone?'

Michael didn't answer.

Had he been as far as Smithies? Perhaps seen Liam's visitor and felt, as she had, a curious jealousy that the artist was not as solitary as he seemed?

She spooned flour into a weighing bowl. Michael dropped the empty can into the swing-bin. 'Will you cut some rhubarb for me, Michael?'

'Where from?'

'From the garden, behind the shed, there's a big clump down there.'

'Sammy doesn't like rhubarb.'

'But you do, don't you?'

He shrugged. 'It's OK.'

Suzannah handed him the kitchen knife. 'Will you cut about five big sticks, and put the leaves on the compost heap?'

'Is it true that slugs won't eat rhubarb leaves?'

'I don't know,' said Suzannah. 'Who told you that?'

'Mum told me.'

The margarine was soft, it clung to the fork, attracting flour like a snowball.

'I expect it's true then.'

'What if I find holes in the leaves?'

Suzannah looked at him. 'What if you do?'

'That would mean it was a lie.'

'Not necessarily. Perhaps it only applies to certain types of rhubarb.'

'Or certain kinds of slug.' The knife dangled from his hand.

'Go carefully with that. Cut the stems as close to the ground as you can.'

While he was gone she rolled out the pastry and cut a star

from the leftovers. Sammy appeared, barefoot, rubbing his eyes.

'Did you have a nice sleep?' She wiped her hands on a cloth and held them out to him. He walked unhesitatingly into her arms. 'Michael's gone to cut some rhubarb. Shall we put on your shoes and go and find him?'

She was upstairs, pulling odd shoes and soft toys from under the bed, when she heard water being drawn from the kitchen tap. She shouted down the stairs, 'Did you get some rhubarb, Michael?'

There was no reply. The water stopped and she could hear footsteps in the kitchen. Hurriedly she undid the knot in Sammy's laces and handed the shoes to him. 'You can do them up, can't you?'

She left him sitting on the floor and went downstairs. There was no one in the kitchen. A bundle of rhubarb had been dumped in the sink, thick, dark stems hanging out on to the counter, twice as much as she needed for the pie.

She took the big chopping board from its hook and laid out the sticks of rhubarb.

'Did you bring back the knife?' she called.

No answer.

'Here it is.'

He was behind her holding out the knife.

'Michael, you gave me a fright!'

She turned on the tap and began to scrub the long stems with a nylon brush. 'This is lovely. Is there any left in the garden?'

'Only thin stalks, I brought all the thick ones.'

'There's enough here to make two pies.'

'I cut too much then?'

Suzannah smiled. 'More than we need, but it doesn't matter. Rhubarb is good for us.'

'During the war people ate the leaves and died.'

She began to chop the stalks.

'Is it true?'

'What?'

'That people ate the leaves and died?'

Suzannah sighed. 'I don't know, Michael.'

'You mean she's lying?'

'Who?'

'Mum, about the slugs and people dying and all that.'

'No, of course not.'

She wanted to scream. Don't try to corner me! Don't try to test me against Ruth!

Michael was silent for a while, watching her fill the pie dish.

'Sammy will only eat the pastry.'

'That doesn't matter. He can have an apple if he doesn't like rhubarb.'

'He always eats the top at home. Doesn't matter what's underneath. Sometimes it's plums and sometimes it's cherries. Cherry pie with almond pastry, she makes it specially for me.' Suzannah laid the pastry over the fruit and trimmed round the edge of the dish with the knife.

'Sammy might not like your pastry. It might not be as good as Mum's.'

She opened the oven door and put the pie inside. 'It might even be better.'

She looked round, smiling, but Michael had gone. There was a new bag of flour in the larder. Once more she stood on the chair.

There was a sudden noise, a series of thuds like fast footsteps on the stairs, and then Sammy's screams. 'Mummy!'

The flour bag flew out of her hands. His screams filled the hall, drowning her cry. 'I'm coming, Sammy, I'm coming.'

Michael was there already, sitting on the landing, trying to hug the little boy against his chest.

He held out one of Sammy's shoes. 'He tripped on the laces.'

'I told him to tie them up.'

'He doesn't know how.'

Suzannah stopped. 'Surely he does?'

Michael shook his head firmly. 'He hasn't got the hang of it yet.'

'I didn't know.' She climbed the stairs towards them. 'I just assumed he could do it.'

Michael's eyes were level with her own. 'He's only had buckles until now – and pull-on sandals.'

At the sight of the shoe Sammy stopped screaming. He grabbed it from Michael's hand and pulled it on to his foot.

The second shoe was on the stair. 'Will you teach him to lace them up, Michael?'

He kicked the shoe towards her. 'You teach him. You're the mother!'

Twenty-four

The seaweed was still there in the morning, a dreadful brown mass rolling in with each sluggish wave.

There was no question of swimming. Henry sat near the tideline in a deckchair, with a straw hat pulled down over his eyes. Above the waist of his trunks Suzannah could see the first trace of fat, a crease of skin, wider than a finger, protruding above the line of elastic. His feet rested on the sand, long-toed, the hair on his legs almost invisible, so that they looked smooth, like his cheeks, as if he were modelled out of clay and lightly tanned, a product of a lotion that smelled of sweet chemicals. Sammy smelled the same; his shoulders, already nutbrown, had been smeared with cream as if he were still pink and vulnerable, as if the days of sun that had turned his skin as brown as Suzannah's had never been. He ran up and down in front of his father, tormenting a tiny crab with a stick.

The last of the cloud was breaking up, wisping and dissolving, a slow side-step that left trails of blue sky in its wake. Further up the beach, Suzannah sat on a deckchair, sheltering in a pool of shade by the rocks. Under her dress her swimsuit felt hot, the sleek fabric clung like a corset. 'Look, I've found a cuttlefish.' It was Michael.

She sat up. The shell felt dry and dead in her hands. 'What are cuttlefish, Michael?'

The boy's face knitted into a frown.

'They're a kind of mollusc,' he said. 'We did them in Science. They have ever so many arms and they let off a sort of inky fluid if you chase them.'

'Do they?' Suzannah was genuinely interested. 'And what part of the creature is this?'

'This is its shell,' said Michael. 'But of course this one is dead.'

Taking the shell from her hand he sat on the sand and leaned his back against the side of her chair. She could see his shoulder bones, straining against the skin, pimples among the freckles.

'Suzannah,' he said, after a pause. 'When you're dead, do you think you'll go to heaven?'

'I don't know, Michael.'

'You must know if you've been good or not.'

'I don't think it's just a case of being good.'

'Mum says you and Dad will go to hell for what you did.'

Taken aback, Suzannah looked at him. He was staring out to sea, holding his head quite still. She could think of nothing to say. She only knew that she must answer. Finally she said, 'Where is hell, Michael?'

He turned round, curling his lip in disbelief. 'Don't you know where hell is?'

'No, you tell me.'

'Down there, of course.'

'Where.'

He looked around for a moment. 'Under the ground.'

'And where is heaven?'

He looked up at the sky. 'Somewhere up there, I guess.' He picked up a handful of sand and let it trickle out between his fingers.

'Maybe.' She leaned forward and adjusted the tilt of the deckchair. 'Maybe it's just a state of mind.'

His mouth hung open, showing the prominent teeth that she would have had straightened if he had been hers.

The cuttlefish had become a trowel to dig a trench around her feet. 'Perhaps it's just a state of being very unhappy,' said Suzannah.

'Like Mum, you mean. As unhappy as she is.'

Her answer came like a squeak, squeezed from a rubber toy. 'Is she?'

'You know, since Dad and you . . . ' He turned to look at his father, playing in the shallows with Sammy. Henry was laughing, loudly. 'It's not fair,' said Michael with sudden force. 'Mum has all the unhappiness, you and Dad don't have to suffer anything.'

'That isn't entirely true,' said Suzannah. 'Your father was very unhappy before he left home.'

'He wasn't,' Michael stood up, holding a scoop of sand on the shell. 'I know he wasn't. He used to play with us every night. He used to play with Sammy in his bath and then he'd come and watch TV in my room. At weekends he used to take us to the park, and he used to fix my bike, and . . . ' He stopped, glaring down at her, panting. A noise came from his throat, not a word, a shriek. Sand flew into her face.

'Michael!' Grains of sand stung her eyes, stuck to her lips.

He was gone, running towards the rocks along the beach, arms and legs flying gracelessly. Henry had heard her cry.

He hurried towards her, pulling Sammy behind him.

'What happened?'

'I don't know.' Her eyes watered and she spat sand out of her mouth. 'One minute we were talking about hell and the next minute it was us, Ruth, how unhappy she is.'

Henry's face altered. They watched as Michael disappeared among the large rocks at the foot of the Head. Seagulls rose up, fluttering into the air like feathers from a torn pillow. 'Let me go to him, Henry.' She used his arm to haul herself out of the deckchair and pushed him gently aside. 'You stay with Sammy.'

Her shadow was short, a dark, fat caricature preceding her across the sand. Michael hadn't gone far. She rounded the first rock and almost cannoned into him, crouched over a pool. She walked around the pool and squatted down on the other side. His face was wet with tears, a line of mucus flowed from his nose, caught where his upper lip angled outward to follow the jut of his teeth. He ignored her, watching his tears drip, rippling into the pool.

It had been a surprise to her, that Michael would cry. At his age she thought that boys had ceased to cry, that they somehow bottled it up as men did.

She took a tissue from her pocket and passed it to him. 'I'm sorry it's not very clean,' she said.

He took the tissue in silence, blew his nose and handed it back to her, slippery and full. She wished he would speak, repeat the things that he had said so that she could refute them. She wanted to tell him that it was not only Ruth who was unhappy; that we are all unhappy, to a greater or lesser extent. Life isn't necessarily happy, you can't expect it to be. The words bubbled in her head, the need to explain, even to exaggerate. She does suffer, but we have suffered too, more than you could understand. It is Ruth's suffering that comes between us, prevents our love; it is entirely destructive. Your father is miserable, anxious; when you are not here the pain of being without you is intolerable to him. She wasn't quite sure if this last part was true, but she wanted Michael to believe it; she could not bear his tears for Ruth.

Instead she put the tissue back into her pocket and rinsed her fingers in the pool. 'Shall we see if we can get around the Head?'

He stood up and waited for her to lead the way. She walked down towards the sea, weaving between the rocks. Once again the seagulls rose, reeling high overhead.

'I'd like to have a gun,' said Michael.

'Would you, to shoot the birds?'

'Anything. I'd like to shoot five in a row and watch them fall into the sea.' He stretched out his arm, imitating a gun and screwed up his face as if to take aim.

'Would you eat them?'

'Seagulls? No thanks, they're vermin.'

He barely noticed that she held out her hand for his as they climbed over the rocks. He was describing the gun that he would own one day. They rounded the Head, chattering like friends, discussing the ethics of killing for pleasure, of killing for food or principle. The subject came round to vegetarianism and Michael said, 'That painter, he's a vegetarian.'

'Is he?' said Suzannah. They perched on the furthest rock, looking north into the village. A fishing boat had come in, they could see the men hauling their catch on to the quay, wooden crates and plastic tubs, glistening with fish.

'He told me he eats fish, though, and sometimes he has a pasty in The Swan.'

'I shouldn't think there's much meat in a pasty.'

'No, but it breaks the rules.'

They sat for a while on the rock, watching the fishermen picking the last of the catch out of their nets. Suddenly Michael sat up. 'Suzannah, will you come swimming with me?'

'I thought you didn't want to swim today – not with all that seaweed.'

'It's not that bad.'

Suzannah looked at the sea; the water was thick with weed, vegetation lay on the beach where the tide had receded, a mass of tangled brown curls, like sweepings from a hair salon. She turned to Michael. His eyes were on her, full of expectancy, looking straight into hers.

'All right.'

He beamed. His ugly mouth spread wide with delight as he took her hand and pulled her up. 'Come on, we can try for the rock again.'

Waving at his father, he led her back to the middle of the bay. She left her dress on the beach and waded in against the waves. Weed, like ticklish fingers, surrounded her thighs. A big wave rolled lazily towards her. She stood and faced it, pressing her feet into the sand. Water splashed up to her shoulders, cold, leaving ringlets of dark weed on her skin. It would find its way inside her costume, be in the folds of her skin when she undressed. For the next wave she turned her back and her breath gasped out as the water swept over her head, swamping her like a douche of cold oil.

Michael came up, yards away, shouting back to her. 'Ugh! It's disgusting!'

She shouted 'Ugh!' too and on an impulse threw a bit at him, a floret of soggy green that slapped into his shoulder and lingered a moment before slipping back into the water.

He shrieked and plunged his hands in. She started to swim, too late, a soggy clump thumped into her back. She turned round, laughing, grabbed an armful and hurled it back at him. He screamed and dived, coming up close to her with his hands full of weed. Droplets of water shone on his hair, his cheeks were pink with excitement. She shouted and giggled, backing away from him. 'No, please don't!' And all the time a quiet voice in her head exalted, this was wonderful, hurling lumps of seaweed, a way of hugging one another. She stopped and turned to face him, panting. 'Pax!' she shouted. 'I give in.'

'Not until I say!' He clutched a great knot of weed, long green tendrils dangling into the water.

'Please, Michael,' she begged, laughing, breathless. 'I can't swim any more.'

'Then you have to have salad for tea!' he shouted and dived on to her, pushing the weed into her face. Choking and coughing, she went down. His arms and legs thrashed over her, a flash of white, then he was gone. She came up, spluttering for air, and saw his two white feet ploughing the water, already yards away.

She followed him out to the rock and let him pull her out of the water.

'Your swimming's miles better.'

'I know,' he smiled, still panting. 'I'll be quite good when I get back to school.'

He lay comfortably beside her, face down on the flat warm rock.

'I wish Dad wouldn't sit on the beach all the time.'

'Perhaps he can't face the weed,' said Suzannah.

'The truth is he can't swim.'

'Of course he can swim.'

'Yes, but only a few yards. He can't get out here.' Michael sighed. 'I used to think he could do anything.'

'That's part of growing up,' said Suzannah. 'Learning that everyone is fallible.'

He rolled over on to his back and raising his arm, flexed a puny muscle. 'If I can swim further than Dad, how come I haven't got big muscles?'

'They haven't developed yet,' said Suzannah. 'Be patient, one day you'll be as big and handsome as your Dad.'

Michael squinted at her. 'Mum used to say that.'

Suzannah was silent. On the shore she could see Sammy sitting in the sand, just short of the incoming water. He was digging a channel and shouting at Henry, who appeared to be asleep.

'Do you think he's handsome?' Michael asked, breaking into her thoughts.

'Oh yes,' said Suzannah.

'Mum says he is, she says that's the trouble.'

Wanting to steer the conversation away from the subject of Ruth, Suzannah pointed up the cliff. 'Look, there's Liam.'

Michael sat up. The artist was walking along the path, a dark figure, almost a silhouette against the bright sky. Michael waved and Liam raised his hand in response. He was carrying a bag.

'He's got someone staying there,' said Michael. 'I saw them walking on the beach last night.'

'Last night?'

'Well, in the evening. While you and Dad were having supper.'

'Who is it?'

'I don't know. A man with a red hat.'

Suzannah watched the figure on the cliff. He walked with hunched shoulders, his free hand thrust into his pocket.

'Do you think he'd like to see my cuttlefish?'

'Why yes, I'm sure he would.'

'He's very nice,' Michael said firmly, as if she had challenged him.

'I like him too,' said Suzannah.

'Mum used to like him.'

'Did she?' Suzannah tried to keep the sigh from her voice. He was determined to talk about Ruth.

'Yes, she used to like him very much. And then she didn't. One summer we came and we weren't allowed to speak to him anymore.'

'Why was that?'

'I don't know.' Michael pulled a face. 'Grown-ups are always going off each other for no reason.'

She saw that though the remark was made casually, he was watching for her response.

'Are they?'

'Dad and Mum,' he said, shrugging. 'Dad went off Mum and on to you.'

'Did that hurt an awful lot, Michael?'

He shrugged again. 'Mum cried such a lot. The garage roof was leaking. She cried a lot about that. If Dad had been there he'd have had it fixed, but it leaked and leaked and I hated you for taking him away.'

Suzannah cleared her throat. It was hard to believe that Henry's house would have a leaking roof; that so soon after his departure the sturdy edifice in Cavanagh Road would start to crumble.

'And then I met you and you were nice,' said Michael.

'Was I?'

'You weren't like Mum said. She hasn't met you so she doesn't know. I didn't know until we came here.'

Suzannah looked at his face, screwed up, struggling with ideas that were too large for his experience. 'What will you tell her when you go home?'

'Nothing much.'

'But she'll ask you what I was like, she's bound to.'

'Oh, I'll tell her you're horrid. Otherwise she'll cry.'

Suzannah smiled.

'It's true,' he said, earnestly. 'Otherwise she'll think Dad won't ever come back and then she'll probably shoot herself.'

'Michael!'

'Oh, she will, she's often said she will. She said it when I failed Maths.'

Suzannah lay back on the rock and looked at the sky. Had she said the same to Henry?

'But we're not going back yet, are we?' Michael asked. 'There's still lots of holiday left?'

'Oh yes, lots.' Suzannah sat up. 'I'm going back into the water. Are you coming?'

He stood up and dived in ahead of her. She waited until he was well away and slipped in, feet first, swimming sideways to keep away from the weed. With a soft, wallowing crawl she turned her face into the water, rolling over on every second stroke to breathe. Her eyes closed against the salt and sun, dazzled by droplets that clung to her eyelashes. She floated for a moment, raising her head to look for Michael. He had reached the beach and was standing in the shallows, picking weed off his arms. The rock and the beach seemed far away, she had swum further than she realised, carried by the tide towards the looming shadow of the Head. A wave came from behind, tossing her gently over, face down. Something scraped her elbow. And again. She turned, tried to swim clear and the same sharp edge scraped her knees. Below, hidden by the water, were the long pointers of rock that spread out into the sand like roots below the Head. She had climbed over them with Sammy at low tide, looking for crabs. Every heave of the water dragged her harder against them, scraping her legs and elbows. Looking down, she saw thin runnels of blood. She whimpered, thrashing out in a high-pitched, childish panic. Again the water pushed her landwards, she shrieked as her knees barked against the rock.

With an effort she made herself lie flat and began a shallow breast-stroke. The needles scraped her legs once more. She had to hold her breath to keep from screaming. After a few strokes she was free, ploughing through shallows. She stood up. Each receding wave exposed more of her grazed arms and elbows, thighs and knees smeared with blood. She called to Henry but he was coming already, running towards her with a towel. 'Suzannah, Suzannah, what have you done?'

The towel was too coarse to bear. The wounds were small, like playground grazes, but the salt stung and they bled profusely. Michael stood with Sammy on the sand, staring at the bloody towel.

'We'll have to take you back up to the house,' said Henry.

'You needn't come,' said Suzannah. Ashamed of her tears, she wiped her face. 'It's nothing – just a few scratches.'

Michael pointed to her legs. 'That's just what happened to Mum, only she really screamed.'

Suzannah looked at Henry. 'This happened to Ruth?'

'Yes,' he said shortly, with a sweeping motion of his hand, as if he would brush away the memory. 'She got caught on the rocks at high tide. She was more shaken up than you are.'

She got to her feet. 'I'll go up and rinse off the salt. You three stay down here and have your picnic, there's no need for your day to be spoiled.'

Twenty-five

The salt on her skin dried as she climbed the cliff steps.

She walked gratefully into the house and filled the bath. The wounds bled a little more, strings of red marbling the cool, clean water. She let them dry in the air, without dressings.

The house was silent, filled with sunlight. Leaving the blood-stained towel in a bowl of cold water, she put on a clean dress and tied up her hair. The french doors whined gently as she pinned them back to let in the fresh air and set up the ironing board in the opening. Soon she was hard at work, her fright forgotten, pushing the heavy iron back and forth across the board. Humming a little, she thought of Michael, of the seaweed and laughter: how he and Sammy had each found their own way to her, making a place for themselves in her heart, more permanent, more welcome even, than Henry had been.

Henry.

She thought of the first days with him, the days he had called the first days of their lives, the beginning of everything; how passionate he had been, exuberant with desire.

'Am I the first?' she had asked.

'You are the first of everything.' His smooth, manicured fingers stroked her cheek.

'You've never had an affair before?' The question was important.

'This is not an affair. You are the beginning of the rest of my life.'

The ironing-board creaked as she pressed. A button was loose on one of his shirts, she hung it carefully to one side, to remind herself to sew it. Once it would have been a joy to her, to find something she could mend, or wash, a kind of triumph in her unacknowledged struggle with Ruth. Now it was simply a task, part of the role he had made for her, substitute wife and now substitute mother, step-mother, unwittingly wicked.

Holding the hot iron above the board, she looked out at the garden, at the blue sea glittering in the bay. Below on the sand she could see Sammy, a small plump bundle running in circles around Henry's chair. Michael was on the far side, sitting on a rock facing the sea. She remembered the picture he had drawn, of Henry as a diligent father, playing with Sammy in the bath, mending Michael's bike. It wasn't true. It wasn't the Henry she knew; but it was Michael's recollection, the father he wanted.

He had left out his grey suit, rumpled from the train. The

smooth, almost silky material carried a whiff of his after-shave and the strong aerosol deodorant he used in the mornings.

Her hand going through the pockets was automatic, an inattentive feeling for handkerchiefs or loose change. Even when she felt the envelope, took hold of it, finger and thumb around the softened corner, she had not thought of prying. It would have rested on the mantelpiece with his wallet and the car keys, until the ironing was done, if her eye had not been caught by the inconsistencies: a handwritten envelope, addressed to his office, a blue envelope, square instead of rectangular, of the kind that is lined with fine tissue. Her mind absorbed these facts without a murmur, as a machine will accept a string of information without response – until it is asked to juxtapose, to add one fact with another, then the machine comes to life and spews out a deduction: this letter is from Ruth.

She went into the sun. The date was a week old, the writing large and chaotic. A chill crept on her skin as she read. Ruth used words she would not think of; begging, pleading, as though she undressed herself on the page. The last paragraph was written more clearly.

'We need you. The boys need their father. I need you. You and I have been through too much together for this girl to make any difference. I have forgiven you before and I will forgive you again. I want you to know that when you and she have finished there will be a home here for you still.'

The garden was full of sound: birdsong, the hum of insects, buzzing and fluttering in the brilliant, purple-blue geraniums that hung like a cloth, carelessly flung over the patio wall.

I have forgiven you before.

Suzannah pressed the jacket carefully, returned the letter and the wallet and the car keys to the pockets. She would ask him. He would explain. He had been planning to tell her of the letter; there had not been a good moment for it. The children took up so much of her time. He would explain it all, even tell her how he intended to reply. Everything would be explained, even the cruel, cold place in his heart that permitted the letter to rest unattended in the pocket next to his breast.

The iron clicked in its cradle. With a rhythmical movement, she ironed his handkerchiefs, pressing and turning them into neat white squares. There was another click, louder than before, that was neither iron nor cradle but like the closing of a door.

She crossed silently into the hall.

'Henry?' Her voice sounded hollow, like an actress on an empty set.

Footsteps in the kitchen.

'Henry?'

Another sound. The back door pulled shut. She ran across. The kitchen was empty. She peered through the glass panel of the door. A movement in the drive, turning into the road, a flick of cloth, a shirt – or the tail of a coat. She turned the big key, took it out of the lock, waited, listening. There was no car, no sound but the quiet tinkle-hum of the fridge and the birds, muted through the glass.

Recalling the open french windows she rushed back to the dining room. It was empty, only the shirts flapping with the movement of air and the iron ticking to itself. She closed the french windows and walked through the house, closing every open window, until she was back in the kitchen with the door key heavy in her pocket.

Flowers in the sink. She had walked past twice and not seen them: the washing-up bowl half full of pink-petalled stocks, flooding the kitchen with a sweet perfume. A note was wrapped around a stem.

I hope you are soon healed.
Liam McGuinness

In the flurry of their coming home, wet towels and swimming trunks, she forgot the vase, the splash of pink on the mantel-piece, the smell of the stocks, almost too sweet to be natural. Michael had filled the green bag with cuttlefish bones. She admired each one and then Sammy, who for once had waited his turn, crept into her arms for a kiss and a plaster for a tiny graze on his knee.

Henry didn't notice the flowers. After supper he called her out on to the patio.

'Suzannah! Come and sit out here, I've poured you a drink.'

The boys were watching television upstairs. She could hear gunfire and sirens and Sammy, higher pitched than the sirens, tormenting his brother.

She sat beside him and sipped her drink.

'I've almost finished the crossword.'

'Good.' Her lips smiled.

'How are your legs?'

She held them out. 'Just a few grazes, they'll heal in a day or two.'

He put out his hand and stroked her calves. His fingers felt cold.

She took a large gulp of brandy. 'Has she tried to get in touch with you, Henry?'

He wrote something in the white squares and then looked up. 'Who?'

'Ruth.'

He raised a finger to his lips.

'It's all right,' said Suzannah. 'The boys are watching TV.'

He nodded. 'Good,' looking at the paper again.

'Well? Has she?'

He shook his head. 'I would have told you.'

The dusk gathered around them. A band of colour had formed out to sea, quickening the sunset. When she touched her arms her skin was quite cold.

'She hasn't written to you – or anything?'

'No.' He shook his head again.

After a moment he wrote a series of letters down the margin of the page. 'Do you know,' he said, 'I think this is an anagram after all.'

Twenty-six

Gouse ate great quantities of potatoes. The crop from Smithies' yard and then Mrs Evans's stock, hauled up from the village in

Liam's string bag. Every day he fried a panful of chips, like thick yellow fingers, and ate them, stinking of vinegar, three at a time, as if he expected the plate to be snatched away.

He waited in the yard while Liam went down to the village, watching from the gate, bird-sharp, for his return.

'You should grow more,' he called, as Liam came near. 'It would save your legs.'

Liam shook his head. 'It would be a waste.'

'A waste of what?'

'Of the soil. I've only a small patch, as you can see.'

'The flowers are a waste.' Gouse pointed to the stocks flowering tall against the fence. 'You can't eat flowers.'

Liam shrugged. 'They serve another purpose.' He took the string bag indoors and came out again.

Gouse followed him around the yard. He had become more adventurous, explaining to Liam that the village would forget him more easily if he were seen from time to time.

'They won't forget you.' Liam bent down and plucked a small red tomato. 'Try one.'

Gouse put it into his mouth and chewed. He nodded. Liam had a glimpse of red skin and seeds before he swallowed. 'Like I said, you should grow more potatoes.'

'Perhaps.'

It was early evening. A faint breeze fluttered the leaves of his plants. Gouse wore his woollen hat and a sleeveless sweater exposing the white, freckled skin of his shoulders that looked yellow in the fading light.

'Shall we walk?'

Gouse nodded. 'But only round the bay, I don't want to be seen in the village.

Liam went ahead.

'Have you forgotten something?'

'What?'

'You haven't locked the door.'

He'd reached the gate. 'It's safe enough.'

Gouse crossed the patch of mud in a single bound. 'Safe! Nothing is safe! Get this into your thick Irish skull, you lock that door every time you so much as put a foot outside the gate.'

'But there's nothing there to steal.'

'How do you know? You know nothing.'

Liam remembered the backpack, the ungiving canvas under his fingers.

'What is it?'

'What?'

'The thing you have stored in my house?'

'You've no need to know.'

'I know a safer place than under your bed.'

Gouse was frowning, small eyes looking hard at Liam, at his lips and eyes and back again. 'Where?'

Liam pointed to the coal bunker. 'The side door is blocked from the inside. You can't open it at all. And you can bolt the lid down, see, and use a padlock.'

'What's inside?'

'Nothing, a few bits of coal.'

Gouse snorted. 'You think that's a good hiding place? A coal hole with a padlock on the cover? You don't think a padlocked coal bunker might arouse suspicion?'

'It's just an idea. It might be safer than keeping it in the house.'

'Safer for us?' Gouse sneered. 'You're scared of being blown up, is that it?'

'It's something to think of,' said Liam, quietly. It was the first time, the first admission that there were explosives in the house. He looked round for Handel's sheep, as if to speak to them, to tell them of this latest madness, but they were far away, at the edge of the field, a flock of seagulls like white litter at their feet.

Gouse stood close to him and patted his shoulder. 'Don't you worry. I'm no amateur.' He kept his arm around Liam as they walked to the kitchen door. 'Now lock it up, and we'll go for our walk.'

'I'll get the key.'

Gouse waited outside. Passing through the kitchen, Liam paused to empty the bag of potatoes into a cardboard box. Gouse's ashtray had overflowed on to the kitchen table. He pulled a face at it, and went upstairs, scowling at the stink of smoke and vinegar.

The Australian was using the same small bedroom that the girl had used. He kept the door locked but Liam had a spare key, finding a moment each day while Gouse was outside, smoking on the step or visiting the outhouse, to inspect the room. It was like a cell: a pile of clothes on the chair, a folded sleeping bag on the bed. Beneath the bed was Gouse's canvas bag. Tentatively, Liam poked it with his foot. The contents were hard and unyielding.

Everything in the room reeked of smoke, even the sleeping bag that Gouse had brought with him. Seeing the soft roll of quilting, Liam wondered if the girl had complained, reported the poor standard of comfort in the safe house?

In a frame on the windowsill was a photograph. Another girl, small, like Gouse himself, wearing a flower behind her ear. Liam leaned across the bed. Her face was round and dull.

'What the fuck are you doing in here?'

He hadn't heard Gouse's boots on the stairs. The little man could be quiet when he wanted to be.

'Looking.'

'Looking at what?'

Liam put his foot against the hard canvas roll.

'That's nothing for you to look at.'

There was fight in the little man's eyes but Liam saw that he was controlling it. Keeping his fists down, Gouse moved between Liam and the bed, forcing him, in the confined space, to back out of the room.

'Let's go for that walk, eh? I want to talk to you about Sunday.'

'What about Sunday?'

'You're going up to London.'

'What for?'

'Carrying. There's something for you to bring back.'

'Not again.'

'Yes, again. You're going up on the train. There and back in a day. Easy.'

'Why don't you go?'

Gently pushing Liam out on to the landing, Gouse pulled the door closed behind him.

'Because that is what you are paid to do.'

'I'm not paid to take risks.'

'There's no risk. I've told you, it's a doddle.'

The wind was stronger on the cliff. Gouse whistled under his breath as they walked along, faces down, hands in their pockets, like a pair of old friends.

'What do you do it for, Liam?' Gouse led the way along the path, turning his head slightly to throw the words back over his shoulder. 'You have no faith in the thing, so why do you do it? Just for the money?' A ring of hair hung below the woollen hat. Liam had never seen him without the hat. Perhaps he was bald, the woollen hat a vanity.

'Well? Is it the money or what?'

Gouse stopped where the path divided, one half leading to the cliff steps and the other along the Head. Above them, hidden by the overhanging rock, was Matilda's Cottage.

'Not for the money itself.'

'What else then?'

Liam stepped round him and started down the steps. 'I want to be a painter. The money pays for my materials.'

'And that's it?' Gouse hurried behind him. 'No love of country, no wish for freedom, just paint pots and canvas?'

'And paper, it all costs.'

Gouse was silent.

'What about you?' They had reached the bottom of the steps, where a patch of shingle merged with the sand. The stones were loud under their boots. In his pocket, Liam turned the boy's pebble between his fingers. 'You're not Irish, what's your motive?'

Gouse drew himself up. 'I'm not confined by petty nationalism.'

'Any war will do then? You're a mercenary?'

'I'm a soldier, my cause is international.'

Liam turned round, scowling at Gouse. 'Blood money, is that what you earn?'

The little man was laughing. 'And what do you call your retainer – an honest wage?' He patted Liam's shoulder. 'Don't look so angry, my friend. Soon we will both have work to do for our money.'

Liam stopped. 'What does that mean?'

'I'll be having some visitors on Sunday.'

'Who?'

'No one you know. You'll be away in London. There's a parcel for you to collect. I want you to be gone before seven and not come back until it's dark.'

'It won't take me all day to pick up a parcel.'

Gouse grinned. 'I'm sure you'll find something else to amuse you.'

Small waves lapped like lazy tongues on the sand; a bank of weed marked the high tide point, a mound of rotting foliage and debris, strips of polythene and driftwood; a strong smell on the breeze.

'Are you listening to me, Liam?'

'These high tides bring in the rubbish from the ferries.'

Gouse stood in front of Liam, but failed, because of his shortness and the slope of the beach, to block Liam's view of the water.

'Are you listening to me, Irishman? Did you hear what I said?'

'You can't have a meeting here,' said Liam, mildly.'The whole village will know of it.'

'No,' said Gouse. 'Our people will be here and gone before the villagers have scratched their heads.'

Liam snorted.

Gouse went ahead, leading them south. His movements were nimble, sure-footed on the uneven ground. Liam shouted at the little man's back. 'Where is the limit, Gouseman? When can I say enough is enough?'

Gouse turned his head, smiling. 'Oh, there's no limit, McGuinness. There's no shallow end for paddlers. Once you're in the water you just have to swim.'

'I only agreed to provide a safe house, nothing more.'

'You're in the deep end, Liam. You're on the payroll.

Hurrying after him, Liam stumbled against a rock that was partly concealed by the sand. A vicious pain shot through his toe. 'Damn!'

'Hurt your foot?'

Liam ignored him. The pain brought tears to his eyes. He sat on the sand and clutched his foot.

Gouse said, 'There's also your brother to think of.'

Liam looked up. 'Will my brother be at this meeting?'

Gouse tapped his nose and turned away towards the rocks. A pair of cormorants took off as he approached the Head, a chorus of anxious cries, a dark clatter of wings against the evening sky.

Liam was awake when they came. It was still dark. He heard Gouse get up, quiet as a cat, only the creak of his bed and the smell of a freshly lighted cigarette marked his movements. They came on foot.

A soft click at the gate and then the door, the scrape of a chair on the kitchen floor. Across the field a dog barked, one of Handel's collies. Smoke drifted up the stairs. Liam dressed in his best clothes: green corduroys and a brown sweater. There were five of them, shadows in the unlit kitchen, three on the chairs and two standing. On the table was an insulated picnic box, like the one he had carried from London.

Gouse was waiting to escort him to the door. He patted his back. 'Until dark, then.'

Liam paused by the door. 'Is Brendan coming?'

'You've no need to know.'

'I should like to see him, if he comes.'

Gouse shrugged.

Liam lingered outside. 'Look,' he said, turning back. Gouse was in the doorway, blocking the view. The doorstep brought the little man's eyes almost in line with his. 'Look, I don't like this.' He fingered a button on his coat. 'It's my house and all that.'

Gouse showed his teeth. 'Go on now.' His hand was on Liam's shoulder, gently pushing him away.

Twenty-seven

'I want to see my father.'

'But you saw him just before we came down here. You went for a whole weekend.'

'Nevertheless . . . '

'He has to get used to being alone, Suzannah. You mustn't let him depend on you for company.'

'That's hardly likely.'

Her voice was bitter but the bitterness was not for Henry. It was for herself, for her own forgetfulness that had permitted days to run into weeks, allowed the preoccupations of being a mother and wife, a substitute Ruth, to shut her father out. More easily than she could imagine, her mother's death had faded, the sharp pain of it eclipsed just as Henry intended. But with it had gone her father's pain, the empty house, the endless ticking of the hall clock, the bottle of sherry at ten o'clock in the morning.

'You sound like an au pair, asking for time off.'

'Perhaps that is how it feels.'

Michael interrupted. 'You're not like our au pair used to be. She used to smoke in her bedroom.'

Henry sent the boys away.

'Don't get angry, Suzannah.'

'I just want to see him. I want to know if he is all right.'

He lay on a deckchair, wearing white swimming trunks that showed off his tan.

'Will you make sure Sammy doesn't get sunburned?'

Henry held his book to shade his eyes from the sun. 'He's much more likely to burn if you're not here.'

Suzannah perched on the arm of a chair. The soles of his feet faced her like a pair of upraised hands.

'It's just for two days, Henry. I'll be back on Sunday night.'

'But you complain when I go away.' His voice was petulant. 'Now that I am here, you want to go.'

Suzannah stood up. 'Is there anything you want? I shall probably take Daddy shopping.'

'Don't go, Suzannah.' Holding out his hand he leaned out of the deckchair. 'How can I manage on my own? What will we do about food?'

'There's a chicken casserole in the freezer, a pizza in the fridge and a chocolate mousse. You'll survive.'

'The boys will pester me to death. I was looking forward to a quiet read.'

The clasp of her handbag closed with a snap.

She would have stayed; she would have let her father wait a while longer. She would have stayed if he had said, 'Suzannah, I need you.' Or spoken of love, or called her into his arms, or done any of the things that a month ago she would have taken for granted. But his complaint was not the loss of her company. He did not wish to be left alone with his children, to play the part that she had been playing since the day Michael had run up the stairs and shouted 'Nothing has changed!'

It was Ruth's part, the role of mother. The more closely she played it, the further she drifted from Henry. As if she was somehow in Ruth's shoes, becoming, by degrees, a little wife, one who could be nagged and used as she now had no doubt he had nagged and used Ruth. His manner estranged her. She was driven towards the children, to Sammy, with his open arms and wet, uncomplicated kisses.

The little boy was standing on the bathroom stool, cleaning his teeth. In the next room Michael lay stretched out on the bed with his arms behind his head. He looked down his nose at Suzannah, between the open collars of his shirt, across the ribby bumps of his chest.

'Will you help Sammy get off the stool when he's finished?'

Michael nodded, stretching himself.

'Mum didn't like the au pair.'

'Didn't she?' Suzannah asked, without interest.

'Mum didn't like the way Dad looked at her.'

Suzannah paused by the bathroom. Sammy was squeezing toothpaste on to a brush, his tongue curling up as he watched the fat blue streak.

'Not too much now.'

He looked up, squeezing involuntarily as he took his eyes from the brush.

'Watch out!' A string of paste oozed out over his fingers, plopped into the basin. She patted his head as he crammed the over burdened brush into his mouth. 'Make sure you rinse it off well.'

'Dad used to look at her legs!' Michael shouted as she went downstairs.

She let the front door slam behind her. No one came out to watch her go. She sat in the car, breathing the smell of sun-warmed leather.

'Wait in the car,' he had said, on that other occasion. 'I'll just pack a bag. I won't be long.' Two hours. The time it took to finish with Ruth.

She drove slowly through the village. A handful of tourists had gathered on the quay, pointing and staring at the pictures spread out along the wall. Liam sat at the end on his little stool. As the car smoothed by, he raised his hand and smiled.

Reaching the main road she found a space in the traffic and pulled out, following the signs for Dover. The car surged forward, purring silently. She felt the cold smoothness of the wheel and the lure of the pedals under her feet.

Two hours she had waited. With the priest's words still fresh in her ears. Two hours. Marooned in his car in Cavanagh Road. She'd left her handbag behind; wallet, keys, dropped everything to answer his summons. 'I'm doing it today, now. Wait for me. Wait in the car. If she sees you she'll know it's for real.'

The curtains had flicked. Ruth's face peering down at her. Not angry. Astonished.

Two hours.

At last the front door opened: Ruth stood against it, pushing her back to the wood as if to brace herself. She wore the bottle-green dress from the photograph. Suzannah remembered it, every detail of her standing there, the dress clinging to her stomach and thighs as she leaned against the door.

And his face. Not pale, or red, or tear-stained, or even frowning; a man being collected, looking out for his driver as he came along the street with his bag. He had changed his clothes.

'Why have you changed?'

She imagined him undressing. Saying it between buttons: I am leaving you. I am going to live with Suzannah. I am going away. And all the while unbuttoning his shirt, stepping out of his trousers as if he had just come home from work and this was an ordinary day.

'She wanted the suit for the cleaners.'

'What?'

'She was making up a load, they do a discount.' He flapped his hand. 'It doesn't matter.'

'Then you'll have to go back for it.'

'Yes.' He had looked away. 'I'll have to go back.'

'I mean soon, straight away.'

'I have others.'

'But you'll want that one.'

Her voice had risen, arguing already, like a wife.

The station car park was full. She drove to the end and, with difficulty, squeezed his car into a space between a rusty Cortina and the brick wall. If he could see it he would be furious; but he could not see it, and the thought of it was obscurely pleasing.

Waiting for her at Victoria, her father was almost unrecognisable. A thin old man in spectacles. She kissed him.

'Oh, Suzannah!' His hands gripped her arms as he led her to his car. 'It feels so long since I saw you last.'

It's only a month, Daddy, she wanted to say. Not as long as all that. But who could say how long a month would be, in an empty house?

The journey home took longer than she remembered. Cyril's driving was hesitant. When they reached the house he went straight to the sideboard.

'I'm not used to all that noise,' he said, clearing his throat as he tilted the decanter.

'So Austin is coming tomorrow?' said Suzannah, reminding him of what he had said in the car. 'Has Gassy made something nice?'

He gulped his sherry and looked up, even his face seemed thin, his spectacles owlish as he smiled at her. 'I took a liberty, my dear, I told her we wouldn't need anything, that you'd make one of your curries.'

'A curry? But Daddy, we should have gone to the shops!'

He waved his hand and emptied his glass. 'All your mother's spices are still in the pantry.'

'What about meat?'

'Chicken. I went to the butcher myself and bought a fresh one. It's ready and waiting in the fridge.'

The hall clock chimed as she took her bag upstairs to her room. Six o'clock. Would Henry warm up the pizza properly? She imagined him struggling with the handle of the oven door. Had she ever mentioned that it needed a special turn? Had Ruth?

The door of the master bedroom stood open; two beds side by side once more. On her mother's bed the counterpane lay flat, signalling the absence of bedding beneath. The dressing-table, too, was bare; the silver-backed hairbrush no longer resting on a lace mat that had been there for as long as she could remember.

Her room felt chilly. She took an old cardigan from the wardrobe and closed the curtains, moving her teddy bear from the windowsill to the bed; its furry head smelt dry and dusty. Returning to the hall she looked at her father through the open door, sitting empty-handed in his chair, staring at the dried flowers in the fireplace.

'I'll make a start on the curry,' she called, falsely bright.

He started. 'What?' And his face smiled to see her standing in the doorway, rolling up the sleeves of her cardigan. 'Anything I can do?' He put his hands on his knees to push himself from the chair.

Suzannah knew the gesture well. Since she was a child, every time her mother announced her next task, he would ask, 'Is there anything I can do?' Joan's answer was always, 'No thank you, dear. I can manage.'

Suzannah paused. He was still holding his knees, waiting for her reply.

'No thanks, Dad. I can manage.'

As if she had released a spring, he slipped back. 'Just as you like, my dear.'

The same reply; she wondered if he had forgotten of whom it was that he asked the ritual question.

The spices were all there; labelled jars and pots in what Gassy called 'that curry cupboard'; even the recipe book was there, that had once belonged to the public library and had somehow, without active dishonesty, found its permanent home among the labelled jars.

Curry on Boxing Day had been her mother's tradition. Until last Christmas when Joan had remained in her chair, already pale, already slipping imperceptibly away as her daughter took her place in the kitchen, with Henry's diamonds glittering by her face, grinding mustard seeds and cumin, soaking tamarind in a bowl like a clump of squeezed dates.

Gassy's apron was too large; she tied the string twice around her waist. The coriander seeds clattered against the glass of the grinder, diminished by the blades to a coarse brown powder that hissed in the hot oil and filled the air with a pungent aroma.

She stood on the kitchen stool to bring down the big brown cooking pot from the top cupboard. The exterior glaze was crazed and the lid had a small chip, but the interior was sound, creamy-yellow ironstone. She had wiped the inside with a cloth and spooned in fried onion puree, mixed with the ground spices and squares of skinned chicken, when the telephone rang.

'I'll get it.' She turned down the gas.

'Suzannah?'

Austin.

'You came home then?'

'Yes.'

'Your father . . . '

She interrupted. 'I'm sorry.'

'No, you go first.'

'Daddy said you would come to lunch tomorrow.'

'He said I should ring to confirm it with you.'

'With me?'

'He said I should only come if you were there to play hostess for him.'

'Oh.'

'Will you?'

Suzannah's fingers twisted her apron string.

'Will you do that for him, Suzannah?'

'Yes, of course I will.' She pulled the string tighter round her finger. 'I've already started the curry.'

Putting the phone down, she released the apron string and felt the blood rush back under her nail.

The lid of the pot slid into place with a faint scraping noise; the oven door closed with a clump. She turned the control to Low and opened the back door to let out the smell.

Cyril had fallen asleep in his chair. The television advertisements came on, louder than the programme had been. She took the control from his hand, adjusted the volume and placed it on the table beside him.

Austin arrived late. An anxious smile as she opened the door.

'I'm sorry, I was held up.'

'No matter – the curry won't spoil. Shall I take your jacket?'

It was made of cotton; as she hung it in the cupboard she caught a whiff of something sharp and sour.

Her father shook Austin's hand. 'Have you been at the hospice this morning?'

He nodded. 'There was a bit of a crisis – that's why I'm late.'

Suzannah retreated into the kitchen. What kind of crisis? She thought of his coat and came out again.

'Would you like to wash, Austin? Please use the bathroom upstairs if you want to.'

He stopped by the kitchen door. 'The curry smells good.'

'Better than your coat.'

He put his hand to his mouth. 'I'm so sorry. I thought they'd sponged it off.'

'I have a strong nose.' She turned away but he waited by the door.

'You're very severe today.'

She said nothing.

He closed his eyes. 'Her name is Eva. She's about your age and she was very sick.'

'Over you?'

He nodded. 'Over me, over everything.'

'What's the matter with her?'

'She has cancer. Almost all the patients there have cancer. You know that.'

'How can you do it, Austin? How can you go there day after day and wallow in all that death?' Her voice had risen. She did not see her father standing behind him.

'Suzannah! What are you saying? That's no way to speak.'

Her hand covered her mouth. 'I'm sorry.'

Cyril's face was contorted.

'I know it's a lot to get used to,' said Austin.

Her father shook his head. 'I don't know what's come over her, Austin. Come and have a drink, with me. Will you have a beer? – we'll be needing something cool to go with the curry.'

As if he had not heard, Austin turned and spoke to Suzannah. 'It's something we'll have to talk about.'

Tears had come into her eyes.

'I didn't mean to speak like that, Austin. I always seem to say the wrong thing to you.'

Her father called from the sitting room.

Austin smiled. 'It's forgotten. Now I shall go and have that wash.'

When he had gone upstairs she went to her father. 'I'm sorry, Daddy.'

He put the back of her hand against his cheek. 'I expect you were thinking of your poor mother.'

Suzannah nodded, though it wasn't of her mother she had thought, but of Michael, sick in McDonald's; the confusion on his face when she had tried to be kind to him.

'Austin helped your mother a good deal, Suzannah. It is noble work that he does.'

She nodded. 'Will you pour me a beer, too?'

She took the glass of beer back to the kitchen and sipped it while the rice came to the boil. Just before it was cooked, she took his jacket from the cupboard and put it in Gassy's new washing machine.

They emptied the pot; emptied too, the bowl of creamy raita that Austin had spooned with such relish over his chicken. He licked his fingers like a child and caught her eye. His were clear blue, warm and smiling; like the Irishman's eyes, but without his lust. She paused, corrected herself, almost without his lust.

'I did enough for six!' she cried, looking into the empty pot. 'I thought we could keep some for Daddy during the week.'

'Too nice to keep.' Austin patted his stomach. 'I'd forgotten how a good curry tastes.'

The meal had gone well. Cyril had made jokes and told long, rambling anecdotes to which Austin listened, laughing unhesitatingly, in the right places. It was four o'clock when finally they rose from the table and Suzannah took the dirty plates into the kitchen. Gassy's machine had completed its cycle, rinsed, spun and tumbled. She put the jacket against her nose; it smelled of warm cotton and washing powder.

'You've washed it?'

He was behind her, holding the empty casserole.

She nodded. 'Do you think it needs an iron?'

He put down the pot. 'It looks fine to me.'

She held it out to him.

'Am I being sent home?'

'No!' She snatched it back. 'I didn't mean that at all.'

'Good.' He smiled.

'Will you stay and have some coffee?'

'Please.'

He remained while she filled the percolator. 'Are you going back to London tonight?'

'Dover.'

He raised an eyebrow. 'Dover?'

'Henry has a cottage along the coast.'

Austin paused. 'How are the children?'

She smiled. 'Delightful. They're staying with us for the summer.'

'Do they like you?'

'Yes.' She turned, defiantly, to face him. 'They like me very much.'

Austin moved towards the window. 'And their mother, how is she?'

Suzannah felt herself flush. 'Henry says she's fine.'

'Henry says?'

'I'm hardly able to tell for myself.' She turned away from him, fussing with the coffee filter. She heard him sigh and then, in a different voice, he asked, 'But you must go back tonight?'

'I'm catching the seven-twenty train from Victoria.'

'Is that a deadline?'

'I want to get back before it is too late.'

'Too late?'

'I mean too late at night,' said Suzannah. 'I've left Henry's car at the station. I don't want to have to drive around in it at midnight.' With a flick of impatience she opened the dishwasher and began to fill the basket with crockery. Austin brought the remaining plates from the dining room. He said no more.

When the coffee was ready she put the cups on a tray cloth that was brilliant with her mother's fine embroidery. Austin peered at it.

'It's exquisite.'

Suzannah smiled. 'My mother made it – years ago. It took the whole of a winter.'

She carried the tray into the sitting room and for a moment it was as if her mother was there again, by the window, holding her needle up to the light.

Be wise, my darling. Don't try to take what cannot be yours.

*

Her father was dozing.

'Coffee, Daddy?'

He stirred. 'Thank you, my dear.' Sounding, as he often did, as if it were her mother to whom he spoke.

'I'll have to go before long, Daddy.'

'Work tomorrow?'

'Yes.' Her voice was bright with the lie.

Austin drank his coffee. 'I'd better be off.'

'No need for you to go.' Her father gestured. 'Why not stay and have a brandy?'

'I must go. They'll be waiting for me.'

Cyril's hand sank back into his lap. Suzannah saw the effort he made to look composed.

'Shall I call on you during the week, Cyril?'

'During the week?'

Austin nodded. 'I'll call by one evening. I can't promise a particular day but I'll come one evening and have that brandy with you.'

Her father beamed. 'I'll get a bottle of something really good.'

Austin shook his head. 'Whatever you have will do, I'm a heathen when it comes to brandy.'

'Nevertheless – ' Cyril pushed himself out of his chair and shook Austin's hand – 'I'll look forward to it, my boy.'

'And so will I,' said Austin.

Suzannah walked out to his car with him. 'That was nice of you.'

He shrugged. 'Your father needs company. This is sometimes the worst part – a few months after a death. People stop making an effort. You get forgotten.'

'Is that the only reason you'll come – because he needs company? Do you never do anything for your own sake?'

'Oh yes.' He smiled. 'I invite beautiful girls to lunch.'

She took a step back but he was laughing as he got into the car. 'Have a safe journey to Dover, Suzannah.'

'I will.'

The plastic upholstery was peeling from the car seat, the paintwork dented and rusty.

'You look very disapproving.'

'I was looking at your car.'

He pulled the seat belt across his chest. 'I suppose Henry drives something smart and expensive.'

Suzannah gave a short laugh. 'Everything he has is smart and expensive.' She held the car door open, resting her fingers against the pitted chrome. 'He will not settle for anything less.'

'And what happens when things are no longer smart? What does he do with his cast-offs?'

Leaving the question unanswered, she banged the car door closed and walked back to the porch.

He wound down the window. 'It is you who must find contentment, Suzannah. You can't make anyone else happy until you are at ease with yourself.'

Twenty-eight

She was late for the train; running across the concourse of Victoria station; a maze of small shops and stalls, more like a street market than a railway station. Clutching her return ticket, avoiding the ticket-office queues that wound like strings of beads among the crowd, she ran harder, boarded the train as the last whistle blew, the guard screaming 'Stand Away', like a parade sergeant.

It was raining. She stared out of the window, at her own reflection, softened by the darkness, the rain like tears on her cheeks.

'It is you, then.'

She hadn't seen him. Hadn't looked around since she had reached up to put her bag on the rack and sank down into her seat. He was across the carriage, empty seats and the gangway separating her from the face leaning forward, raised eyebrows creating tramlines in the heavy flesh of his forehead.

'Will it be all right if I sit with you, Suzannah?'

Without waiting for her answer, he stood up, gathered the big coat about himself, and settled into the seat opposite her own. On the rack above where he had been sitting was a brown paper parcel.

'You've forgotten your parcel.'

His eyes slid. 'I'll leave it there, I can watch it better from here.'

He sat back in the seat, allowing its high back to push his head slightly forward, his bearded chin on to the collar of his coat.

After a minute, during which he looked at her intently, he asked, 'You're by yourself, are you?'

She nodded. 'I've been to see my father.' Her voice was louder than she had intended. 'And you, are you having a break from your painting?'

'In a way.'

There was a pause. He looked at her face, fixing first on one part and then another; eyes, chin, lips – the last so long that she had an urge to lick her lips, to check for crumbs.

'Such bones,' he muttered.

'Pardon?'

'I said you have such good bones. I wish I had my pad.'

She touched her chin.

'Would you let me paint you?'

'You already have.'

'That was nothing but a sketch. I've done that one again, a better version. Now it's a proper sitting I'm after.'

She shook her head. 'It isn't possible.'

'That's a great pity. I'd like to paint you again.' He settled more comfortably into the carriage seat. 'Would he have to be told?'

She looked up, puzzled. 'Who?'

'TeaCoffeeSandwiches.' A steward pulled a trolley into the carriage.

Liam raised his head.

'Coffee, sir?'

'Two, black.'

The steward filled polystyrene beakers from a jug and fitted lids to the top, Suzannah went for her purse but it was too late. Liam had put a pile of change into the steward's hand.

'You needn't have done that,' said Suzannah.

He grinned. 'Why not?'

She didn't answer. Liam put the beakers on a minute side-table fitted beneath the carriage window.

'You didn't want milk or anything?' She shook her head, conscious of the discomfort of being indebted, even so slightly, to the Irishman.

She lifted the lid from her beaker and sipped. The coffee was lukewarm and weak. She pulled a face and Liam laughed. Feeling his eyes on her, she turned to stare once more at the rain-spattered glass.

'You and Henry Alland.' The Irishman leaned forward. She could see him twice, once in the glass and again in the corner of her eye, the face coming closer to hers, eyebrows raised. 'You're not wedded?'

The strangeness of the question made her look up. 'No. He hasn't divorced his wife.'

'Ruth is alone?'

Suzannah nodded. 'Do you know her?'

The Irishman shrugged. 'She used to come to Smithies sometimes.' He took a swallow of coffee and replaced the mug on the shelf. 'I saw her today.'

'Today? Where?'

'I went to her house.'

Suzannah could not keept the astonishment from her voice. 'You went to Cavanagh Road?'

'Is there a rule against it?'

'No.' She swallowed. 'I'm just surprised.' She looked away, out into the darkness, conscious of the sway and tilt of the train. Something of Austin's words, the blunt exchanges of the day, had stayed with her, bringing to her lips the question that she did not want to ask.

'How is Ruth?'

The painter spread his hands. 'She wouldn't let me see her.'

'But you said you saw her.'

'So I did, but it was only through the door. I was not allowed into the house.'

'How did she look?'

'What is it to you?'

Suzannah looked down, fingering the clasp of her handbag. 'I just wondered.'

'She's bad.' The Irish voice came clear across the carriage. His eyes grew wide. 'I've never seen her so.'

Suzannah took a tissue from her bag and blew her nose. There was nothing to blow but she felt a need to cover her face.

The train entered a tunnel, magnifying the noise of the wheels on the tracks; the dark walls wooshed past the window, looming close as the train rounded a bend. The Irishman closed his eyes and settled back once more, resting the beaker of coffee on his knee.

'A girl like you should be married, Suzannah.'

She looked at him. 'Why do you say that?'

'You have a need. It is in your face, you need a ring to say to the world, I am loved.'

She looked out at the rain, avoiding his eyes in the reflection. Austin had said as much, calling through the window of his battered car, his clean, orderly face smiling out at her. She remembered the ring her father wore, one of a pair. Had he kept her mother's? Or had it gone in with the rest of her, consumed by fire with the plush-lined box? His own was too large, lingering loose arund the sinewy skin of his finger. A ring to tell the world he was once loved.

The rest of the journey passed in silence. Suzannah kept her eyes on her own reflection in the glass, ignoring the Irishman who stared at her continuously, eyes moving over her like hands.

As the train pulled into Dover he lifted her bag down from the rack and put it beside her on the seat.

'Will you think about the painting now? I'd be very quick.'

Suzannah shook her head.

He lifted his parcel from the rack on the other side of the compartment and followed her to the carriage door. 'Would you think it a great cheek if I asked for a lift?'

'In Henry's car?'

'If that is the one you have.'

Suzannah paused. He tucked the parcel under his arm. The station car park was dark; street lights shone in puddles on the tarmac. 'All right then, just for once.'

His smile was warm.

She set the pace to the car. They had to cross a wide space

where the ferry buses turned. A handful of travellers waited in the bays by the wall. As they reached the other side a white single-decker bus swung in. The lighted panel above the driver's cab gave the destination as Calais.

Liam loped along beside her, holding himself back to match her steps.

'Shall we be friends, Suzannah?'

He held out his hand, offering it sideways across her path.

She shook it awkwardly, changing hands with her bag.

'And will you sit for me?'

They had reached the car, glossy, discoloured by the artificial light. 'Don't ask me again. I've said no and I mean it.'

'Don't you want to?'

She inserted the key. 'If you go round to the other side, I'll let you in.'

He didn't speak again until they were out of the town, travelling swiftly on the main road. Behind them a low moon smeared the sea with silver.

Liam sat sideways in the passenger seat, watching her as she drove.

'It's pretty hands you have.'

She glanced at the dashboard. The easy power of the car made it an effort to keep within the speed limit.

'And a pretty neck.'

'I wish you wouldn't – '

'Flatter you?'

'Yes. It makes me feel uncomfortable.'

He sat up straight in the seat, pulled his legs up and put his hands on his knees. 'Is that better?'

She said nothing but changed down to second gear for the steep run into the village. Before they reached the High Street he put out his hand. 'This will do. I can walk from here.'

'I can run you to Smithies, it's no trouble.'

'No, I'll walk.'

She pulled up beside the verge. 'As you wish.'

'Don't be huffy now, Suzannah.'

She shrugged. 'It makes no difference to me whether you walk or not.'

He turned to her, the parcel tucked under his arm, holding out his hand. 'Are we still friends?'

She did not shake his hand again. 'Yes, if that is all you want.'

'And will you let me paint you?'

'No!'

He was laughing, holding his hand up in mock surrender. 'A joke.'

His face changed again, eyes turning to pools. 'You should see the new one I've done, it would give you a different view of yourself.'

She watched his back as he walked away.

The Irishman disturbed her. Just as Austin disturbed her; paint on one coat and sickness on the other, and Henry with no blemish at all.

She straightened her skirt and put the car into gear. As she drove past he turned and waved, and in the driving mirror she saw him standing in the road, with the parcel under his arm, looking after her.

Henry came out to greet her on the porch.

'Darling girl, I've missed you so.' His arms drew her against himself, she felt the hardness of his chest against her breasts. Abruptly, the embrace ended. He drew back with an expresion of distaste.

'What's the matter?'

'My God, what have you been eating?'

She smiled, covering her mouth. 'I'm sorry, I'd forgotten, we had a big curry for lunch.'

For the remainder of the evening he kept away from her, turning his face in the bed to read his book.

Twenty-nine

Gouseman's visitors had gone. Liam had to bang on the door and wait for Gouse to slide back the squeaking bolts that before that night had never been used. A row of mugs by the sink, and the bread board, scrubbed clean. Gouse had pushed the woollen hat back off his face, exposing the smooth white bulge of his forehead, as another man might roll up his sleeves on a Saturday afternoon – a sign of relief and holiday.

He smiled at Liam. 'You can leave the parcel with me. Do you want to eat?'

Liam looked at the pan on the stove. The oil in the chip pan had started to move, bubbles rising to the surface, a piece of blackened potato floating at the edge from the last meal.

'No.'

He put his hand on the table. Bright metal filings, fine as dust, clung to his fingers. The plastic box had gone.

'What were you doing here?'

Gouse was peeling potatoes into the sink. 'You'd better use the dustpan and brush.'

'What is it?'

'Dust.'

'What from?'

The peeler clattered into the sink. 'You've no need to know.'

Liam lifted his bag from the corner. 'I'm going to take my coat upstairs. When I come down I want the table to be clean. All those mugs out of sight. I want no sign of it, do you hear?'

Gouse moved towards him, fists raised. Liam spread his legs and waited. At the last moment the hands dropped, the fists relaxed. Gouse turned his palms up, an offering. 'There's no need for us to fight, Liam. We're on the same side. After today, we're winning.'

The pale eyes blinked up at him, eyelids so fine they were transparent, fluttering open and shut.

'I don't like it.' Liam pointed to the table. 'All this. Not in my house. I don't expect it.'

There was a noise from the stove, a lick of flame and then a thick plume of smoke obscured the pan.

Gouse lunged at the cooker, turned off the ring and dived for the sink. Smoke filled the kitchen. Squeezing out a cloth Gouse went back to the stove. A great hiss went up as the cloth covered the pan. The cloth bulged. Coughing and blinded, Liam ran out into the yard. Gouse wrapped his hands in a towel and, taking hold of the red-hot handle, brought the pan, still hissing, into the yard.

'Jesus!' Liam gasped, breath going noisily into his lungs.

Gouse coughed and spat. 'That was fucking close.'

'Is it out?'

Gouse looked at the pan and nodded.

Smoke, thinning to a haze, rolled slowly out of the kitchen door behind them.

'All under control,' said Gouse.

Liam coughed. Tears dribbled down his face.

He wiped his eyes on his sleeve.

'Fucking close,' Gouse repeated.

Liam watched the little man's face; eyes darting, constant glances back at the house, watching the door, the drift of thin smoke wallowing in the windless yard.

'Not just a fire you were afraid of?' said Liam slowly.

Gouse took out his pouch of tobacco. Liam saw the quiver of his hands. Even in his mouth the cigarette trembled.

'Afraid we would end up in the bay?' said Liam. 'Food for the fishes, eh?'

Gouse coughed again as the cigarette smoke filled his lungs.

'Something like that.'

They sat outside until it was dark, on two hard chairs that Gouse brought out when he came back from opening every window in the house. There was no wind. An hour later, the smell of burned oil and smoke still lingered, hanging in the yard like a swamp-mist.

Gouse had a pair of pebbles. He beat them together in his hands. Clack, clack; clack, clack.

'I don't like it,' said Liam. 'I don't like this going on in my house.'

'There's nothing to like or dislike,' said Gouse. 'It's just a fact. There's a job to be done.'

'Why does it have to be done here?'

'Because here is safe.'

The pebbles clacked like solemn castanets.

Liam stretched out his legs. Thrusting his hands into his pockets, his fingers found Samuel's pebble. He rolled it against his palm.

Gouse drew the glowing cigarette close to his lips then stubbed it into the ground with his shoe.

Liam looked down with distaste. The unplanted area of his yard was scattered with tiny paper butts, white in the light from the door.

Gouse followed his look. 'You're lucky they're not filters. A shower of rain and these will be gone.'

'There's been no rain for weeks.'

'No,' said Gouse.

He resumed his play with the pebbles. Clack, clack, clack.

'What have you been up to all day, apart from collecting the parcel?' he asked.

Liam shrugged. 'This and that.'

'I see you wore your good clothes.'

'You don't miss much.'

Gouse grinned.

'I mean with all the visitors coming, I wouldn't expect you to notice what I was wearing.'

'It's the training.'

'Training?'

Gouse tapped his nose.

Liam looked at him. He sat like a bird. Even out here, sitting on a kitchen chair with nothing moving in sight but the trees at the end of the lane, even here he was alert; perched on the edge of the chair, eyes roving the yard and the lane with quick irregular movements. 'Was it the training that taught you what to do with the pan?'

Gouse smiled. 'I learned that from my mother.'

'In Australia?'

Gouse shook his head. 'You're nosy as a woman, McGuinness.'

Liam shrugged. 'It was only conversation.'

The pebbles clacked in Gouse's hands. 'What you don't know, you can't tell.'

'Will you stop doing that?'

'Does it make you nervous?'

Liam shifted in his chair and folded his arms. 'Sure, it just irritates me.'

The evening had grown cool. Gouse went inside for his jacket. Returning, he stretched out on his chair and rolled another cigarette. His hands no longer shook. Liam watched a thin white cylinder emerge from his fingers. 'Would they take just anyone for training?'

'Who do you mean by "just anyone"?'

'Me, for instance.'

'I thought you wanted to be an artist.' Gouse struck a match and dragged on the cigarette.

'But would they? Do you have to be qualified?'

Gouse shook his head. 'Only committed.'

'To what?'

'The cause. Revolution. Whatever it is that you want to happen.'

'You're saying it doesn't matter what it is?'

'The details don't matter.'

'Is it Russians who do the training?'

Gouse laughed. He tapped his nose again. 'Irish nosy, that's what you are.'

The house still smelled of smoke when they went in. Gouse's potatoes were in the sink, waiting to be cooked.

'You'll have to get some more oil in the morning,' he said.

'Will I?' Liam took off his coat.

'What else is there to eat?'

'You could boil them.'

Gouse pulled a face.

Liam used a cloth to wipe the spilled oil from the cooker and floor. He filled a pan with water and lit the ring. The pan-stand smoked a little as the last of the spilled oil burned off.

'Your brother was here today.'

Liam looked up. 'Brendan? Why didn't you tell me before?'

Gouse took out his tobacco pouch. 'I don't want you to speak to him yet.'

Liam put a pinch of salt in the water. 'How is he?'

'Well enough.' With a lighted cigarette hanging from his lip, Gouse carried the chairs in from the yard. 'When will they be ready?' he asked, pointing to the potatoes.

'Ten minutes.' The water was beginning to boil. 'When will I see Brendan?'

'Soon enough.' Cigarette smoke seeped slowly through his nose. 'Young Brendan has been working very hard.'

'Is it finished, then?'

'What?'

'The job. Whatever it was you came to do.'

'It will be soon, when I've gone.'

Liam turned his head. 'When will that be?'

'In a few days.'

The potatoes were ready. Liam's fork slid smoothly from the waxy, yellow flesh.

'You're going for good?'

'For good.' He looked up, grinning at Liam's face. 'That's good news for you, eh? I'll catch a ferry and sail away.' Gouse carefully squeezed the end of his half-smoked cigarette and rested it on the lip of the ashtray. 'Is there any ham?'

'You ate it all yesterday.'

Gouse sighed.

'There's corned beef. Will you eat that?'

He nodded. 'And some of those tomatoes of yours.'

Liam went into the yard. The smoke from Gouse's pan still lingered in the air. Keeping his hand on the wall as a guide, he worked his way around to the side and felt for the plants. The skins were firm and tight. He collected four each and went back to the kitchen. Gouse had re-lit his cigarette and was exhaling smoke over the steaming plates of potatoes.

'When did you say you were going?'

'I didn't say. It'll be in a day or two. I haven't made up my mind.' He began to open the tin of corned beef. 'You'll be pleased to see the back of me.'

'I will.'

'There's one last little job for you.'

Liam slumped into his chair.

The corned beef dropped in a solid lump on to Gouse's plate.

'Do you want some of this?'

Liam shook his head. 'What little job?'

'I'll tell you on the day.' Gouse began to mash the beef into his potatoes.

Thirty

'Your friend keeps himself to himself, Mr McGuinness.'

'He does that, Mrs Evans.'

She was slicing ham; a pink joint rolling back and forth on the machine, depositing a slice with each pass, like wafers of skin.

'He's not vegetarian, then. Not like you.'

'No, Mrs Evans, he's not like me.'

She folded a piece of grease-proof paper round the meat and transferred it to a plastic bag. Her nose pointed down like a beak as she wrote the price on the bag with a black marker pen.

Liam turned to the wall where his pictures had hung. It was quite bare, every one had sold. 'You did well with the pictures, Mrs Evans.'

'I told you they were good. Everyone said they were.'

Liam shook his head.

'We'll do it again, next year. You do some more of those boat scenes – people love boat scenes.' She handed him the bag. 'Will that be all?'

'And a bottle of oil.'

'Again? You only had a bottle at the beginning of the week.' She stood on a low stool and handed him a yellow plastic bottle from the shelf.

Liam took the bottle from her hand. 'Gouse likes his chips.'

'That's a strange name, now.'

Inwardly, Liam groaned. He had given her the name.

'That's not an English name.'

'It's just a nickname.'

She put her hands in her pockets and stepped back behind the meat slicer. 'Why doesn't he do his own shopping?'

Liam paused. 'He's my guest.'

'Funny you never brought him down to The Swan.'

'He doesn't drink.'

The little woman peered up at him. 'There's not much goes unnoticed in a village like this, you know.'

'I'm sure there isn't,' said Liam. 'How much do I owe you?'

Her fingers were quick on the till. 'Two pounds and five

pence.' She tore the receipt off the roll. 'You should stick to your painting, Mr McGuinness, that's where your future is.'

He took the change from her hand. 'I hope you're right, Mrs Evans.'

'My Glyn'll give you a lift up the hill if you like. He's got a letter for Mr Alland, it's marked urgent so he's going up there with it now.'

'No, I'll walk, thank you.'

Mrs Evans looked disappointed. 'It's from London,' she said.

Liam leaned over the counter. 'If you are hoping they'll invite me in and tell me what it says, you'd be hoping in vain.'

The shopkeeper pursed her lips and smoothed her apron. 'Nothing of the sort!'

The doorbell pinged loudly as he went out.

They had finished supper. Suzannah was washing up. 'Henry, there's a van outside,' she called. 'Can you open the door? My hands are wet.'

She heard voices in the hall, then the front door closed.

'What is it, Henry?'

There was no reply. When the washing up was done she made coffee and carried it through, with two small glasses of brandy on a tray.

Henry was sitting in one of the big chairs, holding a piece of paper aloft in his hand. 'It's a letter from Wilson.'

Suzannah put down the tray. 'Dr Wilson?'

He held the letter out to her. 'I want you to read it.'

Without answering Suzannah sat down and put a spoonful of sugar into his cup. Seeing that she would not take it, he read the letter aloud. It was brief and formal. Suzannah sat back, holding a brandy glass in both hands.

'In the bath!' Henry waved the letter in front of her. 'Imagine it, Suzannah! Imagine her there all alone with the bath full of blood.' He gave out a cry. 'On Tuesday, while we played on the beach.'

She could not recall the day. Tuesday had been like all the other days. She'll shoot herself, Michael had said. Instead she had chosen a razor. The pictures came to Suzannah as a series, like frames of a film, frozen, unreal, a room tiled in white; bloody water slopping on to a fleecy white carpet.

Henry grasped her hand and pressed it against his face. 'What have we done?'

Suzannah pulled away. 'Nothing,' she said, through clenched teeth, 'she has done it to herself.'

She left him with his eyes closed, groping blindly for her hand while she took her empty glass into the kitchen and rinsed it vigorously under the tap. 'Ruth made sure someone would come, didn't she!' she shouted. 'I'll bet she timed it to the last minute.'

Mechanically she dried the glass, rolling the tea-towel into a ball to fill the bowl.

'She's bad,' the Irishman had said. 'I have never seen her so.'

Distress on the doorstep. Razor blades in her shopping basket.

Suzannah carried the polished glass into the dining room and put it away in the sideboard. The french windows had been left open. She lifted the tablecloth and shook it out through the doors. Brother Bernard had liked a tablecloth, to remind him of his granny. Austin had put his hands on her shoulders. 'People behave like prisoners, looking only at the square of the world that they can see.'

She folded the cloth and put it in a drawer of the sideboard.

In the sitting room Henry was weeping, single tears oozed slowly down his cheeks. Unable to comfort him, she went upstairs.

'What can I do?' he cried, blundering up after her. 'What can I do?'

'Hush!' she whispered. 'Michael will hear you!'

She reached for his arm and pulled him into the bedroom. Michael's door opened, a shaft of light and American accents spilling out on to the landing.

'What's the matter with Dad?'

'It's all right, Michael. There's nothing wrong,' said Suzannah, shielding his view of Henry with the half-closed door.

'Can I watch the late horror film?'

'All right, but keep the volume down.'

'Thanks.' He closed his door, extinguishing the light and the noise.

Their bedroom was in darkness. She folded her arms and stood by the window. Henry sat on the bed, holding his face in his hands.

'She tried to take her life,' he whispered. 'My Ruthie tried to kill herself.'

My Ruthie. My Ruthie. The words rang in her ears; the unfamiliar endearment like a curtain suddenly parted, a wash of bright light.

'She knew what to do, didn't she?' said Suzannah bitterly. 'She knew what would make you remember her.'

Suzannah stared into the darkened garden. Across the bay she could see a light burning, the artist moving about in his glass studio.

Thirty-one

Henry's suffering was real. An hour passed before she knew it to be so. An hour spent frozen on the window seat, immobilised by a feeling that was like anger but was not anger, but words spilling from her lips, an intonation like a prayer that drowned out Henry's weeping. The white-tiled room, the white bath, the gold taps of her imaginings; blood flowing freely, red-stained water falling over the sides, a pink flood on a fleece-covered floor; an unforgivable drama of running white coats and the rim of red bathwater in the creases of her neck. She would have timed it so carefully, to be sure that someone would come, that someone would drag her out and deliver her ultimatum to Henry.

Through it all Suzannah heard him calling, over and over in the darkness, 'What have we done? What have we done?'

Her anger ebbed away. She crossed the room and switched on the light by the bed. Blindly he turned to her, to bury his tear-wet face against her breast. She held him cradled in her arms, not the Henry she knew, but a child. Looking down she saw that his look was the same as Michael's had been, months before; utterly bewildered, bitterly contrite.

'I had no idea,' he cried.

'But you did, Henry. You knew.'

'I had no idea she would do this.'

'Didn't she threaten it, didn't she say there was nothing left for her to do?'

'Never. I thought she was coping.'

'What about her letters?'

'What letters?'

'The letters from Ruth. I read one.'

He twisted round on the bed, his face contorted. 'You read them?'

'One of them, it was in your breast pocket.'

'That was a letter from my wife!'

'Your wife?' Suzannah's voice was husky with bitterness. 'I thought I was to be your wife.'

He sank back against the pillow, teeth bared as he struggled to speak. 'I didn't think it through,' he whispered, turning again to bury himself against her breast. 'I wanted you so much. You were so lovely, I couldn't bear to think of not having you. That was all that was in my mind.'

'You didn't think of Ruth?'

He whimpered. 'Oh, Suzannah. You cannot understand how it was. Ruth was still there. I could go to the house at any time and she would be there, caring for the boys, being as she always had been. There didn't seem to be any risk.'

'But she was so distressed. She begged you to go back.'

'I didn't want to go back. I wanted you.'

'You wanted both of us,' said Suzannah, pushing him away. 'It's called having your cake and eating it.'

'Suzannah, don't be bitter. Don't be ugly and bitter, don't be like Ruth.' He lunged after her across the duvet but she pulled free and sat once more beside the window. Across the bay the lights in the studio had been extinguished. There was no moon, nothing to see except a grey glimmer of sea under the stars.

At last he slept and she returned to the bed. He turned in his sleep and clung to her, hot breath on her shoulder and his body stirring against her skin. The feel of it kept her awake, with the image of his tear-stained face printed across the darkened ceiling. Not the Henry she knew, but a more lovable man.

It was the foghorn that woke her. His side of the bed was empty. She put on her dressing gown and went downstairs. A white mist hung over the bay, obscuring the beach and the sea. He was sitting on a garden chair, his back to the house. 'You know she used to love this place.' His voice was calm, as if he had been talking for hours. 'She was always asking me to bring her here. She even preferred it to Cavanagh Road. Then suddenly, after Sammy was born, she never wanted to come back.'

Suzannah pulled the sash of her dressing gown tight. The chairs felt cold and damp. Beside him, on a low stone wall, was a train timetable, the pages hanging limp with damp.

'Would you like a cup of tea?'

He didn't answer but when she brought out the mugs he was speaking again. 'It was Sammy, you know. She wanted another baby so badly – ' he sipped his tea – 'but I told her she was too old for it. I was right.' He turned to Suzannah and she saw that his expression was composed, he had brushed his hair, presenting his familiar, handsome face. 'She was far too old. It damaged her body, she lost her shape, she was permanently tired.'

He finished the tea and put the mug on the wall beside the timetable. 'The au pair was no good, what we needed was a really good nanny.'

Suzannah stared past him, out to sea. The foghorn moaned through the mist. Just visible across the grass, the rose bush bore a new crop of buds, tight coils of yellow, slowly unfurling. She remembered the shower of petals on the grass, Michael's white face in the window, looking down at her with such suspicion. A nanny, Henry had said. She felt a bitter smile on her lips. She had made the best nanny of all.

'I'll have to go to her, Suzannah.'

She nodded.

'I can't stay away.' He put out his hand. 'You do understand?'

She nodded again. I understand perfectly, she thought. Ruth has pulled the cord that will return you to Cavanagh Road. You will take the boys and I will be left with nothing, like something forgotten on the beach, like a discarded shoe, waiting for the tide. Henry's family would reassemble, with Ruth's scars to keep his wandering heart in check. And if I should phone, you will wear the face that I have seen so often, and mine will be the shrill voice crying uselessly in your ear.

The foghorn boomed, louder as the mist slowly cleared. She looked down at the sea. The tide was in, a dark, gleamless grey below the cliff.

'They haven't taken it very seriously,' she said.

'What do you mean?'

'If they thought she really meant to do it they wouldn't let her home.'

Henry walked across the patio. The skin of his heel was visible below his pyjamas, exposed by the backless slippers, bald and round, like a skull.

'They'll only let her go if someone is at home to care for her.'

'Couldn't you wait even a day? She'd be stronger tomorrow, more fit to go home.'

Henry shook his head. 'I don't want to wait.' He turned to her, his face pale, holding the timetable so that it covered his mouth. 'This has all been a terrible shock to me, Suzannah.'

She clenched her hands. The Henry of last night had disappeared altogether, he spoke as if his hours of remorse had been nothing but a dream.

'I never expected her to do this,' he continued. 'It's quite out of character.'

He stood up, put the timetable in his pocket and turned to her, drawing in his breath as if he had just had an idea. 'I'll leave you the car.'

'Why?'

'We'll go up by train.'

'But why? Why should I want the car?'

'Because . . . ' He touched her cheek and she saw in his expression, the generosity he felt in what he gave. 'Because it will be a comfort to you.'

She could eat no breakfast. She stood by the sink, pretending to wash up, while Henry, his face sternly composed, made his announcement.

'I'm taking you back to London today.'

Michael frowned. 'I thought we were staying for another week.'

'Your mother has been unwell.'

'Mum? Did she write to you?'

A pause. 'Yes.'

'She never wrote to me.' He sucked his spoon. 'Do you mean you're coming with us?'

'Yes. To see if she's all right.'

He sat up, suddenly alert. 'Will you stay, Dad?' He perched on the edge of his chair, his eyes riveted on Henry's lips. 'Will you stay?'

'We'll see,' said Henry.

'Are you coming too?' Michael spun round to Suzannah, his bottom lip folded under his teeth.

'No, Michael. I shall stay here and look after the cottage.'

Sammy banged down his spoon. 'I want Suzannah too!'

Henry took the spoon out of his hand.

'You'll be pleased to see Mummy again, won't you?' said Suzannah.

Sammy grinned. 'Mummy!' he shouted.

Michael was leaving the table. Henry called after him, 'We're leaving in twenty minutes so you'd better start getting your things together. We're going by train. I don't want any rubbish to carry. Just the things you brought with you.'

'Can I bring my cuttlefish?'

'Certainly not.'

'They don't weigh much.'

'They're rubbish,' said Henry. 'I've just said I don't want any rubbish.'

'I'm going to bring them anyway,' Michael shouted, pounding up the stairs.

Thirty-two

The kettle had begun to boil, a thin column of steam rose from the spout, growing, as Liam watched it, to a great white roar. He reached across and switched the gas off. The steam had clouded the window pane, recreating the mist that had hung outside until the sun came up.

Gouse shouted from his room. 'Will you make me a cup?' Liam could hear him stamping his feet into the high-laced boots and then thumping, like a man much bigger than he was, down the stairs.

'Are you out today, then?'

Gouse nodded. He put his backpack by the door and a small vinyl holdall on the kitchen table. 'Today is the day.'

'But today is Sunday.'

'So?'

'You can't go anywhere on a Sunday. There are no buses.'

Gouse lifted a teabag out of his mug. 'No buses?'

'None,' said Liam firmly.

Gouse dropped the teabag into the bin. 'We'll have to find another way.'

'I thought you were staying until Tuesday.'

Gouse tapped his nose. 'Better at the weekend, more – what do they call them – innocent bystanders?'

Liam got up. 'What?'

Gouse pointed to the mug in Liam's hand. 'Watch that now, you're going to spill it.'

'You can't do that today,' said Liam. 'Not on a Sunday.'

Gouse laughed. 'What have you got, Irishman, an eleventh commandment? Thou shalt not bomb on a Sunday?'

Liam went to the door and looked out. The word had not been used before. Bomb. It was as if something new had entered the picture, as if the saying of the word made true what before had been just a vague idea, a notion, easily set aside.

The grass in Handel's field was silver with dew. Across the bay Matilda's trees waved slowly in the breeze, as if in farewell to the ferries that slid silently across the horizon.

'Why does it have to be a Sunday – there'd be more people about during the week?'

Gouse blew on his tea, making a light bubbling sound. 'It's one of the rules of the game, never do what they expect.'

'But how will you get there?'

'You, Irishman, not me. I shall be away on a ferry.'

'Me? No. You're quite wrong if you think it will be me.'

'Don't start that now. We have been through all this. There is nothing to discuss on the topic.'

'I won't carry any bomb for you.'

'You will.' The Australian laughed. 'You've done it before.'

'Never.'

'How can you say, never? You've carried more than you could dream of. Today's job is a doddle.'

'Why do you have to tell me, then? Why do I have to know?'

Gouse laughed again. 'You crease me, Irishman. Everything's all right as long as you don't know, is that it?'

Liam stared out over the bay. The sheep were in the far field. He could hear Handel's dog barking.

'You can't ask me to carry a bomb for you.'

'Not just carry, Irishman. It will be you who plants it.'

Liam clenched his teeth. 'Is there no end to it?'

Gouse waved his hand. 'Relax, Liam. After this you'll be left in peace. You're a gem of an operator. We'll want to keep you safe. You won't hear from us for a good while.'

Sucking in his breath, Liam sat opposite Gouse at the table. He rubbed his face, covering his mouth with his hands as he spoke. 'How will we get to Dover?'

'If necessary, we'll hitch a lift.'

'You can't hitch a lift!'

'Why not?'

'Not carrying . . . that luggage.'

'It's quite safe.'

'I thought you were a professional. I thought you'd been taught to do things properly.'

Gouse pulled his woollen hat more firmly down over his forehead. 'Keep calm, Irishman. Would you want us to go in a taxi – would that be more discreet?'

'It's hardly discreet to go hitch-hiking around the countryside on a Sunday morning. The driver would remember us. He'll remember the bag.'

'You'll be bringing the bag home with you.' Gouse unzipped the brown holdall. Inside was a yellow plastic carrier bag, daubed red with the logo of a Duty Free shop. 'It's only the carrier you'll be leaving.'

Liam cleared his throat and rose once more from the chair. 'I want no part of this.'

Gouse ignored him.

Liam raised his voice. 'I said I want no part of this.'

'You are already part of it.' Gouse began to re-thread the laces of his boots. He spoke quietly. 'You have been part of it from the beginning. You have harboured our members, transported arms, permitted your home to be used for the manufacture of an explosive device.' His pale fingers wove the laces in a neat criss-cross pattern. He looked up and smiled. 'You're one of us, Liam, like your brother.'

Liam bit his lip. 'After this you'll leave me in peace?'

'For a long time.'

'And the money?'

Gouse smiled. 'You'll still get the money. More if you do well.' He leaned forward. 'I tell you, it's a doddle. You just take the bag on the train and leave it at Victoria.'

'Victoria?'

Gouse nodded, draining the last of the tea from his mug. 'The target is Victoria station. Your instructions are very simple. There is a photo booth at the back of the newsagent's stall. You will leave the carrier behind the little stool in the booth.'

'Someone will find it there,' said Liam, forgetting for a second the purpose and thinking only of the plan.

Gouse shook his head. 'Nobody will go near it. There is a large sign saying 'Out of Order'. Leave the carrier behind the stool and then walk away – and don't forget to bring the holdall back with you – we don't want to leave anything they can identify.'

'I'll be seen. They'll remember me.'

'You? They won't remember your face, Liam. There are too many tramps on Victoria station for them to pick out a man in a paint-stained coat.' Gouse took out his pouch of tobacco.

'Should you do that here?' asked Liam.

The other man looked up, raising an eyebrow.

'I mean, with what's in the bag,' said Liam.

Gouse smiled. 'It's better built than that.'

'How long before it goes off?'

'Long enough. We're not amateurs.'

'It might go off on the train.'

Gouse shook his head. 'It won't.'

'You can't be so sure.'

'We can be sure. We can be certain. There is a science to it.'

'But you could get it wrong.' Liam gestured vaguely at the holdall. 'You could get the timing wrong.'

With a cigarette clenched lightly between his teeth, Gouse grinned. 'What do you think? We'd send you on the train with an alarm clock ticking in there?' Smoke dribbled out of his mouth. 'The only thing that can go wrong is you. It is only you who could let us down.'

'And if I do?'

'There is a science for that, too.'

They reached the top of the lane; Liam's arm ached from holding the bag away from his body.

'You needn't nurse it now,' said Gouse. 'It won't go off before time.'

Nevertheless Liam tried to keep the bag from banging against his legs.

'Easier than a coolbox, eh?' Gouse laughed.

'I didn't know what was in the coolbox.'

Gouse pulled a face, simulating sympathy. 'It's a simple life for the innocent.

Liam trudged on, slightly ahead of him, wanting the journey to be over.

They reached the main road.

'Well, if it isn't our happy family,' said Gouse.

Liam looked back. Henry Alland's limousine was pulling out of Matilda's drive.

Gouse stuck out his thumb.

'Don't!' Liam cried.

'Why not?'

The car pulled up beside them. 'Where are you going?'

'Into town,' Gouse answered. 'It would save our legs if you're going that way.'

Henry turned to the boys and told them to make room on the back seat. Sammy climbed on to his brother's lap and Henry got out to unlock the boot. Suzannah heard the stranger laugh as they loaded the bag that Liam had carried. 'Watch that one, he's got his granny's china in there.'

She turned to the stranger as he sat behind her. 'Are you going away?'

The man grinned, showing a row of little teeth that were somehow in line with the thick ribbed band of his woollen hat. 'Liam here is going to London.'

Suzannah smiled as Liam got into the car.

Michael and Sammy both chattered at once. 'We're going to London, too.'

'On the train.'

'You're going on the train?' Liam repeated.

Suzannah saw him turn to his friend as if to speak. The stranger looked at him hard, stopping him with a slight shake of his head before he turned to Michael. 'Why are you going to London?'

Suzannah noticed his accent, Australian perhaps.

'To our Mummy!' cried Sammy.

'Isn't this your Mum?' asked the stranger.

'Yes, but – '

Michael interrupted his brother. 'She's our other mother.'

Suzannah's heart lifted. She smiled at Henry but he was watching the road.

'Your holiday's over, is it?' asked the Australian.

Sammy answered. 'My Mummy wants us to come back home,' he said, solemn for a moment.

Liam turned to him. 'She misses you, does she?' Suzannah noticed how he looked at the little boy, studying every inch of his face, drinking it in.

'Will you be here next time we come, Liam?' Michael asked.

As the car swung down into the station she heard the Irishman's reply. Barely a word. 'Maybe.'

The station was busy. A queue of holiday-makers stood in the bus-shelter, red stickers on their luggage: Ostend, Zeebrugge, Calais. Above them flower baskets hung like inverted helmets, trailing bright blue lobelia.

Henry opened the boot and let the Australian heave out his rucksack and bedroll.

'Thanks, mate,' he said and turned to smile at Suzannah. 'Thanks for the lift.'

Liam put out his hand. 'Gouse, wait.'

The Australian started walking towards the bus shelter. Liam went after him, took hold of his arm.

'Piss off, Irishman.' Gouse nudged him away. 'You're going to miss your train.'

Liam spoke under his breath. 'I'm not going on the train.'

Gouse stopped, shrugged the rucksack higher on to his back. 'Don't give me that.'

Liam muttered through his teeth. 'I'm not taking any bomb on any train.'

Gouse put down the bedroll and stood very close to Liam. 'We've been through all this. You will take the bag to Victoria and you will do as instructed.'

'I will not.' Liam put his hands in his coat pockets. The pebble was there, falling neatly into his palm.

Gouse hissed, 'You'll fucking do as you're told!'

Liam shook his head. In the corner of his eye he could see Henry Alland taking the brown holdall out of the car. 'I'll do nothing.'

'You think you can back out now? You think we can work for months setting this thing up, paying you money, keeping you clean and innocent, only to have you screw it for us?'

'I'm not going,' said Liam. 'It's as simple as that.'

'As simple as getting shot,' Gouse spat.

'I'm not taking the bag.'

Gouse snarled. 'You won't live twenty-four hours, yellow-belly.'

Liam shrugged. 'So be it.'

Suzannah knelt down to button Sammy's jacket.

The Australian was coming back. He smiled at Michael. 'My Irish friend has changed his mind, you'll have me as a travelling companion instead.'

Suzannah looked for Liam. He was on the far side, walking

up towards the road. His gait was peculiar, shambling, as if he was ill or drunk.

'Is Liam not going to London?'

'Slight change of plan.' The Australian grinned. 'I'm going in his place.'

'We'll be travelling first class,' said Henry in a clear voice. He had put the Alland luggage on a station trolley.

'Can't we all go in the same carriage?' asked Michael.

Released from Suzannah's arms, Sammy ran towards the stranger.

'We must get a move on,' Henry said, ignoring Michael's question.

The Australian turned to pick up the holdall. Sammy was kneeling by it, poking his fingers into the gap where the zip was not quite fastened. Suzannah heard a noise like a cough. The Australian was lifting Sammy bodily away from the bag.

The little boy giggled. Suzannah held out her hand. 'You mustn't touch that, Sammy. It isn't your bag.'

The man picked up the bag, still grinning. 'I'll be off to the steerage, then.'

Suzannah took a step forward. 'I'm sure Henry didn't mean . . .'

The man laughed. 'No sweat, lady.'

Henry slammed the car boot. 'We should hurry and get our tickets or we'll miss the train.' He turned to her. 'You needn't come with us on to the platform, Suzannah.'

She followed them into the ticket hall thinking how cool he sounded, how unlike the weeping man of the night before.

There was no sign of the Australian. Henry's voice was loud and confident as he asked for the first class tickets. Michael stared at the posters that lined the walls: Awaydays, Weekend Breaks, Golden Rail holidays. Sammy hung on her arm. 'Choo, choo!' he cried. 'Choo, choo!'

'Bring those bags, will you, Michael.' Henry folded the tickets into his wallet. He looked at Suzannah. 'The train is already here, it's due to leave in a minute.'

Turning away from him, she bent down and gave Sammy a hug. Michael picked up the cases, looking away, as if one of the wall posters was of immense interest.

'Goodbye, Michael,' said Suzannah. 'I know you're too big

for a kiss, but why don't we shake hands?'

He put down the bags and came towards her. She held out her hand but he kept on coming and planted a wet, toothy kiss on her cheek.

Then they were hurrying on to the platform, Henry with a pale smile and the two boys, pausing frequently to wave.

'Henry!' He had gone through the barrier, his shirt collar a bright white line above the dark cloth of his jacket.

'Henry!'

It was Michael who turned, looking back, his face full of questions. He pulled Michael's arms, pointed.

Henry turned, woodenly. She ran forward to the barrier.

'Ticket, miss?' The collector's arm blocked her path. Sending Michael in ahead, Henry lifted Sammy into the train and followed him, closing the door. A whistle blew. The last she saw of him was the sleeve of his coat against the glass.

'HENRY!'

Thirty-three

Gassy had made a fruitcake. A slab rested on the plate at the side of Cyril's tray. Abandoning the chicken, warmed in the microwave, Cyril turned to the cake. Idly, with his free hand, he pressed the TV remote control. A picture of the Thames swivelled into view, the loud gong of Big Ben announcing the news. A presenter's eyes stared glassily into the camera, she read her prompt with great solemnity, and then her face was replaced by a film, the concourse of a railway station; the rubble remains of a newspaper stall, ahead of it a gaping space where the Departure board had hung, a girder hanging twisted from the roof. The bomb had gone off in the afternoon. Experts believed it had been planted earlier in the day. A man had been seen with a bag near a photo booth that was out of use. Cyril leaned forward as the camera panned. The station looked like a film set; arc lights and cables, men in yellow jackets scrambling between piles of books and scattered newspapers. The camera singled out a ticket collector's cap, lying in a dark pool. Then the viewers were led to one side; to where men were carrying stretchers, waiting their turn to load sealed black bags, large and small, the bodies of adults and children, into a white van.

Cyril shook his head. Briefly he thought of the families; the grief that would be suffered. Like his own grief, bottomless, incurable. He took a sip of wine and turned back to the fruitcake. It was dark and moist; the crumbly texture of the sponge combined with raisins in a rich chewy mass. Cyril followed the last morsel with a mouthful of wine.

Another presenter appeared, aglow with life, as if she had just come in from the piste, to read a more cheerful item of news. Cyril picked up his tray and carried it through to the kitchen. It would remain on the counter until Gassy came in the morning. He re-filled his wine glass from a box in the fridge. The uninhabited kitchen was full of noise; the hot whirr of the gas boiler, overhead the hum and tick of the strip-light and in the corner the light buzzing of the big chest freezer. He peered through the opening in the face of the boiler; a wall of blue flames; such a lot of fire, he thought, to heat one man.

The phone rang in the hall. Taking his glass, he hurried towards it.

'Hello?'

'Daddy? Daddy, it's me.'

'Suzannah?'

'Daddy, can I come home?'

'Of course. You can always come home. You don't have to ask.'

Her cry burst along the line, noisy, whooping sobs.

'Suzannah, what is it? What has happened?'

'I'm alone. Henry's gone. He's taken the children.'

Bewildered, Cyril groped for the hall chair, slipping between the narrow, carved arms. What could she mean, what children? Henry who?

This had happened to him before. Since Joan had gone his memory was not to be relied upon. Steering for caution, he asked, 'When are you coming, Suzannah?'

'Tonight, I'm coming tonight.'

'Are you in trouble, dear?'

'No. But it'll be a while before I'm with you. I'm driving up from Kent.'

'From Kent?'

But she had gone, the receiver burred in his ear.

Rubbing his face, he went back to the kitchen to re-fill his glass. What could have happened to upset her so? He finished the wine and went back to his chair. The presenter's face was wishing him goodnight. Cyril closed his eyes. He could have a little nap, be fresher when she came, better able to advise.

Advise? He thought of his daughter, of the bright colours, the make-up, the glittering laughter, so fragile a shell for the little girl she had been.

The hall clock was chiming midnight when he heard a car turn into the drive. Hurrying through the hall, he saw a gleam of headlights through the glass, heard the clunk of a car door. She was struggling with something. He switched on the porch light. In the drive was a shiny black limousine with the door open, his daughter almost hidden behind it, hauling something from the rear seat.

'Whatever is it, Suzannah?'

'It's a picture,' her voice was muffled.

'A picture?'

'It was given to me as a present.'

'By whom?'

'By the artist who painted it.' At last the parcel was out of the car; a frame wrapped in a newspaper. Cyril took the weight of one side and helped her carry it into the light.

'Here, we can unwrap it here,' said Suzannah. They lowered it gently on to the floor.

'Who is the artist?' Turning to look at her in the light, her appearance took his breath away. Not his daughter; no longer his butterfly girl. A woman in a blue dress, smudged mascara in the lines beneath her eyes.

She knelt down on the polished floor and with unpainted nails began to undo the string that held the cloth. The back of a canvas appeared, stretched taut upon its frame.

'It's me,' she said, turning the picture over to lean against the wall.

He bent down. Nothing but a blur. 'I'll have to fetch my spectacles.'

He hurried back. A beach scene; a woman in a red costume, a coil of hair caught between the blades of her shoulders, the cheeks of her buttocks bulging into soft sand. All around her lay the playthings of the beach, a bucket and spade, the tower of a sandcastle, a gathering of cuttlefish shells. The woman was turning her face to the onlooker, the face of a child, painted to appear as an adult.

'It's me,' Suzannah repeated. 'Me as I have been this summer.'

Cyril patted her arm. 'Did you go to the coast? I didn't know where you'd gone. I was afraid to ask.' He looked up into her face, at the pale, streaked eyes. 'You look tired, Suzannah.'

She stood up and took hold of his arms. 'Come on, Daddy, you'll get sore knees on this hard floor.' She smiled. 'You look tired, too.'

'Me? I've been dozing since you rang.' He rubbed his eyes. 'I was watching the news, there's been a bomb in Victoria station.'

'At Victoria?' Suzannah's eyes widened. 'When?'

'Late this afternoon.'

'Oh . . . thank God.'

Cyril looked at her, mystified.

'I mean . . . ' Suzannah left the sentence unfinished.

Leaving the picture against the wall, he led her into the warm sitting room. 'Is there anything I can get you, my dear?'

She shook her head. 'No, Daddy, but let me make you some cocoa.'

Her father beamed. 'Cocoa would be a lovely treat, I haven't had any for a long time.'

She squeezed his hand. 'You wait in here and I'll bring it to you.'

Cyril dropped into his chair. Through the open door he could see her in the kitchen, her slender outline in the plain blue dress. She seemed so much changed.

When she came back into the room, carrying a mug of steaming cocoa, he said, 'I hope you won't think I'm prying, my dear, but with your coming here suddenly like this, I have to ask. Have you been in some sort of trouble?'

Her voice was faint as she sat on the carpet in front of his knees. She had sat in just that way when she was a child, laying her long hair in his lap. 'I was,' she said, smoothing the stray strands over his knee, 'but it's over now. I've come home.'